Emma was tempted almost beyond bearing.

The idea of being the woman to bring warmth to Joe's cold eyes, to bring happiness to his bleak face, to bring a smile to his hard mouth, was heady indeed.

But thinking it possible was dangerous to her own barely healed heart.

For Joe wasn't the only one with old hurts. She'd already lost as much as she could stand to lose.

She was surviving.

But instinct told her she might not survive loving— and losing—a man like Joe.

Dear Reader,

Welcome to Silhouette *Special Edition* . . . welcome to romance.

Last year I requested your opinions on the books that we publish. Thank you for the many thoughtful comments. For the next couple of months, I'd like to share quotes with you from those letters. This seems very appropriate while we are in the midst of our THAT SPECIAL WOMAN! promotion. Each one of our readers is a very *special* woman, as heroic as the heroines in our books.

This month, our THAT SPECIAL WOMAN! is Kelley McCormick, a woman who takes the trip of a lifetime and meets the man of her dreams. You'll meet Kelley and her Prince Charming in *Grand Prize Winner!* by Tracy Sinclair.

Also in store for you this month is *The Way of a Man,* the third book in Laurie Paige's WILD RIVER TRILOGY. And not to be missed are terrific books from other favorite authors—Kathleen Eagle, Pamela Toth, Victoria Pade and Judith Bowen.

I hope you enjoy this book, and all of the stories to come!

Sincerely,

Tara Gavin
Senior Editor

QUOTE OF THE MONTH:

"I enjoy characters I can relate to—female characters who are wonderful people packaged in very ordinary coverings and men who see beyond looks and who are willing to work at a relationship. I enjoy stories of couples who stick with each other and work through difficult times. Thank you, Special Edition, for the many, many hours of enjoyment."

—M. Greenleaf, Maryland

PAMELA TOTH

WALK AWAY, JOE

Silhouette®

SPECIAL EDITION®

Published by Silhouette Books

America's Publisher of Contemporary Romance

This book is dedicated to the rural mail carriers and substitute rural carriers at the Marysville, Washington, post office with great appreciation for all your help and encouragement. Thank you!

 SILHOUETTE BOOKS

ISBN 0-373-09850-2

WALK AWAY, JOE

Copyright © 1993 by Pamela Toth

Books by Pamela Toth

Silhouette Special Edition

Thunderstruck #411
Dark Angel #515
Old Enough To Know Better #624
Two Sets of Footprints #729
A Warming Trend #760
Walk Away, Joe #850

Silhouette Romance

Kissing Games #500
The Ladybug Lady #595

PAMELA TOTH

was born in Wisconsin, but grew up in Seattle, where she attended the University of Washington and majored in art. She still lives near Seattle with her husband, two teenage daughters, a dog and four Siamese cats. Having recently left her job as a substitute rural carrier at the local post office, she spends her time reading and traveling when she isn't seated at her computer. One of her books, *Two Sets of Footprints,* won the *Romantic Times* WISH award and has been nominated for two *Romantic Times* Reviewers' Choice awards.

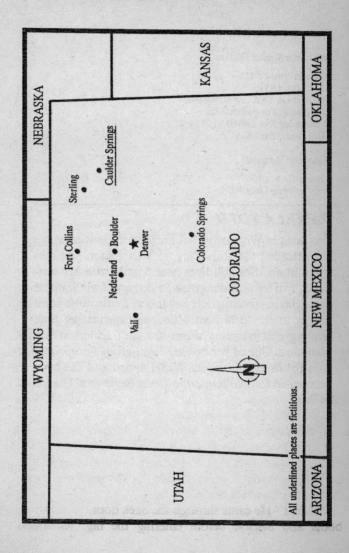

All underlined places are fictitious.

Chapter One

"Let the men know that I want to get an early start tomorrow," Joe Sutter told his foreman as the two of them walked out of the barn. "First light." Joe paused to rotate one aching shoulder. "There's still a lot of fence to check."

Daniel Sixkiller's tone was resigned. "Among other things."

Joe rubbed the side of his neck, where a branch had scratched him. "Not enough hours in the day." He lifted one hand in a laconic gesture of dismissal as his foreman turned toward the bunkhouse.

Even Daniel's strong shoulders drooped beneath his sweat-stained chambray shirt. It had been a long day and both men were tired, hot and hungry. Joe hoped his mother had supper ready; there was a pile of paperwork waiting for him before he could call it a night.

"Mom?" He came through the back door, shedding his boots and Stetson before entering the big, remodeled kitchen. The room was empty, and the usual mouth-watering aromas from his mother's cooking were notice-ably absent. Joe frowned at the silence. From the floor above, where the bedrooms were, he heard the sound of coughing.

He crossed the kitchen and raced up the stairs.

"Mom? Are you up here?" he shouted as he went down the hall to her room. He was answered by more coughing and a scratchy voice calling his name. Pausing in front of her closed door, he knocked and then turned the knob without waiting for an invitation.

His mother was in bed, an unusual-enough occurrence at this time of day to bring Joe to a stop. What really upset him, though, was her pallor. Marian Gray was hardly ever sick.

"Joe," she said with a wan smile, "I'm glad you're here." Another fit of coughing rattled through her body. She looked alarmingly frail as she held up one hand. "Don't come too close."

Ignoring her, he advanced to the bed with a worried frown. "What's wrong? Shall I call the doctor?"

She shook her head and coughed again. "No," she gasped. "It's just a cold that's settled into my chest."

"You were okay this morning," he observed.

"I didn't want to say anything. I thought it was a sniffle that would go away. I'm sorry about supper. I—"

"Don't worry about that. I can feed myself." He'd been doing just that until last year, when his mother's second husband had died and she'd come back to Colorado. To the Blue Moon Ranch to keep house and cook for Joe, who was divorced. He had sensed that she needed to be useful and, after minor adjustments on both their parts, the arrange-ment had worked out pretty well.

"I'll get you some medicine," Joe told her, "and then I'll fix us both something to eat."

Her hands fluttered, and she coughed again.

"I'm not hungry," she objected.

He studied her pale cheeks. "You need to eat. If you don't feel better in the morning, I'm calling Doc Armstrong."

Marian started to argue again, knowing her son had to be tired after a long day on horseback, but he frowned at her over his shoulder.

The words died on her tongue. "Thank you, dear," she called after him instead. Time enough to tell him about tomorrow when he came back. He'd be annoyed, as he always was when she did things without telling him—even when they were for his own good.

This time she'd really done it, inviting a guest to stay at the ranch for half of the summer. But Marian hadn't known she'd be sick tomorrow, too sick to drive to the bus station at Fort Morgan and pick Emma up. Marian had expected to tell Joe about her in the morning, when he was in a hurry to leave, bolting down his breakfast just as he always had since he was a little boy, in too much of a hurry to talk. She would have mentioned that she was picking up the daughter of an old friend, who would be staying for a while. He would have told her in his usual distracted way to enjoy herself—and probably have asked her to stop by the freight office or the co-op and pick something up for him, since she was going to town anyway. By the time he really thought about the visitor, he would have been in some distant pasture on his horse and she'd be meeting Emma's bus.

That was how things were supposed to happen. Now, all because of this blasted cold, she had to tell Joe about Emma's arrival while he was tired and hungry, with nothing but canned soup to fill the void in his stomach and nothing to distract him from the realization that he would have to miss a half day's work to meet the bus himself. He'd think that Marian had planned it—inviting an attractive young woman to the ranch as part of some plot to marry off her only son.

Marian suppressed a smile and coughed into her tissue. If anything did develop between Joe and Emma, it would just be a happy coincidence, not the result of some nefarious scheme of hers. Not really.

After a little while she heard the thud of his feet on the stairs and pulled herself up to a sitting position. It would be difficult enough to tell him without getting a crick in her neck while she did. Perhaps she'd let him eat his soup first. Maybe he wouldn't get angry at all. And maybe there was a magic elixir that would make this blasted cold disappear.

"Do you want anything else?" While Joe watched his mother spoon up her soup, he'd drained his own bowl and swallowed the last bite of the ham sandwich he'd slapped together. Finally she laid down her spoon and sighed. At least now she wasn't coughing so much.

"No, thank you, dear. I've had plenty. I hope you were able to find enough to eat yourself. I really should have—"

"I'm fine," he cut in. "Don't worry about it. Tomorrow I'll eat at the bunkhouse. I'll have Cookie bring your meals and there won't be anyone or anything else for you to worry about. You can rest all day."

He noticed that she'd begun to pleat the top of the sheet with nervous fingers. Now she bit her lower lip. Something was obviously bothering her.

"What is it, Mom? Is there anything else you need?" He braced himself for whatever she had to tell him. She'd overspent the grocery account, or wanted to redecorate one of the rooms in the big old ranch house or have someone over for a visit. He had told her not to worry about things like that, but she did, anyway. He only hoped it wasn't about her health, something she'd kept from him. He hated it when she kept things from him.

"Are you terribly busy with the ranch work?" she asked, surprising him.

He nodded. "Yep. There's lots of fence to fix, calves to check on, as well as everything else that needs doing this time of year. Why? If you need anything, tell me. If you want a woman from town to stay with you, I can call—"

She shook her head. "It's not that. I need you to run an errand for me. Tomorrow afternoon."

Joe tried to keep his impatience in check. "Can't one of the men—" He broke off what he'd been about to say when she shook her head. Her expression was both sheepish and defiant.

"I need you to go," she said. "To Fort Morgan to meet the bus from Denver."

Joe's self-protective instincts kicked in with a thud. "Why?"

Marian began pleating the top of the sheet again, while Joe barely resisted the urge to still her hands and shake her, cold or no cold.

"What have you done?" he coaxed, still thinking she must have bought something for the house that had to be bused in. Something she didn't think he was going to like. She'd been talking about replacing his worn-out recliner in the den. No, it would have to be something smaller to be coming by bus.

She took a deep breath and coughed until her eyes teared. Joe handed her a glass of water and tapped one foot.

"I invited a friend to come for a visit," she said quickly, without looking at him.

Joe let his body relax. She'd finally decided to have some company. Well, that was good. He knew the late spring days could be lonely, even though she insisted they weren't. He could deal with having a stranger in the house for a little while, even a couple of weeks.

"About time you did," he said. "Too bad about this cold, though. You'll have to hurry and get better so you can enjoy her visit." A sudden thought stopped him. "It is a woman, isn't it?'' He didn't think she'd been conducting any long-distance romances, but one never knew.

She nodded, obviously relieved. ''Oh, yes,'' she agreed. ''It's a woman. An old friend.''

Joe relaxed even further. Another middle-aged woman wouldn't be any trouble. The two of them would probably gossip while Marian cooked and tended her vegetable garden. As soon as she felt better they could take the car and see the local sights.

''What's her name?''

''Emma Davenport,'' his mother replied. ''Emma's from Seattle. Her marriage broke up and she seemed to be at loose ends.'' She made a vague gesture with her hand. ''She needed a place to stay. I hope you don't mind. I intended telling you.''

''Before or after you met Emma's bus?'' he teased her with a grin.

She had the grace to look embarrassed. ''Before, of course.''

He leaned back, crossing one foot over the other. ''So, tell me,'' he coaxed. ''What time does our Emma's bus arrive?''

Emma stared out the bus window and wiggled in her seat, trying to find a position that didn't aggravate the nagging ache in her back. Too bad the flight from Seattle had been delayed, making her miss the earlier bus. Making it necessary for her to call the ranch—only to learn that Joe Sutter and not his mother would be picking Emma up.

''A visit on a working cattle ranch will be a nice change from life in a big city,'' remarked Jane Benson, the middle-aged woman in the next seat. They'd talked off and on during the long bus ride.

Emma agreed. She still had her doubts about spending such a long time with a woman who'd been more her mother's friend than her own. But the invitation had been a god-send in its own way. It got Emma out of Seattle and gave her time to decide what to do with her life, now that her divorce was final. Go back to teaching? Try something different? Stay in Seattle or move elsewhere?

"Maybe you'll meet someone while you're here." Jane had discovered early in the ride that Emma wasn't married. "Pretty girls like you will always be welcome where the warmest thing a man has to cuddle is a cow." She chuckled at her own humor.

Emma forced a smile. She wasn't about to admit knowing that Marian's son, Joe, was also divorced. Emma had been kept abreast of all the milestones in his life. Marian had written about college football, Joe's graduation, his wedding and later, the ending of that marriage. Emma knew that the ranch he owned and ran himself had been left him by his father, Marian's first husband.

"I'm not here to find a man," she told Jane. "I just wanted a break, a little vacation."

Her traveling companion nodded, and her eyes twinkled behind her glasses. "You never know," she said. "Our men are a handsome lot, with their rugged tans and tight jeans."

Emma's eyes widened at her words.

"Oh, I'm not too old to notice," the other woman continued. "I've been widowed for ten years. What's this fella who's coming for you look like? Handsome?"

"I don't know. We've never actually met." Emma knew about Joe's appearance only from the occasional snapshots Marian had sent. Since the last of his school pictures, his face had always been hidden by the shadow from his Stetson or by sunglasses or both. She knew only that he was tall and broad shouldered. When she'd called Marian about her delayed arrival she hadn't thought to ask what Joe looked like. But then, how many men who were built like him could there be waiting for her bus when it pulled in to Fort Morgan, anyway?

The countryside rolled by outside the window but she barely noticed. She was wondering, instead, where she would be and what she would be doing at the end of this summer that stretched before her like an unmapped road.

Emma needed a break from responsibility and life-altering decisions. She needed time to recover from the wrenching upsets in her life, time to gather the strength that had always seen her through and was, even now, she hoped desperately, waiting just beyond her reach. Maybe here, in the wilds of Colorado, she could regain touch with that inner resilience that had so far managed to elude her.

When the bus rolled into the terminal Emma said good-bye to Jane and followed her down the center aisle of the bus. As Emma stepped onto the pavement, a man she might have taken for Marian's son approached the older woman and touched his fingers politely to the brim of his Stetson.

"Are you Emma Davenport?" Emma heard him ask. She watched as Jane shook her head and turned to point.

"I believe you're looking for her," Jane told him with a wink at Emma. "Have a nice vacation," she added before turning away.

"Thanks," Emma called. Then she looked up at Joe Sutter, only to wonder at his forbidding expression. She'd been right; he was tall and his shoulders were almost impossibly broad beneath his Western-cut shirt. His features, except for a grim mouth, the tips of intriguing sideburns and a square jaw, were shadowed by the brim of his hat. Just not shadowed enough to disguise the unfriendliness stamped on his weathered face.

"Are you Emma?" he demanded, lifting his chin so she could clearly see narrowed gray eyes beneath brows that were currently bunched into a frown.

She attempted a smile and held out her hand. "Yes, I am. You must be Marian's son?" Her voice rose at the end, turning the statement into a question.

He ignored both it and her outstretched hand. "You're supposed to be a friend of my mother's," he stated instead, as if something about her appearance completely negated that possibility.

"Actually, she and *my* mother went to college together," Emma explained, holding on to her patience and her smile as she let her hand drop back to her side. Hadn't she heard stories about Western hospitality and the courtly manner in which cowboys treated women? Apparently Joe Sutter hadn't heard the same stories.

"Where's your mother?" he asked, glancing around.

Emma blinked, taken aback by the blunt question. "Hasn't Marian mentioned that my mother passed away seven years ago?" Good grief, did he intend to keep her standing here for an inquisition? Already, other passengers were pushing past them to reach their luggage.

Joe's expression softened fractionally, and for a moment she got a glimpse of how attractive he would be without the frown. "I'm sorry," he said gruffly. "I should have remembered."

"Thank you." She stared into his eyes, wondering if they ever lost their chill. Was he always this unpleasant or had she managed to do something to irritate him?

"I'm sorry you had to come and get me," she said hesitantly. "I imagine that you're very busy."

"Yes, I am. I've been waiting two hours for your bus to get here."

"I'm sorry," she repeated. "My flight was late. I called the ranch but you'd already left. I'll get my luggage."

He brushed past her. "Show me which one is yours."

She pointed at two matching suitcases and a large tote. She'd had to pack carefully to get enough clothes for the extended visit into the three bags.

"All of them?" he asked, obviously startled.

"I'll carry one," she said defensively. Apparently everything about her was going to annoy him. Well, she was through apologizing!

"Never mind." He hefted the bags effortlessly and started walking toward a large blue-and-white pickup truck. Emma watched him go, fascinated by the shifting muscles in his wide back and powerful legs. And Jane was right about those tight jeans.

After a half-dozen steps he stopped and turned. "You coming?"

Embarrassed to have been caught gawking, she hurried after him. "I'm sorry," she said again, breathlessly.

Rain spattered against Joe's shoulders as he crossed the street to the truck. Instead of throwing the bags into the unprotected back as he had intended, he yanked open the passenger door and stacked them inside. He should have brought the car, but he'd been too annoyed at the disruption in his workday to think about it. He circled the truck as Emma followed.

"Perhaps you'd rather I just took the next bus back to Denver," she suggested in a belligerent tone.

Joe stopped and stared down at her. She was a little thing, with a cloud of curly black hair and blue eyes so dark he'd call them indigo if he was trying to be poetic. He'd expected to pick up a contemporary of his mother's, not a siren who looked as if she'd just stepped from the pages of a high-fashion magazine. Unwelcome awareness had already replaced his first dumbfounded shock at her appearance.

For a moment her offer to leave again tempted him unbearably. Then reality took over.

"My mother would kill me if I came home without you," he grumbled, opening the driver's door and stepping back.

"I beg your pardon?" Her delicate hands were splayed on trim hips sheathed in a skirt that was black, narrow and short. He liked the way she had paired it with a blue-and-black-plaid jacket hanging open over a blouse that matched her eyes.

His pleasure in her appearance only served to deepen both his frown and his mood. He had no business being attracted to Emma Davenport or anyone else. It was important he remember that.

"Mom would climb out of her sickbed and box my ears if I showed up alone," he admitted when she gave no sign of budging. "Get in." He held out a hand to assist her.

"I didn't realize your mother was sick." Emma hesitated, worrying her full lower lip with her teeth. "Maybe I'd better go back."

The last thing Joe wanted was to have to convince her to come to the ranch. Deeply honed survival instincts were screaming at him to buy that return ticket and hustle her onto the bus before it pulled out.

"It's only a cold," he heard himself explaining. "That's why she sent me to fetch you instead of coming herself."

"I wondered," she murmured. "But she didn't say on the phone." The rain started to fall harder.

"Come on," he urged again. "We're both getting soaked standing here.

Raindrops shimmered like diamonds in her dark hair while she eyed his already damp shirt and shrugged.

"Okay." She moved toward the truck without taking his hand, but hesitated when she saw how high the cab sat off the ground. He noticed her chin jut out as she finally accepted his assistance. The warmth of her touch sent an electric charge sizzling up his arm to the elbow. Obviously it had been too long since he'd made one of his infrequent visits to Sterling.

He could see her calculating the distance between the ground and the cab, and he almost regretted having removed the running boards because he hadn't liked the way they looked. But he didn't often give rides to women. Especially ones in tight skirts.

She gripped his hand harder and he glanced down, noticing that her short nails were painted light pink, like the inside of a seashell. A tremor went through him. He hoped she'd blame it on the rain.

Emma hiked up her skirt with her free hand and gave him a look that dared him to so much as peek at her exposed thighs. When he did, blatantly, she gasped. He forgot all about his regret over the running boards as he eyed her shapely legs in sexy black nylons. Before she could attempt the step he released her hand and grasped her around her small waist, propelling her upward. He thought he heard her choke back a scream and he barely registered the warmth of her body against his palms before she was in the truck, scrambling quickly past the wheel to the middle of the wide bench seat.

"Thanks," she murmured. Her voice sounded breathless, but it was undoubtedly just his own rioting imagination. A woman who looked like Emma wouldn't be attracted to a grumpy jerk like him.

As he climbed in after her, Emma fastened the seat belt with hands that shook. Joe had lifted her as if she weighed no more than her purse and shoved her into the truck with unflattering haste. No doubt he was eager to be on his way. He must figure that he'd wasted enough time on his mother's unwelcome errand.

She bit back another apology. Instead she asked, "How far to the Blue Moon?" as he shut the door behind them. His hard arm brushed against hers as he twisted the key in the ignition and put the truck in gear. She tried to move closer to the wall of luggage, but the seat belt held her fast.

"It's about an hour's drive," he said without turning his head. An hour spent trapped with her in the confines of the cab. He turned the radio on to a country station without asking what she cared to hear. And without analyzing his deliberate rudeness.

"You okay?" he asked grudgingly, staring straight ahead.

"Just fine, thank you." It was the last thing either of them said for quite a while.

He could have pointed out things along the way, but he didn't. He told himself she could have asked if she was really interested, but he knew she wouldn't. After a while he began to regret the gruff way he'd acted. She was undoubtedly tired from the long trip. Maybe cold and hungry, too. He turned on the heater.

One by one he thought of and discarded attempts at small talk. Finally he settled on asking her how long she had lived in Seattle. Before he could force out the words, he felt a soft bump. Startled, he glanced down.

Emma had fallen asleep and her head was resting against his arm. For a moment he allowed himself to enjoy the feel of her cuddled next to him and the idea of her trusting him enough to nap while he looked after her.

Then, abruptly, the corners of his mouth turned downward. As the truck ate up the miles he sucked in a deep breath and filled his head with the same sweet honeysuckle fragrance he'd noticed when he had lifted her into the cab.

Joe froze like a deer that had scented some threat to its very existence. Before he could think what to do, a small red car pulled onto the road directly in front of him, shattering the spell that had been reeling him in. Swearing, he hit the brakes hard to avoid smashing into the other vehicle. Beside him, Emma was jerked abruptly awake.

"What—?" she cried.

"It's okay," he reassured her as the car accelerated out of their path and Joe took his foot off the brake. He glanced at Emma while they regained speed. She was blinking like a baby owl. "Idiot cut in front of us, is all."

She rubbed a hand across her eyes. "I must have fallen asleep," she murmured. "Are we almost there?"

Joe wondered if she realized what she'd been using for a pillow, then decided she probably didn't. Not that he was about to mention it.

"Ten more minutes," he said as he signaled and turned off the main road. He told himself he'd be glad to hand Emma over to his mother. And he'd be careful not to get caught alone with her again. If this woman was part of another ill-advised matchmaking scheme, the plan was doomed to failure. Joe's divorce had driven him to his knees and taught him a painful lesson. He had no intentions of getting involved again.

Emma barely glanced at the outside of the big farm-house as she followed Joe up the sidewalk. He was no friendlier on his own turf. At least Marian would be glad to see her. The two of them had always gotten along well.

"Mom's room is the first one on the right," Joe told her when they topped the carpeted stairs. "Why don't you say hello while I put your bags in the guest room?"

Emma watched him disappear through an open door down the hall without waiting for her to answer. She had noticed as soon as he removed his hat that his hair was a medium brown, several shades warmer than his personality. For such an attractive man, he was certainly disagreeable. No wonder he was divorced.

"Emma?" called a familiar voice. "Is that you?"

She broke into a smile and pushed open the door Joe had indicated. Marian was sitting up in bed, a box of tissues and a book next to her and an answering smile on her face.

Without thinking, Emma reached down to give her friend a hug.

"No, don't get too close," Marian cautioned, holding up her hands in warning. "I don't want you catching my cold. Sit down at the end of the bed and let me look at you, though."

Emma perched there self-consciously while Marian studied her. "You look great," she said finally. "I'm sorry for all you've been through."

"I'm recovering," Emma said lightly, thanking her. She was vaguely aware of the sound of Joe's booted feet descending the staircase. She felt her tired body shed some of its tension.

"So how was the trip?" Marian asked, reaching for another tissue.

"Long," Emma replied. "I'm really beat. If you don't mind, I'd like to turn in early."

Marian nodded her understanding. "You must be hungry, too. Let me ask Joe to fix you something first."

Emma rose, shaking her head. She was starving, but would never admit it if it meant accepting anything else from Marian's son. Perhaps later she could sneak down and fix herself some toast.

"Oh, no," she said. "I don't want to take up any more of his time."

Marian frowned. "You and Joe got along okay, didn't you? I know he can be a little, well, quiet, but he's really not..."

The door opened and Joe walked in, carrying a loaded tray. On it were steaming bowls of soup and a pile of sandwiches.

"Joe's not really what?" he asked as he positioned the tray in front of his mother.

Emma swallowed to keep from drooling at the aroma of the hot soup. "I was just telling Marian how grateful I am that you picked me up," she said. "I know you're much too busy to be playing taxi."

Joe shot her an enigmatic look. "No problem. I had Cookie make some soup and sandwiches and I thought you two would like to eat together while you visit."

"Thank you, dear," Marian said. "That was very thoughtful. I'll bet Emma is famished."

He set up a small table in front of a side chair and indicated that she sit there.

"Aren't you eating?" she asked, noticing that he had brought up two of everything.

"I'll have something in the kitchen." He straightened. "Don't let the soup get cold. I'll be up in a while to collect the tray."

Emma smiled at him but his expression remained cool. "I can bring it down when we're done," she offered.

His firm lips relaxed into what might have been meant as a friendly response. "Thanks."

As she eyed the chunks of vegetables and chicken in her bowl, he left the room. This time she was puzzled to feel both relief and disappointment that he was gone. A lot of the energy in the room had seemed to depart with him. Emma dismissed the thought—probably only a reaction to her extreme hunger. She was here to visit Marian and think about the future, not to speculate on her friend's grown son.

"So, dear, what do you think of my boy?" Marian asked with a smile, spoon poised.

Chapter Two

Emma wasn't sure what woke her. It was barely dawn beyond the curtained window of her room. Her stomach growled and her mouth was dry, so she decided to steal downstairs. Perhaps she could make some tea and toast. Slipping on her red silk robe and her slippers, she fluffed up her curly hair and tiptoed out of her room. She stood in the hallway and listened intently but, except for a few tired groans, the old house was quiet.

When Emma padded down the stairs and approached the kitchen she saw a strip of light beneath the closed door. Cautiously she pushed it open.

Joe, leaning against the counter, turned to look at her over the rim of his coffee mug. He wore jeans and a work shirt with a denim vest, and his hair was damp from a recent shower. In his boots he towered over Emma, who wore flat black slippers trimmed with ostrich feathers. At that hour of the morning Joe looked better in his rugged clothes than any man should.

"G-good morning," Emma stammered. "I didn't think anyone else would be up yet."

Joe set down his mug and rubbed his finger along one sideburn.

"The day starts early around here," he said as his gaze traveled over her clinging robe. "But I didn't think you'd be downstairs for hours."

Emma wished she'd taken the time to throw on some clothes. Joe's perusal was making her nervous. Without his hat to shield it, his face was riveting, with his flashing gray eyes and sensual mouth. Everywhere his gaze lingered, her body warmed in response.

"I could make you some breakfast," Emma offered, surprising herself.

Apparently her sudden offer surprised Joe, too. His eyes widened slightly.

"You cook?"

She pulled the belt of her robe tighter. "Of course I cook. What would you like?" Circling him cautiously, she opened the fridge and peered inside. It was well stocked.

"Nothing. I can't take time, but thanks for offering." He was watching her through narrowed eyes, his expression unreadable.

"You have to eat." Emma had no idea why she was arguing, why she wanted to keep him here. His presence was disturbing; better to let him leave so she could scurry back upstairs and get dressed. She was much too wide awake now to go back to bed.

"I'll eat at the bunkhouse." He glanced at his watch. "I'd be obliged if you'd fix Mom's breakfast when she wakes up, though," he added. "If you don't mind. I was going to have Cookie send something over, but he's pretty busy with the men. And help yourself to whatever you want."

"Of course I don't mind," Emma exclaimed. "Do you think I expect to be waited on when Marian is sick and you're so busy?"

His silence told her that was exactly what he'd expected. He turned to gaze out the curtained window as she fumed. This was never going to work. He obviously despised her, whatever the reason, and he made her as nervous as a balloon seller in a sticker patch.

"I'd be glad to help out," Emma said, "especially while Marian is sick." She moved closer to where Joe stood with his broad back to her. His damp hair was slightly wavy and needed trimming. She wondered what it would feel like against her fingers. She swallowed and went on.

"I think you and I got off on the wrong foot. Could we start over? Then, when your mother is better, I can go home with a clear conscience."

Joe turned, surprised to find Emma standing barely an arm's length away. The thin wrap she wore didn't disguise the fact that she would make a nice-size armful, either, slim but tempting. He needed another shower, a cold one.

With an effort Joe cut off his wandering thoughts and paid attention to what she was saying. Her offer to help and her suggestion that they begin again made his face heat with discomfort. Some host he was, so inhospitable that she thought he wanted her to leave. Well, he did, but it wasn't really her fault he felt that way.

He glanced down at her outstretched hand, remembering when she had offered it before and he had ignored the gesture. The last thing he wanted to do now was to touch her, but he couldn't refuse. Not twice.

Slowly he wrapped his fingers around hers. Her bones were so finely made he could have snapped them with little effort.

"Agreed," he replied as the warmth and softness of her skin melted into him. He would have loved to pull her closer, to find out if she still smelled of honeysuckle. Instead he forced himself to release her hand.

She smiled and something burst inside him, like a fireworks display. His gaze touched her full lips and then strayed back to her dark eyes, as blue as a night sky on the range. Whatever secrets shimmered there were screened by her black lashes. If his mother had meant to tempt him, she was doing one hell of a fine job.

"Thank you, Joe." Emma's voice was soft, without guile.

"Thank *you*," he echoed, liking the way his name sounded on her lips. "For offering to help out. Once Mom's better, you two can have a nice visit. She has friends on some of the other spreads she'll want you to meet, too."

Emma's hand still tingled from its contact with his. "Of course I'll help out," she said. "I wouldn't expect to stay until the middle of the summer and not do whatever I could."

She watched, dismayed, at the shock that froze Joe's face, then at his belated attempt to hide it.

"The middle of the summer?" he stammered.

It was her turn to look uncomfortable. Clearly, he didn't want her here. But why? Did he think she was after *him?* The thought almost struck her dumb. Then she grasped wildly for some way to get the idea across to him that she wasn't interested—without humiliating herself if she was wrong.

"Your mother insisted that I stay that long," she said with a helpless shrug. "I thought you knew."

"Actually, no." He clapped his hat on his head. "But that's, uh, fine. I've gotta be going now."

"Wait." Emma wasn't sure what to say next but she was determined to set him straight. "I just went through a rather painful divorce," she blurted.

His eyes narrowed, but he didn't move. "I'm sorry."

She searched her mind for the right words. "It's going to be a long time before I want to try that again." She forced a false breeziness into her tone as she took a cup and began looking through the cupboards for a tea bag.

"There's coffee on the stove," Joe said.

"Thanks, but I really prefer tea if you have any." Emma smiled at his grimace of distaste. He probably lived on coffee. "Marian was kind enough to invite me to stay here while I figure out what I want to do next," she continued, taking a tea bag out of the brightly painted tin Joe handed her. His expression had turned to one of polite curiosity.

"I used to teach school." She filled the kettle from the tap. "I might go back to that, but I'm not sure."

Thoughts of children still brought with them a flood of painful emotions.

"What I really want, though, is to be on my own for a long time," she said, putting the kettle on the stove and turning up the burner. "Five years of marriage was enough to last me for quite a while. I'm really too independent to be tied down." She glanced at him again, expecting to see relief. Instead, scorn edged his expression.

"I see."

"So don't feel that you have to introduce me to any of your friends," she finished hastily, puzzled at his reaction. Had she read him so incorrectly? "Because the last thing I'm looking for is another man."

When she was finished speaking he nodded abruptly and turned away. "I'll keep that in mind."

Emma dragged in a deep breath. She had done her best to reassure him. When Marian had asked what she thought of Joe, Emma had given some vague reply, but the truth was she found him darn attractive. Good thing she wasn't looking for involvement, because Joe's feelings toward her were painfully obvious.

"Wait!" she called out as she heard the back door click open. "What time do you want supper? I'll fix something."

He told her and then left without saying goodbye. Behind her the teakettle began to sing. Now that Emma had tried to defuse any possible concern on Joe's part, what was she to do with her own unasked-for and unwanted attraction toward him?

"Oh, dinner smells wonderful," Marian said late that afternoon when she came downstairs after a nap. "I can hardly wait."

Emma checked the bubbling casserole in the oven. She had found everything she needed in the freezer and pantry. "You must be feeling better if you can smell it," she said with a smile.

Marian had donned a lavender sweatshirt and matching pants in a cozy-looking knit. There was a little more color in her cheeks and she had brushed her gray hair.

"The nap helped," she said, pulling a tissue from her pocket. "Except for my nose, I do feel much better. And I *am* hungry."

Emma assumed a scolding expression as she put the finishing touches on a salad of orange segments and sliced red onion mixed with torn greens. "That's because you only picked at your lunch."

Before Marian could reply, they heard footsteps on the porch and then the sound of the back door opening. Moments later Joe poked his head in, saw his mother and grinned.

The transformation to his hard face made Emma swallow a gasp. Good thing for her peace of mind that he didn't smile more often.

"You look a lot better," he told Marian.

While she replied, Emma quickly turned her back and busied herself at the stove. She told herself she was only saving him the effort of having to speak to her politely in front of his mother.

"Something smells good," he said from directly behind Emma as she lifted the lid on the pan of rice with raisins and peanuts. "I hope you made a lot of food."

Emma felt his warm breath on her cheek. Maybe the idea of starting over hadn't been such a good one.

"There's plenty," she replied.

"Hurry and wash up so we can eat," Marian urged him. "I told Emma she didn't have to cook, but she's fixed some lovely chicken."

"Great," Joe called back as he clumped up the stairs. "I love chicken."

It had been a long, difficult day but he felt better after a quick shower and a change of clothes. Emma had looked so cute with her cheeks flushed from the stove heat that he could have taken a bite out of her. He didn't want to think about that, though, preferring instead to look forward to a good, hot meal and the knowledge that his mother was getting better. When he found himself lingering in front of the mirror, combing his hair carefully, he threw down the comb with a muttered curse and hurried from the room, refusing to dwell on the fact that washing up for supper didn't usually include a shower and clean clothes.

Joe might love chicken, but it was obvious he didn't care for Emma's chicken. She had watched his face when she set the casserole dish of poultry cooked with peaches on the table. His expression had been more confused than ecstatic. The rice and raisins had been next. He'd frowned. When she had set the salad bowls down a little harder than necessary, he and Marian had both looked up, surprised.

Emma had been quiet during the meal, but Marian had kept telling her how good everything was, and asking Joe how he liked it. He'd been polite, but Emma was sure that after a long day on the range a hungry rancher usually ate more than he did.

Finally Joe shoved back his chair and excused himself, carrying his dishes to the counter. He scraped the food left on his plate into the garbage. Then he dug out a loaf of bread, spread peanut butter on several slices and made himself a couple of crude sandwiches.

"I've got paperwork to do," he said, pouring himself another cup of coffee. "Thanks again for dinner."

Before Emma could reply, he was gone.

Marian rose and began clearing the table.

"Sit down," Emma told her. "I can do that."

Marian didn't meet her eye. "You fixed such a nice meal, dear. No one expects you to do the KP, too."

"Joe didn't think it was such a nice meal," Emma said before she could stop herself. She looked at the food that was left over and wanted to chuck it all in the garbage.

Marian began to stack the dirty plates. "He's just used to plainer dishes, I'm afraid. I've been pretty conventional in my cooking since I came back, so I guess part of it's my fault."

"Nonsense," Emma snapped, surprising both of them with her vehemence. "Your son just doesn't like me, or anything I do." Appalled at what she'd said, she glanced hastily at her friend and then began banging the pots and pans around.

Behind her, Marian sat back down at the table. "That's not true!" She sighed. "I'm glad you're here," she said softly. "Give Joe a chance, and he will be, too."

Emma sent her a disbelieving glance before opening the dishwasher and arranging the dirty dishes inside. "Don't set your heart on it."

"Don't take his attitude personally," Marian replied. "He's been a little moody ever since his divorce, but he'll come out of it."

A little moody! Like the Grand Canyon was a little hole in the ground. Emma wondered which of them the other woman was trying to convince. Not that *she* cared what Joe thought.

"I hope you're still planning to stay," Marian continued with a worried frown. "I've been so looking forward to your visit. It gets a little lonely here, with Joe gone most days."

Emma smiled. It was nice to have someone who wanted her company. "Of course I'll stay," she said, making a sudden decision. "But I insist on taking care of the kitchen duties until you're completely better. I can cook meat and potatoes as well as the next person."

Marian chuckled. "I'm sure you can."

"And, as long as I stay, I insist on helping out as much as possible," Emma continued. "I'm sure there's a lot to be done on a ranch like this."

"Well, there is that," Marian concurred. "Sometimes more than I think I can possibly manage, so your help will be greatly appreciated." Her expression sobered. "How are you doing, really?" she asked.

Emma squared her shoulders. "I'm doing fine. For all intents and purposes, my marriage was over two years ago. The divorce was more a relief than anything else." She blinked back tears of regret for all that might have been. "Thanks for asking, though."

Marian's smile was gentle. "You'll be fine, I know. You're a strong girl."

"I hope so."

It was time to change the subject. "Do you know how to ride?" Marian asked.

"I love horses," Emma replied. "I rode a couple times as a kid, but it's been a long time."

Marian's eyes gleamed and a shiver of warning slipped down Emma's spine. She knew that one more thing needed saying. Uncomfortably, she forged ahead.

"And don't worry about Joe and me not getting along," she said. "We probably won't see that much of each other anyway."

Marian's expression became more thoughtful. "I'm sure you're right," she agreed mildly.

"So, what's the lady who's visiting your mother like?" Daniel asked Joe as the two of them repaired a section of fence.

Joe bit back an ironic laugh. "Nice enough, I guess. Younger than I expected."

Daniel straightened. He had known Joe's wife, had been working at the ranch when she lit out for Denver. "How young?" he asked.

Joe glanced at his foreman, then began to study the horizon as if he found it fascinating.

"Young enough. Maybe you'd better come up to the house for dinner one night. She's quite a cook—a little fancy for my taste, though. But she's easy on the eyes." If Daniel and Emma showed any interest in each other, perhaps Joe's mother would back off.

The foreman held up a detaining hand, dark eyes narrowed in his sun-bronzed face. "No, thanks, boss. If you're after some guy to entertain your house guest, you'll have to keep looking."

Joe hid his grin. At least he had successfully distracted the other man. Joe knew that Daniel's life was almost as empty of female companionship as his own, but he wasn't sure why. Daniel was a handsome man, with black hair and dark skin. It was easy to see he had Indian blood in him, but even though they had worked together for years Joe realized he didn't know much about Daniel's background.

Well, a man was entitled to his secrets. Lord knew, Joe certainly had his.

Emma set the huge pot on the table with a defiant thud and removed the lid. Inside was a steaming, savory beef roast that swam in its own juices. She didn't look at Joe to see his reaction as she returned with dishes of mashed potatoes, cooked carrots and biscuits. If this didn't meet his idea of a traditional meal, he could send out for pizza for all she cared.

After they had all three served themselves, Emma toyed with her mashed potatoes as she waited for his comment. He'd loaded his plate. After a couple of cautious bites he was dispatching the food efficiency.

"Did you put the mail on my desk?" he asked Marian between mouthfuls.

"Yes, dear," she replied as he washed down a biscuit with a swallow of milk. "I didn't see anything from the feed lot in Greeley, though."

Joe frowned. "Okay, maybe tomorrow." He returned his attention to his plate.

Disgusted, Emma buttered a biscuit and took a bite. It was light and flaky. Did Joe realize she'd made them from scratch or did he assume she had popped them from a can? Was he even aware of what he was eating or was his mind on his cows? Stubbornly she bit back the questions that danced on her tongue, telling herself she had no interest in his opinion of the meal, anyway.

After complimenting Emma on the dinner and thanking her again for fixing it, Marian turned her attention back to her son. "I don't think I should go outside for another day or so," she told him. "Just until I'm entirely over this cold."

His gaze lifted for a moment as he cut a piece of meat. "I agree."

Something in Marian's smile set off alarm bells in Emma's mind. What was the older woman up to now?

"I thought you'd want me to stay in until I'm better," she continued. "While I'm trapped inside, would you take a little time to show Emma the ranch? She hasn't seen anything but the inside of the house since she arrived."

Emma tried to swallow her mouthful of carrots so she could make some excuse not to go with him. Instead, she began to choke.

Instantly Marian handed her a glass of water.

"Are you okay, dear?" she asked, concerned, when Emma had taken a sip and finally stopped coughing.

Emma nodded, embarrassed by the tears rolling down her cheeks. "It just went down the wrong way," she croaked, wishing she was close enough to kick Marian under the table for asking Joe to take more time away from his work. The way Marian had put her request sounded as if Emma was already getting bored and needed to be entertained. It was the last thing she wanted!

Before she could speak again, Joe cleared his throat and looked directly at her. "How does tomorrow after lunch suit you?"

Emma gaped at him for a moment until she realized he was waiting for her answer.

"Uh, tomorrow afternoon would be fine," she stuttered. "If you really can spare the time."

His nod was brusque as he helped himself to more roast beef. "I'll make the time." Then he glanced at her again, fork poised. "Dinner's good."

Emma was still smiling when Joe had excused himself to work in his office and Marian had gone back upstairs for a sweater. Joe had eaten two big helpings of everything. It was useless to tell herself she wasn't pleased. At least now he knew she could cook.

As she put leftovers away, loaded the dishwasher and wiped off the counters, Emma refused to think about why that gratified her. Or why she was so looking forward to the next afternoon.

"It's beautiful out here," Emma said as she studied with pleasure the luxurious green of the rolling pasture that spread like a shaggy carpet toward the west and a line of trees that Joe had told her were aspens and conifers. Pioneers had crossed these plains well over a hundred years before, their eyes on the same mountains she was looking at now.

Emma took a deep breath. Even the air was sweet and unspoiled.

After showing her the barns and the bunkhouse, Joe had driven his truck along the fence line, pointing out some of his cattle in the distance. They had stopped and gotten out as a magpie flew overhead.

Now Emma breathed in more of the pure air and tried to relax. She was still uncomfortable that Marian had asked him to show her the ranch, but she was doing her best not to react to his presence next to her, tall and masculine in his Stetson and boots.

Joe pointed off to the left as Emma shielded her eyes. "More of the herd's out there," he said. "The horses we raise are in closer, off the other way. We can go see them, if you'd like."

Emma smiled. "I'd love to."

Back in the truck she tried to draw herself unobtrusively toward the passenger door while she chattered lightly about the ranch and what he had shown her. Joe remained silent as he drove slowly over the road that was no more than two worn ruts in the grass.

"You must wish you were out with your men," Emma blurted. "Instead of playing tour guide when you have so much work. I'm sorry that Marian suggested this."

To her surprise, Joe stopped the truck in the middle of the crude road and turned to look at her.

"Why do you say that?" His voice was deep, his arm resting on the wheel as his gaze held her fast.

Around them the silence, except for the cry of a bird, was absolute. Emma swallowed. She hadn't expected him to question her comment. She looked out the windshield, searching for inspiration. None came. She looked back at Joe. Abruptly he smiled. Her heart slammed against her chest.

"We're starting over," he said. "Remember? Why would I rather be around a bunch of scroungy cowhands and stubborn cattle instead of a beautiful woman?" His thick brows lifted. "Do I look that stupid?"

Emma was vaguely aware that he was trying to dispel the awkwardness that had wedged itself solidly between them from the time they'd first set out in the truck.

"Do you think I'm beautiful?" The words left her mouth without her permission as she stared into his compelling face.

Something in Joe's eyes darkened. His easy smile faded. He turned and shoved the truck into gear before he answered.

"A woman like you doesn't need to ask for compliments," he said in a cool voice. "Let's go look at the horses."

Emma didn't begin to relax until they got out of the truck again. Joe's abrupt mood changes were annoying as well as confusing.

"These are some of the horses we breed," he said, as he hooked one foot on the lower rung of a split rail fence.

They'd driven back in the direction of the ranch house and stopped beside a pasture containing a half-dozen mares. Each had a foal at her side.

"Oh, they're wonderful," Emma exclaimed, almost forgetting about the maddening man next to her. The horses before her were a colorful collection—black- or brown-and-white pintos, as well as one mare that was pure white. Several of them came toward the fence, obviously curious.

Emma froze as Joe grabbed her hand. Reaction sizzled through her like an electric charge as she turned to face him. Then she realized he was trying to give her something.

"Feed the mares some of these," he said as she gazed down at the chunks of carrot he had placed in her palm. He was holding a plastic bag she hadn't noticed before. "I always bring some along with me. They expect it. Just hold each piece out on the palm of your hand."

When Emma looked their way again, the horses had crowded closer. One youngster whose face was half black and half white, his mane striped, poked his head through the fence and boldly nibbled at her clothing. Laughing in delight, Emma tried to touch him but he skittered away.

"That's Jester," Joe said. "His momma was a champion barrel racer before my sister retired her."

"How's Ashley doing?" Emma asked. She knew that the girl was actually Joe's younger half sister, from Marian's second marriage. She had been a serious competitor for several years now, traveling the rodeo circuit.

He shrugged. "She's doing well, but she doesn't visit often enough. I know that Mom misses her."

"Is she still single?" Emma asked as she held out a piece of carrot the way Joe had told her. One of the mares lipped it delicately from her outstretched hand.

Joe scratched the horse's forehead as she chewed the treat. "Oh, yeah. Ashley's got an apartment in San Antonio but

I doubt she'll ever really settle down until she's too old to compete.''

Her life sounded empty to Emma. She wanted to ask Joe if he ever felt like traveling or if he was happy to stay at the ranch. Instead, she held out another piece of carrot. A spotted colt sniffed at it curiously, his breath tickling her hand, but he pulled back when she moved. Another mare took his place.

Emma fed the rest of the horses that vied for her attention, talking softly to them all as she admired their big dark eyes and silky coats. When she was finished, the plastic bag empty, she rubbed velvety noses and warm necks as the tame animals searched for more treats.

"They're all so gorgeous," she exclaimed, patting a foal that moved closer. "And the young ones are adorable."

Leaning against the fence, Joe watched her with his ladies, as he called the mares. It was clear that Emma loved animals. She had a real way with the normally skittish colts.

"We breed them for color, among other things," he said. "People buy them for the rodeo or for flashy pleasure mounts." The white mare, one of his favorites, hung her head over the fence and butted his chest, as if to scold him for not bringing more carrots.

Emma's laughter at his involuntary step backward was like the sound from a music box. "I see they have a lot of respect for the boss," she teased.

Joe found himself returning her dazzling smile. For a moment, at least, the constant tension between them seemed to have disappeared.

"Do you ride?" he asked.

"Not very well," she replied. "But I'd love to learn more."

Her comment hung between them until the silence grew awkward.

"Maybe I can have one of the hands teach you," Joe finally muttered, wishing he'd never brought up the subject. What was wrong with him, anyway? One glance from her jewel-like eyes and his common sense fled.

Tired of being ignored, the horses began wandering back to their grazing. Instead of taking Joe up on his less-than-enthusiastic offer, Emma stepped back and jammed her thumbs into the tooled leather belt she wore with slim jeans and a long-sleeved plaid shirt.

"I've been trying to figure something out," she said, head thrown back. "Perhaps you'd be kind enough to enlighten me."

Joe braced himself, instinct telling him her question wasn't going to be an easy one to answer.

"Shoot," he said, feeling as tense as if she were aiming something more lethal than mere words in his direction.

"Just tell me flat out," Emma demanded. "What have I done to make you dislike me so much?"

Chapter Three

Emma watched a string of emotions flicker too rapidly for her to identify across Joe's face. Then a shutter slammed down, masking his feelings, and she knew he wasn't going to answer her question. Wasn't going to say why he disliked her.

"I'm sorry you've gotten that impression," he told Emma without meeting her gaze. He swept his hat off with one hand and raked the other through his brown hair before setting the Stetson back in place and tugging down the brim. "I get preoccupied with ranch business, and I guess I'm not as friendly as I could be."

No, he wasn't going to tell her, and she didn't feel like standing around while he did his best to snow her with trite phrases instead. She shifted impatiently and glanced at the pickup. What had she expected to find out when she'd voiced the blunt question? Joe might be distant, even inapproachable, but she'd seen no evidence that he would be deliberately cruel.

"I'll have to try harder," he said after a pause while they watched two of the spotted foals scamper after each other.

"Of course." Emma turned toward the truck, only to stop again when Joe's hand closed abruptly on her arm. His expression was so markedly earnest that it put her on her guard.

"Believe me," he said softly, "you haven't done anything wrong." His gaze flickered and Emma's mouth warmed as if he'd pressed his lips to hers. "Don't pay any attention to me, okay? Just enjoy your visit." For another moment his eyes bored into her, and then he let her go. Before Emma could word a reply, he'd opened the door of the truck and stepped back, waiting for her to get in.

Her ascent was easier in jeans than it had been in the short skirt. She didn't need Joe's assistance, but he gave it, anyway, cupping her elbow with his hand to boost her up. Part of Emma took delight in the heat that radiated from him like some kind of dark force. The other, more sensible side of her wanted to grab the next bus back to Denver.

When they pulled up in front of the house Joe made an excuse about an errand in the horse barn and drummed his fingers on the steering wheel, waiting for Emma to get out.

"Thanks for the tour," she told him in her most polite tone as she held the door open. "I enjoyed everything, especially seeing the horses."

Joe nodded without speaking, a ghost of a smile softening his mouth but leaving the chill in his eyes intact.

"Well," she said, "I'd better not keep you any longer. See you at dinner."

Again he surprised her. "I'm looking forward to it."

By the time Emma had gone into the house and crossed the kitchen she had convinced herself that he could only be referring to the food itself.

"How was your afternoon?" Marian called from the living room where she sat with a book. A Strauss waltz was playing on the radio. Emma was amazed. She'd thought the airwaves of Colorado carried only country music.

She stopped in front of the couch. "Can I get you anything?" She was glad to see that Joe's mother didn't sound as congested as she had over lunch. She looked better, too.

"Oh, no, dear. I'm fine. But I'd love to hear what you thought of the ranch. It's Joe's pride and joy, you know. His father was always so pleased that Joe wanted to carry on here in his footsteps. I like to think that made it easier for Barnett in the end, knowing how Joe felt."

Marian's first husband had died of pneumonia and its complications after being stranded in a freak snowstorm. His foresight in taking out a generous life insurance policy on himself had enabled Marian to keep the ranch going with hired help while Joe attended college. Emma wondered how much his father's early death had affected Joe's quiet, even taciturn personality, but she didn't ask. Instead she told Marian about the foals Joe had shown her.

After she had excused herself to start dinner, she returned to describe to Marian in glowing terms the rest of what she'd seen.

"There's so much more for you to look at," Marian said, eyes sparkling. "I'm sure that Joe will—"

"Please," Emma interrupted, "don't ask Joe to take me out again. He's been very nice, but I know he's really too busy to show me around."

"Nonsense," Marian told her with a dismissive gesture. "I know he loves to work alongside the men, but he's said before that the ranch could practically run itself without him. He's got a good crew working for him, and Daniel Sixkiller is the best foreman around. Joe can easily spare the time for you."

Emma hesitated, not sure what to say. She had to get Marian to stop throwing the two of them together, had to convince her that nothing was going to work if her aim was to spark an interest between them. Nothing short of a love potion for Joe, anyway.

Emma almost grinned at the mental image of her pinching his nose while Marian poured a vile concoction down his throat.

"Joe and I don't get on that well," Emma began. "I know that he's your son and he's a fine man, but—"

It was Marian's turn to interrupt. "I'm glad you think Joe's a fine man. He has many admirable qualities. But he's been alone for too long, nursing old hurts. He needs the right woman to bring him out of his shell."

For a moment Emma was tempted almost beyond bearing. The idea of being the woman to bring warmth to Joe's cold eyes, to bring a smile to his hard mouth was heady indeed. And she knew that thinking it was somehow possible for her to do so was dangerous to her barely healed heart.

Joe wasn't the only one with old hurts. She'd already lost as much as she could stand to lose. And she was surviving. Healing. But a deeply rooted, self-protective instinct told her she might not survive loving and losing a man like Joe. It was important she remember that.

Marian frowned worriedly. "Unless you aren't over your former husband yet," she said, a question in her voice.

Emma sat beside Marian and took the worn hand in her own. "I've been over him for a long time," she said gently. "But I'm not the right woman for your son."

Marian looked unconvinced.

"I'd hate for you to think I was and end up disappointed," Emma continued. "Better you forget about any more matchmaking, okay?" She smiled to soften her words. After a moment Marian smiled back sheepishly.

"I guess I was pretty obvious, huh?" She gave her gray head an unremorseful toss. "I hope that I haven't embarrassed you."

Emma got to her feet. She wanted to check on dinner, another haunch of meat she thought Joe's untutored palate would appreciate.

"No, of course you haven't embarrassed me." She laughed lightly. "Joe's a nice man, don't get me wrong. But he and I really don't have much in common." She thought for a moment, trying to conjure up a fantasy man who was the total opposite to Marian's son. "I'm afraid it would take more of a city type to catch my interest," she said, hoping to discourage her friend's meddling without hurting her feelings. "Perhaps a business tycoon. A man who wears a custom-tailored suit like a second skin. One whose idea of a challenge is a hostile takeover. A civilized man who *appreciates* chicken cooked with peaches."

Marian sighed, smiling. "I see."

Emma began to warm to her fantasy. "I'd like a man with polished edges," she continued. "A man who spends his time with computer printouts and stock market ticker tapes, not livestock." If she laid it on thick enough, perhaps Marian really would give up.

"I guess you aren't into square dancing and weekend rodeos," the older woman guessed.

Emma pretended to ponder the question. "I don't think so." In truth, both activities sounded like fun. She stuck her nose in the air and said in her haughtiest tone, "I'm afraid that tennis at the club and a dip in the heated pool after is more to my taste."

Marian chuckled.

Emma's saucy grin was unrepentant. "My dream date would have to be a city boy with styled hair and a sports car, one who wears his power like a good cologne, not a man who drives a pickup, reads the cattle breeders' weekly and smells of—''

"Cow manure?"

At the sound of Joe's deep voice, Emma spun toward the kitchen doorway. His face was an expressionless mask. Dismay wiped away her own playful smile. How much had he heard? Too much—that was obvious.

Mortification flooded Emma as she tried to remember her exact words. She hated hurting anyone or anything. And she was afraid her thoughtless prattle had hurt Joe's feelings, despite the denial of his carefully blank stare. She glanced back at Marian, whose expression was a mixture of lingering amusement, dawning regret and unhappy sympathy.

There was nothing Emma could say to Joe. No explanation she could make that would wipe out the sting of her careless words. Humiliated, afraid she was going to make the situation infinitely worse by bursting into tears, she rushed past him to the stairs and the sanctuary of her room. She'd taken no more than half a dozen steps when she heard the slam of the back door.

In the living room Marian sat back down, picked up her book and smiled to herself. Joe was a man, after all, and what man could ignore a challenge like the one Emma had just unwittingly given him? Marian was greatly encouraged.

As soon as she was sure that Joe hadn't lingered, Emma went out and worked off some of her tension by watering Marian's large vegetable garden. She'd offered to help with the weeding and cultivating, too, and Marian had accepted gladly.

"I love to garden," she had confided to Emma. "But I like flowers, things that bloom, and I don't mean pea vines. Much as I understand the need to grow and put up our own vegetables, I'm afraid I can't work up much enthusiasm for hoeing carrots and hills of potatoes.''

There wasn't much time today for Emma to do more than water the parched garden before she had to stop to finish cooking dinner. She was fixing scalloped potatoes and peas to go with the ham she'd started earlier.

The next day she planned to attack the weeds. She enjoyed gardening, liked working in the fresh earth and watching green things grow. There had never been much time for it while she was working. Besides, she and her ex-husband had lived in an apartment until partway through her pregnancy. By the time they'd bought a house she'd lost interest in the flower beds.

Emma knew that Marian was almost ready to take back control of her kitchen. Unless Joe came through with riding lessons, which Emma doubted, she would have nothing but time on her hands for the next several weeks. Plenty of time to devote to the vegetables.

Dinner that evening promised to be an awkward affair. Joe had come in and greeted both women, then headed for the stairs to wash up. Emma dished up the food, alert for the sound of his returning footsteps. When she heard his familiar tread she glanced at Marian, who seemed preoccupied with setting the table. Emma slipped quietly from the room, letting the door swing shut behind her.

She almost ran into Joe in the hallway. The scent of some outdoorsy after-shave reminded her painfully of her earlier words as he stepped aside, no doubt assuming she wanted something from the second floor. When he would have gone around her and continued into the kitchen, she held a detaining hand to his hard chest.

"Wait a minute, will you?" she pleaded softly, aware of his mother on the other side of the door.

Joe's dark brows rose and he looked pointedly at her hand splayed against his shirt. Emma snatched it back as if she'd been singed.

"What do you want?" he asked as she moved past him down the hall, motioning for him to follow. His voice was gravelly. "Did you burn dinner?"

She glanced back to see if he was kidding. He wasn't.

"I need to talk to you."

He followed her as she led the way into the living room. "What about?"

Emma gripped her hands together hard. "About what you overheard earlier."

Joe waited silently for Emma to continue, wondering what she had to say. His chest still tingled from where she'd touched him so unexpectedly. What was she playing at now? Advance and retreat? Cat and mouse, with him as the unsuspecting rodent? He'd heard what she had said about the kind of man she liked. It hadn't really surprised him. His reaction, the sharp burst of disappointment, had. So what was she after now?

"I wanted to explain," she said, worrying her full lower lip with her teeth as her eyes searched his.

For a moment Joe felt as if he was going under, sinking beneath the surface without a struggle. Then he remembered who she was. Who *he* was. And *what* he was. He frowned.

"I didn't mean anything by what I said," she continued. "I didn't want you to think I did."

Joe nodded impatiently. He knew he had been a fool to let her teasing words get to him. She had meant nothing personal. The sudden ache he'd felt had been quickly replaced by a flare of anger. A fury at the injustice life sometimes dealt out. Then he'd stalked back outside, needing to get away. Not thinking how his retreat might have looked to her.

"Don't worry about it," he said now. "What you want in a man has nothing to do with me."

Her cheeks bloomed with color, increasing her attractiveness. "Of course not. I didn't mean to imply that it did. I told you before that I'm not looking for a man, any man."

He rubbed his sideburn with one finger while he contemplated the look of concern in her face.

"But a rich man—a successful man—might make you change your mind?" he guessed, perversely pleased when her concerned expression turned to a glower.

"No, I didn't mean that at all." She let out an exasperated sigh. "Oh, forget it. I just didn't want you to think..." Her chin jutted out in a gesture that was already becoming familiar to him. It made him want to bait her further, to see if he could make her eyes flash.

"That you're not immune to me?" he finished for her.

"Of course I'm immune to you," she snapped. "As you're so obviously immune to me. So I guess we're even." She started to step around him. "We'd better go. The food will be getting cold."

Joe ignored her words. To hell with dinner. His appetite for food had fled. Instead, some devil urged him to do something totally out of character. He grabbed her arms and hauled her against him. Hard.

"And are you?" he muttered in a voice that revealed nothing of the feelings that churned inside him.

Emma peered into his face, her body flush with his. "Am I what?" she squeaked.

He lowered his head until his mouth was almost touching hers. Until he could see the violet rings around her dark blue eyes. And each individual curling eyelash. "Are you really immune to me?"

He could feel her quickened breath on his lips, could smell her scent, could feel her body begin to mold itself against his. He pulled her closer, and she stiffened. Then she began to struggle. Instantly he let her go. So abruptly that she almost stumbled. He put his hand back out to steady her, and she flinched away.

"Just forget the whole thing," she said through gritted teeth. "Obviously, your ego is much too strong for me to waste any concern about denting it."

She stalked away, slamming back the kitchen door as Joe stared after her. He almost laughed out loud at her parting shot. Instead, he trailed her out to the kitchen.

As he pushed open the door his smile faded. It had been a mistake to hold her like that. A mistake his body was already making him regret with a fierce ache. But if he didn't go through a pretense of eating, his mother's suspicions would flourish. He already had enough to deal with. Besides, now he was the one who owed Emma an apology, and he didn't like it one bit.

The three of them had been eating for a few minutes when Emma surprised Joe by asking Marian if she could take the car to town the next day.

"We need a few groceries," she explained without looking at Joe. She had done her best to ignore him through most of the meal, even though his appetite had returned with the aroma of the food, and he had complimented her on everything more than once. "I thought I'd do a couple of personal errands while I was there, too."

Marian glanced at Joe before answering. "It's not that I mind you taking the car," she said hesitantly. "I just don't want you getting lost. This isn't Seattle, you know, with a market down the street."

Emma swallowed the protest she'd been about to make. Marian was just concerned for her, she knew. But, with directions, she was confident she could find her way to Caulder Springs, the nearest town, without any trouble.

"I have to go to the co-op tomorrow," Joe said. "I can pick up whatever you need at the store."

Emma thought of the feminine products she hadn't remembered to bring with her. No way was she going to ask him to pick them up.

"Maybe I could follow you," she said brightly. "Then I wouldn't hold you up."

Joe's expression was resigned. "I guess you'd better ride in with me," he said, pushing the peas around on his plate. "No point in taking two vehicles when one will do."

Emma was determined not to keep him waiting for her. She was up early, dressed in jeans and a cotton sweater in a blue-and-white print. While she was eating a quick breakfast of cold cereal and sliced banana with her tea, Joe walked into the kitchen.

"I'm almost ready," Emma said, sliding back her chair.

"Whoa, there." He gestured for her to stay put. "Finish your breakfast. I'd like another cup of coffee before we head out."

Emma returned her attention to her cereal, not sure what to say. Since yesterday, when he'd pulled her close and she had thought he was going to kiss her, she hadn't been able to relax around him. His action had surprised her, but she hadn't been repulsed by it. Quite the contrary—she had wanted his kiss. Had wanted to discover what he would feel and taste like. And the thing that bothered her most was not knowing if any of that sharp yearning had shown in her face.

Had Joe guessed what she was feeling? Was that why he'd stopped, pushing her away so abruptly? Or had she read him wrong altogether? Maybe kissing her had been the farthest thing from his mind. Maybe he'd just wanted to prove a point. And he had. Proved that the smartest thing for Emma to do would be to stay away from him.

So why was she looking forward to riding into town with him this morning?

No common sense, she decided as she finished her tea. Joe hadn't sat at the table, preferring to drink his coffee standing with one hip braced against the counter. He hadn't removed his hat, and she was reminded of the first time she'd seen him at the bus terminal, with the expression in his eyes shielded from her view.

Maybe it was best she didn't know how he felt about taking her with him today.

"Well, I tried to keep out of your way," she blurted when the silence between them began to drag. She rose and carried her dishes to the counter. Joe straightened when she reached to open the dishwasher, setting his mug on the rack next to hers. At least he didn't seem to expect her to pick up after him, as some men would.

She grabbed her purse and looked up. "I'm ready if you are," she said.

"Go on outside," he replied. "It's a pretty morning. I'll say goodbye to Mom and be right with you."

His voice stopped her again as she crossed the mudroom and reached for the knob to the back door.

"But don't think you're getting away without explaining that last remark." Before she could react, he'd left the kitchen.

"So," he said when he'd climbed into the cab beside her, "what did you mean about keeping out of my way? If it had anything to do with our confrontation last night, I want you to know that I'm sorry it happened."

His apology surprised her. She wanted to ask him what exactly he was sorry for. That he'd grabbed her? That he hadn't followed through and kissed her? She turned and looked out the side window of the truck, not sure what to say. Joe touched her arm and she jumped, startled.

He put his hand back on the wheel. "Are you nervous around me?" he asked in a challenging voice. "If I scared you, I didn't mean to."

Emma continued to stare at the passing scenery, not sure how to reply.

"Emma!" His voice was like the crack of a whip. She wrenched her head around. He glared at her before returning his attention to the road. "Don't worry about anything like that happening again," he continued in a softer voice. "I promise I won't touch you unless you want me to."

Her eyes widened at his words. He must have seen the longing in her eyes when he had held her. Now she would find out if people really could die of embarrassment.

Joe's sigh was heavy with exasperation. "Emma, say something. Please."

She continued to look at him as she licked her lips nervously. "You didn't have to apologize," she murmured finally. "You didn't scare me. And I guess I provoked you."

He glanced at her again, his eyes unreadable. "Shall we declare a truce?" he asked.

"We always seem to be getting off on the wrong foot with each other." She turned away.

"Don't you know why that is?" he questioned.

She shook her head without looking at him. "No."

His chuckle was wry. "Sure you do. Just think about it for a while and you'll come up with the answer. Meanwhile, tell me what you need to get in town."

Emma was grateful for the change of subject. "I have a list of groceries," she said. "And I need a few things myself. Is there a drugstore in Caulder Springs?"

"Sure," Joe said. "Maybe you could pick out a couple of those historical novels Mom likes so much, and a bag of

M&M's for me. I'm almost out. Just put everything on the ranch account.''

"I have money," Emma protested.

His eyes crinkled and his mouth relaxed for a moment. "I'm sure you do. But, unless you're buying out the place, I think I can manage the bill this time. You've been a big help since you got here, after all."

Glowing from his praise, Emma began to argue further. One glance at his expression stopped her. He looked immovable.

"Thank you," she said instead. Moments later they pulled up in front of a feed store with faded paint and peeling letters over the door. Emma noticed several other pickup trucks parked in the lot.

"You can stay here or come in with me," Joe said. "I'll be a few minutes loading stuff up."

Emma scrambled out her side of the truck without answering. And without waiting for his help. The sun's warmth was getting serious and she wished she had worn a short-sleeved shirt instead of the sweater. Meanwhile, she didn't want to sit in the cab and roast if she didn't have to.

She followed Joe up the wooden steps and into the high-ceilinged wooden building. The older man behind the counter greeted him like a long-lost friend and then glanced curiously at Emma. She smiled and he gave her a ready grin, revealing several broken teeth.

"Who you got with you, Joe?" he asked with a gleam in his eyes behind wire-framed glasses. "I've never known you to allow your social life to spill over into the middle of the workday before."

If the man's assumption that Emma was a girlfriend bothered Joe, he didn't show it.

"Emma, I'd like you to meet Red McCoy," he said easily. "Red was a rodeo clown before he had to quit. Landed on his head too much. Scrambled what little brains he had."

Red guffawed and slapped the counter. "That ain't true, Joe."

"He's still got a line a mile long, so watch yourself around him," Joe continued.

"Now, is that any way to be?" Red protested, his faded blue eyes darting between Emma and Joe. "I'd never poach on someone else's territory."

Emma flushed at his words and didn't dare look at Joe.

"This is Emma Davenport, from Seattle," he said calmly. "She's visiting my mother."

Red stretched out his hand and Emma shook it. Before either of them could say anything more, two men came in the front door. They were dressed like Joe, in work clothes, boots and cowboy hats. While Joe greeted them and introduced Emma, another man who obviously knew him walked up from the back of the store. After Joe introduced him as a neighboring rancher, he explained yet again that Emma was a friend of his mother's. This latest arrival, a calendar-handsome hunk named Cal Banning, kept her hand trapped in his.

"In that case," he said with a warm smile, "perhaps I could call you sometime. I'd like to take you out to dinner."

Emma didn't know what to say, with Joe standing over her like a protective maiden aunt. She glanced at his expressionless face and then back at Cal. What better way to show Joe she had no personal interest in him?

"That might be nice," she told Cal.

He squeezed her hand more tightly and then let it go. "Good," he said, cutting a triumphant glance at Joe. Then Cal touched his hat politely. "I'll look forward to it."

Emma managed another smile, already regretting her impulse. Had Cal hoped somehow to get at Joe?

"Me, too," she said. With a last smile, Cal said something to Red about coming back when his order was in and left. He seemed nice enough, but the last thing she needed was to start seeing anyone here in Colorado. Besides, Cal's touch had done nothing to her pulse rate—while being in the same room as Joe made it skip like a flat stone across smooth water.

Red began helping the other two men and, for a moment, Emma and Joe might as well have been alone.

"I've got some supplies to pick up," he said shortly. "Amuse yourself while I get them, but don't wander off. I don't want to waste time looking for you."

Emma ground her teeth furiously as he turned his back and moved down a narrow aisle. He'd made it sound as if she were a little child who couldn't be trusted not to get lost.

Emma glanced around. Amuse herself with what? All she saw were rows of feed sacks, cardboard boxes, bottles of veterinary supplies, work clothing and other items she couldn't begin to identify. Then a row of gleaming saddles caught her attention and she forgot all about Cal and Joe as she went to look more closely at the beautiful leatherwork.

Three aisles over, Joe was fighting unexpected pangs of jealousy at the way Cal Banning had casually expressed his interest in Emma. Joe knew that Cal, married and divorced at least twice, had a reputation for success with the ladies. Joe thought about warning Emma, and then clamped his teeth together. He couldn't say anything, not without giving her the wrong impression. Or was it the right impression? If things had been different, would Joe be the one to ask Emma out, to take her to dinner? To hold her close afterward? An image of Cal kissing her was enough to send his blood pressure soaring.

Emma's voice floated over to him, and he looked up to see her by the show tack, talking to Red. The old man looked as smitten as Cal had been. Joe clenched his fists until his knuckles turned white. He had to face facts. If Emma ever found out the truth about Joe even Red would have a better chance with her. And Joe would do well not to forget it.

Chapter Four

The first night that Marian cooked, Emma insisted on cleaning up the kitchen afterward. By the time she finished, Marian was engrossed in a program on television. Joe had disappeared right after a roast chicken dinner that Emma could freely admit was delicious.

"Come and sit down," Marian invited when Emma poked her head into the living room. She could see that the program had already started and knew it was one of Marian's favorites.

"Thanks, but I think I'll go upstairs and get my book instead," she said. "I'm right at the good part."

Marian smiled with understanding as she returned her attention to the screen.

Emma ascended the staircase and went down the hall. The door to Joe's room stood open and she wondered where he'd gone. Not back outside, of that she was sure. Then she saw light coming from the partly closed door to his office. He was probably working on the ranch account books, an activity that seemed to take up a lot of his evening time.

She was walking by quietly when she heard a groan of disgust, followed by a string of mild curses and the thud of something hitting the wall. Emma hesitated, and then knocked softly on the door.

"Come in." Joe's voice sounded less than welcoming.

Emma pushed the door open. "Something wrong?" she asked hesitantly. He probably wouldn't appreciate the interruption, especially from her, but a fresh cup of coffee might help his mood.

Emma hadn't been in his office before. It was cluttered without looking messy. Joe was sitting at a massive wooden desk, his big body sprawled in an executive chair with padded leather arms and a swivel base. He made the room look cramped. Surrounding him were floor-to-ceiling bookshelves and several file cabinets. One paneled wall was covered with framed pictures and photographs. In front of him on the desk a computer hummed softly, the amber glow of its monitor lighting his face. Next to it was a bowl of M&M's. On the floor was a software manual. From the way it was lying open, Emma guessed it was responsible for the thud she had heard.

Joe punched a couple of keys and glanced at the monitor before turning back to Emma.

"You don't know anything about computers, do you?" he asked. "I've been fighting with this one for an hour and I think it's winning." His thick brows were bunched into a frown above his gray eyes, the usual storm in them temporarily subdued. His hair looked as if he'd been running his hand through it, the brown strands sticking out in several places.

Emma's first instinct was to go over and smooth his tousled hair. Her second was to stand her ground, one hand gripping the doorknob tightly. Even sprawled in the chair as he was now, Joe reminded her of a powerful predator, unmoving but hardly relaxed. Ready to spring at the slightest provocation.

"As a matter of fact, I do know a little about computers," she confessed. "What software program are you using?"

Joe told her. It was the same one she had used to keep their financial records when she and Bob had been married. She had even taken a class to learn it. No doubt the program had been updated since then, but it was probably still basically familiar to her. She crossed the room and looked down at the screen.

"What's the trouble?" she asked. "I know this program pretty well."

Joe straightened in his chair, leather creaking. A grin curved his mouth.

"That so?" he asked, eyes narrowed. "Well, well. Pull up a chair, teach." He pointed to a steno chair on wheels in the corner. "Sounds like you're just the person I need."

"If I had known how time-consuming this would be, I never would have begun putting my records on computer," he grumbled at one point as he munched a couple of candies. "The salesman who sold me this system told me a chimpanzee could run it."

Obviously realizing what he'd just admitted, he turned and met Emma's startled gaze. His expression was sheepish, and it was all she could do to contain her laughter.

"Maybe I should hire a chimp," he said with a self-deprecating grin.

Emma knew she was on dangerous ground and should think carefully before she plunged ahead. Tossing away caution, she smiled and asked, "Would I do, instead?"

Joe's eyes darkened with interest. "Would you be willing to help me get this started?" he asked. "I think I could run the thing once I got the hang of it."

Emma leaned back in her chair and studied him carefully. What was she getting herself into? Joe's gaze slid back to the screen and she was grateful that he couldn't read her mind.

"Am I asking too much?" he questioned without looking her way. "I know you came to visit Mom, and you've already helped out more than I expected."

She bit back a heated reply to his last comment. He probably didn't deserve her help, after he'd made it so clear that what he *expected* was for her to be a useless parasite. Not once had he actually admitted how wrong he'd been. She considered carefully while he studied the monitor and punched in a couple of numbers. The screen went blank except for a flashing message.

Fatal error.

Joe threw up his hands and glanced helplessly at Emma, who couldn't suppress her grin. She'd thought of something she wanted from him, something worth bargaining for.

"I could help you," she said slowly as she nibbled on an M&M, "but my services don't come cheap." Her instinct for self-preservation was screaming inside her head, but she ignored it.

Joe's face darkened with embarrassment. "Of course I'll pay you for your time. I didn't expect—"

Emma shook her head adamantly. "I don't want to be paid. I had more in mind a trade of services."

He looked so distrustful that she almost laughed out loud. What kind of women had Joe Sutter been keeping company with, anyway? She didn't want to know.

"What sort of a trade?" he asked.

Now Emma did smile. "I'll teach you to use the computer and I'll post your records into the system. In return, you teach me something *I* want to learn," she told him, watching his expression alter from deep suspicion to puzzlement.

"I'm listening." She had the impression that his relaxed posture was a ruse.

Emma took a deep breath, hoping she wasn't making a bad mistake. Common sense told her to stay away from Joe but she was unable to resist the opportunity he had presented to spend more time with him. No doubt she would have plenty of opportunity later to regret her weakness.

"Riding lessons," she said on an expelled breath. "I'll help you get your system up and running, and in exchange, you give me riding lessons."

Whatever Joe had been expecting, his expression indicated plainly that this wasn't it. His hands tightened on the arms of his chair.

"Riding lessons?" he echoed. "Horseback riding?"

A tiny thread of satisfaction began to unfurl inside Emma. "That's right. Computer training in exchange for horseback-riding lessons."

"You told me you knew how to ride," Joe said accusingly.

Emma shook her head. "I said I'd ridden a few times, but I wasn't very good." A sudden thought struck her. "Would you have the time?" she asked worriedly.

Now a grin softened Joe's mouth. If it was meant to be reassuring, it failed miserably. Instead, he reminded Emma of a fox who had just discovered that the henhouse door had been left unlocked and the chickens were eager to see him.

"I'll make the time."

Emma glanced away from his smoky gaze.

"Shake on it?" he asked as she stared dumbly at his outstretched hand. As she slipped hers into it, absorbing the warmth of his leathery palm, she wondered at what point she'd lost control of the bargaining.

Joe released her hand and stood. "If you have the time now, we could get started," he suggested.

Emma tipped her head back and looked up at him. A long way up. "With the riding?" she asked.

"Not tonight. It'll be dark soon." He wore an expression of exaggerated patience, as if to say, *City slickers!* "What I had in mind was some work with the computer."

She blinked in surprise. She'd all but forgotten her part of the deal they'd just made, instead picturing herself racing across the range with Joe in hot pursuit.

"Oh, sure," she agreed, cheeks warming beneath his gaze. "Good idea."

His smile was brimming with satisfaction as he leaned over her. When she pulled back, his eyes locked on hers for a breathless moment and then he picked his empty mug up off the desk.

"I'll fetch some more coffee and a cup of tea for you while you look things over, okay?"

"Okay," she echoed, feeling like a skittish virgin. When he left the room she drew in a couple of deep, shaky breaths and rose to scoop the manual from the floor. The small room seemed a lot bigger without Joe in it.

In moments he was back, carrying two steaming mugs. Placing hers at her elbow, he sat next to her and reached for another handful of candy. His chair groaned beneath his weight as Emma muttered a breathless thank-you.

For the next hour she did her best to ignore his nearness as she went over the computer's operation. She was relieved to see that the software had changed little and she was able to familiarize herself with the updated version as she explained it to him. He didn't say much, only asked an occasional question.

Finally Emma logged off the computer and pushed her chair back with an exhausted sigh.

"That's enough for tonight. I feel brain dead, and I'll bet you've absorbed all you can for one session."

Beside her, Joe drained the last of his cold coffee and then stretched his long arms out in front of him. There were fine brown hairs on his muscular forearms.

"Thanks," he said, his voice a few degrees warmer than usual. "I couldn't have managed anywhere near this much without you."

Emma picked up the empty mugs and stood, taking a step backward to put a little space between them as he rose beside her.

"I hope you still consider this a good bargain when you see me on a horse for the first time," she admitted. It had been years since she'd ridden and, suddenly, she was nervous. About the only thing she remembered was that she had loved the feeling of freedom that even riding at a sedate walk had provoked within her.

"Tomorrow morning, okay?" he asked, expression unreadable. "Come down to the horse barn at nine, and we'll get started. Do you remember where it is?"

They had been by there when he'd taken her on the tour of the ranch. The long building was much newer than the house or the other, older barn, and remarkably clean and well organized.

"Sure, I remember. I'll see you then." She turned to leave, needing to get away from his overwhelming presence for a while.

"Emma." His voice stopped her in midflight. She turned, curious.

"What?"

"Thanks again for your help tonight." He didn't exactly smile, but she would have sworn that the habitual stern expression on his face was noticeably softer.

Flustered, she shrugged. "You're welcome. I'll see you in the morning."

She thought she heard a muttered reply as she went out the door. Perhaps it was just as well she hadn't been able to make out the words.

While Emma was walking out to meet Joe the next morning she looked all around at the blue sky over her head, streaked with faint white clouds, and the rolling pasture-land that stretched out before her, dotted with grazing cattle. As a warm breeze ruffled her dark curls she realized that, for the first time, her waking thoughts hadn't been about her failed marriage, her ex-husband or the uncertainty of her future. Even the memory of the baby girl who had been born to her silent and unmoving two years before, while still bringing deep sadness and regret, didn't hurt as much as it had.

Now a feeling of near contentment stole over her. She was beginning to heal, and it felt pretty good. Not that she would ever forget Alicia Marie. But now, perhaps Emma was ready to tuck the memory of the child she had never had the chance to know into a quiet, safe spot in her heart—and truly put the husband who had subsequently grown more and more distant into the past. And get on with her life. Soon, too, she would have to make some major decisions about where that life was headed.

A bird trilled in a nearby tree. Soon, Emma thought, but not on this glorious day. She increased her stride as her arms swung loosely at her sides and a smile tugged at the corners of her mouth.

When she got to the stable she looked around outside, but didn't see anyone except the Irish setter she'd met before.

"Hi, Dolly," Emma said, holding out her hand for the dog to sniff. Dolly's feathery, rust-colored tail began to wag and her brown eyes squeezed shut as Emma scratched behind her ears.

"Seen Joe?" Emma asked, but Dolly only gave her a doggy grin and remained silent. Poking her nose into the dim interior of the stable, Emma called out timidly, "Joe? Are you in here?"

She heard a horse exhale noisily and, Dolly at her side, she stepped farther into the wide aisle that ran the length of the building.

"Joe?" she called again. A couple of horses poked curious heads over the walls of their stalls.

Emma spoke to them as she walked through the building, absorbing its blended aroma of animals and manure and leather. Before she got to the open door at the other end of the barn she heard Joe's voice.

Dolly's ears perked and she trotted on ahead. The lifting of Emma's heart as she followed the dog was purely involuntary.

Joe was in the corral on the building's far side. With him were a stocky chestnut with tall white stockings, and a slightly smaller mare, coal black from nose to tail. As Emma approached, Joe heaved a saddle onto the mare's blanketed back. The chestnut horse shook his head and jangled his bridle impatiently.

"Hi," Emma said, battling a sudden acute attack of shyness.

Joe glanced over the black mare's back. He was wearing a battered gray Stetson, and his wide shoulders were covered in blue chambray. Beneath the horse's belly Emma could see his long legs in worn jeans above dusty work boots. He looked like a cowboy straight out of a Western movie.

"Hi," he answered as she tried to swallow her guilt at taking him away from his ranch work. His brows rose in question, but he didn't say anything more before he bent his head and tightened the cinch around the horse's belly. The animal shifted its weight without protest.

Joe glanced again at Emma, glad to see she was wearing jeans and sensible boots.

"Come on over here so I can adjust your stirrups," he said. After his first sight of her, he had tried to keep his attention scrupulously on her mount. Damn, Emma looked good in dark blue jeans that hugged her hips, a Windbreaker and a T-shirt with a picture of a red apple and the word Washington scrawled across the front where it clung lightly to her breasts.

Why had he agreed to this bargain, anyway? He must be a true glutton for punishment to subject himself to several hours a day in Emma's company after he'd vowed to keep his distance. One look into her navy blue eyes and he was probably lucky he hadn't offered to deed the ranch over to her, besides.

Joe bit back a groan of dismay and turned to where she'd climbed gracefully over the fence. She was eyeing the mount he'd saddled for her with open admiration.

"She's beautiful," Emma said, smiling.

Joe had to yank his attention away from her face to look at the horse.

"Yeah, she's got good bloodlines, and she's a sweetheart, too," he said absently "Her name is real long and kinda pretentious, so we call her Belle. Lost her foal during the birth or she'd be pastured with the horses I showed you the other day."

"That's too bad," Emma said softly as she went around to the mare's head. "Hello, Belle."

"Let her smell you," Joe told her, watching carefully. "Do you need help mounting?"

After Emma had made friends with her horse, she came back to where Joe was waiting.

"I don't know," she admitted. "As I told you, it's been years since I was on a horse."

"Let me help you, then," Joe said, holding the stirrup. Emma put one foot into it and, with a little hop, managed a shaky ascent into the saddle. When she was settled, her grin was triumphant.

"Maybe I've remembered more than I thought."

Joe let her take Belle's reins and led his own larger gelding, named Tulsa, outside the corral. Then he came back inside, shutting the gate behind him. For the next few minutes he put both Emma and Belle through their paces, assessing Emma's riding skill as she walked Belle in a circle and followed his commands. Dolly watched the proceedings from outside the corral, her head resting on her front paws.

When Joe was satisfied, he opened the gate wide and went through to mount his own horse.

"Come on," he said without looking at Emma. "We'll go for a short ride and see how you do."

Emma might have been hesitant, but she followed him down the dirt road without protest. Secretly, Joe thought she had the makings of a born rider, and he was pleased to discover that she already knew the rudiments. In no time at all she would be able to gallop alongside him almost anywhere he wanted to go.

The thought pulled him up short. He didn't want her with him. Didn't want to spend time with her. So why did the idea of her accompanying him as he rode about the ranch bring an almost foolish grin to his lips? It was a question he dared not examine too closely.

Emma allowed Belle to pull up beside Joe's horse. "Is this okay?" she asked when he glanced at her, his smile fading.

"Sure. We won't go far. You'll be sore after using unaccustomed muscles, anyway. You might want to soak in a warm tub when we're done. It could save you some discomfort." The image of Emma's nude body hidden by a mound of bubbles danced before his eyes like sunspots.

Beside him, Emma watched his gaze darken before he suddenly turned away and clucked to his horse. The big gelding broke into a trot. Belle followed suit, and Dolly came along behind them.

Emma's first impulse was to grab the saddle horn, but she resisted. After a couple of uncomfortable bounces she began to pick up Belle's rhythm and move with her.

"That's right," Joe said approvingly beside her. "You catch on quick."

Pleasure at his praise flooded Emma's cheeks, but she didn't dare glance at him. She was too busy concentrating on what she was doing. Way before she was ready, Joe slowed and turned his horse's head.

"Time to head back," he announced.

Emma swallowed a protest, knowing he was right about aching muscles. Besides, he probably had other, more pressing things to do than trot along with her like two kids at the pony rides. The temptation to release him from his end of the bargain rose, but she forced it back down. If she learned quickly enough, perhaps she could go riding without him. The thought of long, peaceful forays over the ranch cheered her until they returned to the corral.

Joe dismounted and then watched carefully while Emma did the same. As much as she tried to prevent it, her legs trembled from the unfamiliar strain when she was back on foot.

"Be sure to take that bath when you go in," he ordered as he bent to loosen Belle's cinch.

"I should unsaddle her myself," Emma protested, not ready to thank him and leave. She felt a special kinship with her mount, too, another mother who had lost a baby.

Joe looked surprised. "We'll deal with the tack next time, okay? We'll start from scratch, and you can saddle her up."

Emma nodded reluctantly. "Okay." Wondering when next time would be, she went around to Belle's head, patted the horse's silky black nose and told her what a good girl she was. Without warning, Belle lowered her head and butted Emma playfully, pushing her into Joe.

Emma stumbled as his arms came around her in a reflex action. She turned her head to look into his face. Turbulence disturbed his usually stoic expression as he pulled her around to face him. His strong arms tightened, and he bent his head.

He meant to kiss her! Without thinking, Emma lifted her chin. Before her eyes could flutter shut, Joe released her with unflattering haste and stepped back, frowning darkly.

"I have to ride out and find Daniel, my foreman," he said. "Go take that bath while I finish up with Belle."

Mortified by what had almost happened, Emma stuttered out a shaky thank-you for the lesson and hurried away toward the house and refuge from her embarrassment. She didn't understand Joe, didn't know if he hated her or was unwillingly attracted. But never again, she vowed later as she sank into the tub full of blissfully warm water, would she let him put her in such an embarrassing position!

Emma attacked the vegetable garden and its weeds with singular fury that afternoon. The dull ache in her thighs had almost disappeared after her soak. The straw hat she had borrowed from Marian covered her head, but she had forgotten to ask for a pair of work gloves. The hoe she wielded like a sword of justice was raising blisters on her hands, but the discomfort wasn't enough to slow her down. She was determined to finish weeding the whole neglected garden and she didn't question her motives, just knew she wanted to get it all done before supper.

Soon the ache in Emma's back from repeatedly bending over began to take her mind off the stinging of her hands.

Later, when Joe walked past the garden toward the house, she was so engrossed that she didn't even look up. Watching her silently, he decided against telling her it was almost time for dinner. He'd wrestled with a couple of calves that afternoon and was filthy with dirt and sweat. He'd see Emma soon enough, sitting across the kitchen table from him as tempting as a sugary dessert must be to a diabetic. And as bad for his health.

"Is that you, dear?" Marian called as he came into the mudroom and shed his boots and hat.

"Yeah, Mom. I need a shower, so I quit a little early." He padded into the kitchen in his stocking feet.

Marian grinned as she began to set the round table. "Looks like you lost the argument with whatever you were wrassling," she told him. "You've got dirt all over your face."

Joe put his hand to his cheek. "Looks like Emma's whipping the garden into shape," he said. "I'm glad she had the sense to wear a hat."

His mother straightened and glanced out the window. "That girl's a hard worker," she replied, setting out silverware.

Joe hastened to agree, wishing he hadn't brought Emma into the conversation. "I'm going to grab that shower now."

"You don't have to hurry." Marian followed him to the kitchen doorway. "Dinner won't be ready for a good half hour. Why don't you sit down at the table and have a cup of coffee before you go up? I made some fresh."

Joe hesitated. He really wanted to get cleaned up. Then he looked into his mother's eyes and relented. They hadn't talked much lately. As long as she didn't want to talk about Emma.

As soon as she'd filled their cups Marian glanced out the window again and then sat down across from him.

"Rough day?" she asked.

Relaxing slightly, Joe began to tell her about the calves that had given him trouble. "The last little fellow would have been fine if his dim-witted mother hadn't bawled her head off and frightened him," he finished on a note of disgust.

"That's what mothers do," Marian said. "Fuss over their children."

Joe grinned at her. "Yeah," he agreed. "Like you still fuss over me." He meant to tell her in no uncertain terms that nothing was going to happen between him and Emma and to stop pushing her at him. Before he could, she spoke again.

"Did Emma tell you about her divorce?" she asked, toying with the handle of her cup.

Joe remembered what Emma had said about not looking for a man. Had she been trying to warn him off? Could she tell how drawn to her he was despite his determination to resist? Joe vowed to fight the relentless pull even harder.

"Yeah, she told me. Guess she got burned pretty bad." Stubborn pride wouldn't let him ask questions, but he was curious as to why any man would let Emma go. Perhaps her husband hadn't been given a choice—perhaps she'd upped and left, the way Stephanie had left Joe when she lit out for Denver.

His mother smiled sadly and shook her head, taking a sip of her coffee while Joe waited impatiently for her to continue.

"It was a tragedy," she said after a moment. "Did she tell you about the baby?"

"Baby?" Joe echoed, stunned. "What baby?" He hadn't pictured Emma with a child. Hadn't thought about it at all. But wasn't that what most women wanted? It had sure as hell been what Stephanie wanted. More than she wanted him, that was for sure.

"Emma and her husband had a baby two years ago," Marian continued, watching Joe. "A little girl. Something went wrong, and she was stillborn. The doctors couldn't save her.''

"Damn. Poor Emma." Joe looked away. "Losing a child must be rough."

"Yes, and to make things worse, that was why her marriage broke up, too," Marian continued. "After they lost the baby she told me that she and Bob drifted farther and farther apart. They never were able to really talk about it, even though Emma tried. She even suggested counseling, but Bob refused to go. Finally he got involved with a woman from work and Emma left him. That was why I invited her to come here. She seemed at such loose ends."

Joe stared into his coffee cup and shook his head. "I'm sorry." He felt bad for all the times he'd been less than friendly toward her. She'd been through a lot and still she managed to smile and act cheerful, never letting him guess what she might be feeling inside.

"Yes, Emma's had a hard time of it the last couple of years," Marian agreed as she rose and looked out the window again. "Despite whatever she told you, I think what she really needs is another family."

Joe jerked his head up and stared at his mother. "What are you saying?" Why did the idea of Emma remarrying cause such a chaotic reaction in him?

Marian smiled. He knew that expression. It was what he privately thought of as her scheming smile.

"What I'm telling you," she said carefully, "is that Emma's a sweet, pretty woman who needs another husband. She's got too much love in her to stay alone for long. She'd make some lucky man a terrific wife."

Joe was already shaking his head, knowing where she was leading, when she delivered the final blow. "I think the best thing for Emma," she continued firmly, "would be to get married again and have more children. Not that another baby would ever take the place of the one she lost, but a woman like her needs children to care for. Don't you agree?"

Joe was groping for an answer, one that wouldn't reveal the turmoil inside him, when he heard the back door open.

"I don't know what's good for Emma," he said, feeling trapped. "I only know that *I* don't want any children. Not ever."

His mother's mouth fell open. "Joe!"

"I have to get that shower," he said, rising abruptly. Before his mother could say another word he was out of the kitchen and headed up the stairs, the things she'd said about Emma pounding through his brain. Yes, he agreed silently as a glowing light inside him flickered and went dark. A woman like Emma needed children. Deserved children of her own. And that was why Joe had no right to touch her, to want her, to even think about her.

He stalked into his bedroom, hands bunched into fists. Then, with a low growl of pure pain, he whirled and slammed the door behind him.

Chapter Five

Emma walked into the kitchen in time to see Joe disappear through the door to the hallway. Seated at the table, Marian looked shaken by his announcement.

"He doesn't want children?" Emma echoed, surprised. Why would he feel that way? Surely not from anything in his own childhood. Emma's mother had told her how Marian and her first husband, Barnett, had doted on Joe. Barnett had been a quiet man, but a proud, loving father to Joe until his tragic death. Had the early loss marked Joe in some way, turning him against wanting children of his own? Had Marian's second marriage influenced him?

It didn't really make sense. Emma would have liked to ask Marian, who was staring at her clasped hands, but didn't. While she was thinking, the other woman rose and put the dirty mugs in the dishwasher.

"First I've heard of this," she said. "I can't imagine why Joe feels that way, unless it's some holdover from his marriage to Stephanie that I don't know about. Of course, the two of them never had children.''

Emma felt guilty for discussing such a personal aspect of Joe's life behind his back. What if he came down to the kitchen and overheard them?

Besides, her own back was aching, her hands were smarting, her legs throbbed dully from riding Belle and she wanted a shower before dinner.

"I'd better get cleaned up," she said, feeling inadequate. It was easy to see that Joe's remark had upset Marian, but there was nothing Emma could say to make her feel better.

"Sure, go ahead." Marian made a dismissive gesture. "Supper won't be ready for a while, anyway."

Emma went upstairs. The door to Joe's room was firmly shut. There was evidence in the bathroom that he had showered recently, but he'd picked up after himself as he always did. As usual, when Emma stood under the spray and let it sluice down her naked body, she felt a little uncomfortable knowing that Joe had been in there before her. As she dried herself off she tried hard not to imagine him with the water hitting his wide shoulders and muscular chest, but it was no use.

Afterward, as she crossed the hall to her room, wrapped in her red satin robe, Joe's door burst open. Emma jumped and caught her breath, but he merely looked at her with an unsmiling expression.

"Hello, Emma."

"Hi," she answered, trying to sound normal. "I guess I'll see you at supper."

"I hope you'll have some time to help me with the computer tonight," he said, his gaze never wavering from her face.

"Sure. That would be fine." She wondered if he had noticed that she'd weeded the entire vegetable garden, but there was no way to ask. Perhaps Marian would bring up the subject while they were eating.

"Well," Emma said, gripping her dirty clothes more tightly, "I guess I'd better get dressed."

For a moment a flash of humor lit Joe's eyes. "It's okay with me if you'd rather eat in your robe," he drawled. "I like you in red."

Before she could think of a reply he'd turned away, long legs striding toward the stairs.

Later, when they had eaten and Emma had helped Marian clean up the kitchen, the older woman straightened from putting leftovers into the fridge.

"I'm sure Joe didn't mean that about not wanting children. He was upset over something I'd said, but I know he doesn't really feel that way."

Emma wondered what the two of them had been discussing that upset him, but was too polite to ask.

"I'm sure Joe would make a good father," she ventured.

Marian's expression relaxed. "Yes, I think so, too. I hope he'll have a family of his own and give me some grandchildren. Lord only knows if his sister will ever settle down." Obviously satisfied, she closed the refrigerator door and began to wipe off the kitchen counter. "Thanks for your help," she said. "Are you going up to work on the computer with Joe now?"

Emma nodded, doing her best to ignore the gleam in Marian's eyes. "I'll see you later."

She mounted the stairs and took a deep breath before pushing open the door to Joe's office. He was already seated at the desk and the computer was on. When he heard her come in, he slid back his chair.

"I'd like to work on ledger entries first," he said. "If that's all right with you."

"Sure. Good idea." Emma sat next to him and concentrated on the screen. They worked companionably for a couple of hours. Her back was beginning to ache again, so she leaned forward and rubbed it absently. Joe looked up from the data he was entering into the program.

"Back sore?" he asked.

She nodded. "A little, but it will be okay."

He continued to study her as she shifted her gaze to the glowing computer screen.

"How do your legs feel?" he asked.

"Fine. The bath helped a lot." She didn't meet his eyes.

"Perhaps you overdid it this afternoon," he suggested. "No one expected you to weed the entire garden in one day, especially right after your first riding lesson."

Emma flushed. Now that he'd brought it up, her desire to impress him seemed foolish. She shrugged.

"I guess I just lost track of the time and didn't realize how long I'd been at it." She reached for another pile of receipts. Maybe she should ask him for a back rub.

Joe grabbed her hand. As soon as his rough fingers touched hers, one of her blisters broke. Emma jerked free of his grasp, crying out sharply.

He froze. Then he caught her by the wrist and turned her hand over carefully.

"Good God," he exclaimed when he saw her palm. "What the hell have you done to yourself?" He snatched up her other hand and examined the blisters on it. When Emma didn't say anything, he raised his head. His eyes glittered.

"Didn't you have the sense to wear work gloves?" he asked as one finger brushed across her tender skin.

She felt like a child who was being scolded. "I didn't have any."

Joe muttered an oath that made her flinch, and shoved back his chair.

"These need to be attended to," he said, rising. "Or they could become infected. I'll get some first-aid cream." He shot her a look that pinned her in place. "Stay put."

Still tingling from the gentle stroke of his finger across her palm, Emma could do nothing but wait for his return. She glanced at the computer, but the information on the screen made no sense.

When Joe walked back into the room he seemed to have banished most of his annoyance. His expression was less forbidding as he sat next to her.

"Did you wash your hands thoroughly when you came in from the garden?"

Emma's chin rose. "Yes, mother. I washed them in the shower."

For a moment he held her defiant stare. Then he set down a box of bandages and uncapped the tube of antiseptic cream as she held out one hand.

"You're supposed to be here visiting Mom," he scolded as he smoothed the medicine carefully over the blisters, patting it gently on the worst of them. "Not working yourself half to death."

"I think you're exaggerating," Emma said in a shaky voice. Joe's hand, holding hers, was warm and reassuring. His touch was doing strange things to her breathing. He was so close that she could see the individual whiskers that were beginning to darken his chin. He didn't say anything more while he doctored her, but Emma thought she saw his own hand tremble as he reached for a bandage.

"No more hoeing until these are healed," he said gruffly. "And no more gardening without gloves. At least you had the brains to wear a hat, or I might be treating you for sunstroke, as well."

"I'm not a complete idiot," Emma retorted. It was all she could do to keep from snatching her hand away from his. How much longer could she stand to be this close to him without revealing her attraction? She stared at the rich brown hair on his bowed head as he smoothed the second bandage on her palm.

He was being so patient and gentle. He would make a wonderful father. She almost told him so.

When he was finished, he lifted her hand and pressed a kiss to her wrist where the blood flowed close to the skin. Emma's heart began to race at the totally unexpected gesture, and she wondered if he could feel her pulse fluttering beneath his lips.

When he looked up, his eyes were dark and unreadable. Her breath had lodged in her throat. Her lips parted as her gaze slid helplessly to Joe's mouth and then back to his eyes. She lifted her chin, sure now of what she wanted.

"Joe," she murmured.

"I said I wouldn't touch you unless you wanted me to." His voice was hoarse. She saw him swallow, the muscles working in his tanned throat.

"I want you to." If he didn't kiss her this time she would scream with disappointment. He hesitated as if torn with indecision. Then he lifted his hand slowly and cradled her cheek. He leaned toward her.

The first touch of his lips was as gentle as a sigh—and yet it exploded along Emma's nerve endings. Before she could begin to get enough of his kiss he broke the contact with her mouth. Moaning a protest, she curled one hand around his neck, urging him back. She threaded her fingers through the hair at his nape. As she did, he groaned and slid his free hand up her arm to grip her shoulder. His chair squeaked as he shifted, and his knee bumped hers. He put his hands on her legs to pull her chair closer, spreading his thighs to nestle hers between them. She was surrounded by his warmth.

His mouth lifted into a sensual grin that faded as he slanted it across hers. As he kissed her in earnest, Emma became lost in the sensations spinning between them.

Joe's tongue traced her lips and she opened to his possessive exploration. Greedily she strained closer as he slid one arm across her back. Both of her arms went around his neck and her breasts pressed against his hard chest. Heat poured through her. She whimpered.

Joe changed the angle of the kiss, frantic for more of Emma's taste and the touch of her mouth under his. She was sweeter even than he had imagined, soft and intoxicating in her responsiveness. He urged her more tightly against him, wishing they were standing so he could feel the press of her body all down the length of his. His blood was racing, his masculine senses alive with need.

He plunged his tongue deep and felt her arms tighten around his neck as she responded. Her tongue stroked his and he almost lost control. The need to be inside her grew stronger. He was moving his hand to her breast when, through the fog that was rapidly closing in around him, he heard a light tread on the stairs.

He realized dimly that he hadn't shut the door when he'd brought back the bandages and antiseptic cream. It stood wide open to the hallway.

Releasing Emma took every ounce of his shaky control, but he managed. Barely. At the desertion of his arms, her eyes fluttered open. She looked bewildered. Her mouth was slightly swollen from his kisses. His own breath rasped in his throat like a hot, dry wind and his lips were on fire from the touch of hers.

"Mom's coming," he muttered hoarsely, pushing her chair away.

Emma blinked as if awakening from a trance. Her lids looked heavy and her eyes glowed a deep and mysterious blue from beneath the curtain of her thick, black lashes. As she gazed at him, a slight smile curved her soft lips.

Before Joe could say anything else, a knock sounded against the open door. He looked up to see his mother standing there.

"Working hard?" she asked.

Beside him, Emma straightened in her chair.

"We've just now stopped," she said, voice slightly breathless. "But Joe is picking things up very quickly." She didn't look at him, but he saw color spread across her cheeks.

"Yeah," he said, amusement in his voice. "Emma's an excellent teacher."

"I'm glad to hear it." Obviously, Marian was unaware of the undercurrents in the small room. "I'm going to read for a while before I go to sleep. See you both tomorrow."

After they had wished her good-night, Joe looked back at Emma. He wondered if, for her, the spell had been broken.

"How about a cup of tea before we turn in? I could use some more coffee." He picked up his empty cup and stood. If he stayed there in the office with her any longer, they'd end up on the floor with him all over her like a teenage boy with hormone problems.

She deserved better.

At first he thought she was going to refuse the tea as she looked into his eyes, but then she smiled instead.

"Tea sounds good."

Emma stood on slightly shaky legs. At first she thought Joe might take her in his arms again, but he only leaned over to turn the computer off and then stepped back to allow her to exit the room ahead of him. All the way down the stairs she felt his burning gaze on her back. Once she stumbled, but his arm shot out to steady her.

"Are you okay?"

Feeling embarrassingly awkward, she nodded. He let her go and she went hastily to the kitchen. Once they were seated, steaming mugs before them, she searched anxiously for something to talk about. All she really wanted was to crawl up into his lap and kiss him again.

Or to ask why he felt the way he did about children.

Joe leaned back in his chair and studied Emma carefully in the bright overhead light of the kitchen, wondering what she was thinking. Wondering what it was about her that set him on fire and seared away his common sense. Was it the black hair that waved softly around her small face or the dark blue eyes that were so enticingly framed by curling lashes? Her full mouth with its slightly swollen-looking lower lip or that way she had of thrusting out her chin when she thought she was being challenged?

Emma squirmed and took a sip of her tea, and Joe realized he'd been staring.

"Sorry," he said briefly. "You're so pretty that I can't help looking at you."

Her cheeks grew pink, and she dropped her gaze.

"Thank you." It was obvious that she was uncomfortable with the compliment. Joe wondered if the failure of her marriage had made her unsure of herself.

"How long have you been divorced?" he asked, even though he knew the answer. His mother had told him it had been only a few months.

"Not very long," Emma told him. "But the relationship was already pretty dead by then." She hesitated and he waited, hoping she'd elaborate, but she didn't.

"You're over him, then?"

She bobbed her head. "Totally."

"I'm sorry things didn't work out for you." In truth, he wasn't the least bit sorry. If she had still been married, would he have wanted her any less? "It must have been rough."

She studied his face and he thought how soft and smooth her skin was, and so fair against her dark hair.

"What about you?" she asked. "You were married, too."

Joe chastised himself silently for not realizing that, if he asked personal questions, she would have the right to ask them of him.

"Yeah," he agreed shortly, "I was married for six years." The subject still brought with it a crushing sense of failure, although he and Stephanie had been reasonably happy until she had decided it was time to start a family. Joe shifted uncomfortably in his chair.

"If you don't want to talk about it, you don't have to," Emma said, taking another sip of her tea.

"Not much to say." He remembered clearly the day Stephanie had told him it was over—and the reason she had given. Her eyes had been full of tears and he had never felt less like a man.

"We got to the point where we wanted different things," he told Emma. "Finally, one day, she upped and left for Denver. I can't say I was really sorry to see her go." He lifted one shoulder. "I heard she's remarried. End of story."

Not the whole story, though. Joe's mind veered away from that, hating even to think about it.

His fault, totally his fault. He slid back his chair and got to his feet.

"If you're done with your tea," he said pointedly, needing to be alone, "it's getting late."

Emma's smile became strained. "Sure." She took one last swallow, then got up and put both mugs in the sink.

Watching her rinse them, Joe berated himself for his brusqueness. He wasn't sure what to do next. Tell her his sudden bad mood wasn't her fault? Warn her off? Kiss her again and test his badly frayed self-control? Or throw her over his shoulder and take her out to the barn, to the soft hay in an empty stall? Maybe that would warm the icy chill deep in his chest.

He banished the fanciful thought as his body went taut
with wanting. Grimly he took in a deep, slow breath and
willed his libido to behave.

After she'd rinsed out the mugs and set them on a folded
towel Emma turned back to Joe. If she noticed the strain on
his face, she must have decided to ignore it. Instead, she
wished him good-night and left him and his dithering
thoughts about kissing her in the dust where they undoubtedly belonged.

The next morning was Sunday and Emma found a pair of
work gloves outside her door. She looked up and down the
hallway and then took them into her room. Stroking the
sturdy fabric, she laid them on her dresser.

After breakfast she accompanied Joe and Marian to the
church in town. They hadn't attended the week before when
Marian had been sick and Joe was busy with the cattle.

Today both Marian and Emma wore flowered dresses.
Emma's was covered with red and orange poppies and belted
at the waist. She thought Joe looked almost absurdly handsome in a cream-colored Western shirt with dark topstitch-
ing, a string tie and dark pants with his brown boots and
matching Stetson. Sunglasses hid his eyes.

He drove them to church in the car, a dark sedan he'd
washed before breakfast. They went through Caulder
Springs and parked by a quaint white building with col-
ored-glass windows and a tall steeple. He was unfailingly
polite to both women, holding the door and helping them
out of the car and then escorting them up the front steps,
one on each arm. On their way through the open double
doors he and Marian greeted several other people but didn't
stop to visit.

As Emma followed Marian down the center aisle, Joe
right behind her, and slid into a pew, she heard several
hushed comments. Feeling self-conscious, she managed to

keep a casual smile pinned to her face. After they sat down, Emma in the middle, Marian turned to her.

"They're probably all wondering who you are," she whispered. She had greeted a couple of families sitting near them. "We don't get many strangers here," she added.

When two more people entered the pew, Joe moved closer to Emma. He looked down at her, his silvery eyes glittering between narrowed lids. She wondered what he was thinking, and whether he regretted kissing her.

He'd removed his hat and set it on his lap. With his athletic physique, Emma thought he would have looked equally at home in a tuxedo or a sweatshirt.

"You okay?" he whispered.

She shook off the spell that watching his mouth was spinning around her, and nodded.

"Yes, thank you." Before either of them could speak again, the choir filed in and a hymn was announced. Joe handed Emma a book to share with Marian and then took one for himself. As organ music filled the church, his voice blended with those around them.

At first Emma was too intrigued listening to his rich baritone to sing herself. When she realized what she was doing, she joined in softly, amazed at the sense of peace that flowed through her. For a moment she was tempted to pretend that she was attending the service with her family, that she and Joe had something special going between them. Then the hymn ended and a lovely blonde in the row ahead of them turned and spoke to him as the minister walked out. Joe returned her enthusiastic greeting with a subdued one of his own. The minister began to speak and the woman rolled her eyes, then turned back around and sat down.

From the corner of her vision Emma saw Joe glance her way, but she kept her gaze glued to the short, graying minister who was telling them about a man who was jealous of his neighbor's material wealth. The only thing Emma was jealous of was the avaricious way the blonde had smiled at Joe.

After church Emma stood with Joe and Marian while they introduced her to what must have been most of the congregation, as well as the minister and his family. The blonde who had been sitting in front of them walked by and smiled at Joe again, but she and the tall man with her didn't stop to talk.

"That's her fiancé," Marian muttered to Emma under her breath.

An older couple came up. Marian introduced them as Grover Granlund, who owned a neighboring ranch, and his wife, Ruby.

"Joe's father was Grover's best friend," Ruby told Emma.

"Their son, Rob, was my best friend all through high school," Joe said. "We lived at each other's houses when we weren't doing chores."

"And Rob was best man at Joe's wedding," Grover volunteered in a loud voice.

Emma saw Ruby dig him in the ribs with an elbow. She almost smiled at Grover's dawning comprehension and the color that filled his sagging cheeks.

"Where's Rob now?" she asked him as he glanced apologetically at Joe.

"He's teaching in Alaska," Ruby said.

"Emma's a terrific teacher," Joe replied. "She's been coaching me on how to use that computer system I bought."

Grover shook his head. "I'll stick to pen and paper, thanks."

Emma smiled at his leery expression. While Marian asked Ruby about the upcoming bake sale and Joe and Grover speculated about beef prices, Emma took the time to glance around them as the bright sun warmed her arms below her short sleeves.

A towering blue spruce stood by one front corner of the church, surrounded by neatly trimmed grass and some pink flowers she couldn't identify. Everywhere Emma looked, people were talking in small groups. Children ran around them, chasing each other and laughing. A stray dog had wandered over and a white-haired woman stooped to pat its head. Everyone seemed to be smiling.

When Emma had attended church in Seattle with her husband, the congregation had been large and they hadn't known many people. Bob had always wanted to leave as soon as the service was over.

Belatedly Emma realized that Ruby was speaking to her.

"It was nice meeting you," she said. "Have Marian bring you over for coffee before you leave."

"Thank you." Emma was touched by the friendly gesture. "I'll try to do that."

"Have Joe bring you by to see my breeding bull," Grover told her in his booming voice. "Thunder's as potent as he is ornery."

Once again, Ruby's elbow connected with Grover's ribs. As Emma looked away, trying not to grin, Joe caught her eye and winked.

"Thank you for the offer," she managed to tell Grover while maintaining a straight face with effort. All around them, the crowd was thinning out as people left. The Granlunds said goodbye, and Joe followed Marian and Emma to the car.

"I'll have to take you by the Granlunds' to see their breeding bull," he told Emma in a bland voice. "I think you could tell that it's Grover's pride and joy now that Rob's left home."

"Joe," Marian admonished him, "don't make fun of Grover."

"Yes, ma'am."

After dropping him off at home, Emma went with Marian to visit a young friend of hers who was expecting her first child. Marian took a loaf of nut bread, and the three women visited over coffee.

Emma found that being around a pregnant woman gave her mixed emotions. The sadness she always felt over the loss of her own baby was still there, but blended in with it was the realization that she was ready to go on and not look back.

As Marian drove to the ranch she explained, "Tricia's mother lives in Maryland and isn't well enough to make the trip out. Chuck adores Tricia, but she needs another woman now and she's too shy to make friends easily. I like to keep in close touch."

"I'm sure she appreciates your friendship," Emma said. "She's very nice."

Marian nodded. "I told her to call me when she has the baby, and I'd come over to help her out. If you're still here, I won't even feel guilty leaving Joe to fend for himself."

Emma didn't say anything, but a sudden burst of reaction raced through her at the thought of being alone in the house with him. She wasn't afraid. Not of Joe. He would be a perfect gentleman if that was what she wanted. It was her own growing attraction to him that worried her.

"When's Tricia due?" she asked in a strained voice.

Marian smiled. "Oh, not for a couple of months."

When they drove into the yard Joe, who had changed into work clothes, was coming from the barn. Emma thought he looked even better in his faded jeans and plaid shirt, sleeves rolled up, than he had in his Sunday finery.

"Have a good visit?" he asked as he followed them into the house.

"Yes. Tricia's very nice," Emma replied as he took off his hat and hung it on a peg by the back door. "I enjoyed meeting her."

In the kitchen Emma offered to help Marian, but was shooed out.

"Dinner will be ready in a little while. Go talk to Joe while you're waiting."

Emma colored at Marian's ploy, but she trailed him out of the room.

"I'm sorry about that," he said quietly, stopping in the hallway. "I hope she doesn't embarrass you."

Emma gazed at his serious expression and wondered how much Marian's manipulations bothered him.

"Don't worry," she said.

For a moment he looked as if he wanted to say something else. Then the phone rang. Marian answered it in the kitchen.

"Emma," she said. "There's a call for you."

Joe pointed to the phone in the living room. "You can take it there if you want."

"I don't know who it would be," Emma murmured as she picked up the receiver.

As he watched her, Joe's chest tightened. He had a good idea who was on the other end of the line—and he didn't like it one bit.

The softening of Emma's voice told him he was right.

"Hello, Cal. How are you?" she asked, glancing at Joe.

He knew he should leave and give her some privacy, but his feet seemed nailed to the floor. Emma turned away, cradling the receiver to her shoulder as Joe eavesdropped unashamedly.

"I'm fine," she said. Joe could hear a faint voice coming from the receiver.

"Tonight?" Emma glanced at him again, then hastily dropped her gaze. She lowered her voice. "Dinner?"

Joe clenched his fists, shocked at the violent emotions that coursed through him at the idea of her spending the evening with another man. Outrage. Betrayal. Searing jealousy. And a terrible frustration that he had no right to any of those feelings. Not after kissing her just one time.

Suddenly he realized that Emma wasn't accepting the invitation. She was turning Banning down.

"Tonight isn't a good night for me," she said. Again the tinny voice came through the receiver. Joe imagined he could hear the frustration in Banning's voice.

"Of course you can. And thank you for asking me," Emma murmured as Joe grinned broadly. "No, don't apologize for calling so late. I'll talk to you another time, then." She listened for a moment. "Thanks again," she said. "Goodbye."

Hastily Joe wiped the smile of triumph from his expression.

"That was Cal Banning," Emma explained unnecessarily after she had hung up.

Joe couldn't tell if she was annoyed that he hadn't given her any privacy, but he didn't care. He wasn't about to admit he hadn't been able to make himself leave.

"Did he invite you out?" he asked in what he hoped was an innocent tone. To his surprise, Emma looked uncomfortable.

"Yes, he did. But I didn't accept." She glanced at her hands as she twisted them together absently. "I've been a little tired. Maybe I've got a touch of your mother's cold or something." She looked up again and her expression was serious, even anxious. "Anyway, I just didn't feel up to dinner out."

Joe kept his tone equally grave. "I understand," he said. "And I think you did the smart thing."

"You do?" Emma eyed him carefully, as if looking for clues.

"Yes."

"Well," she said after a moment, brightening, "I think I'll read until lunch is ready."

Joe watched her go up the stairs. He took in a deep breath that expanded his chest, and then it deflated again just as quickly when he remembered that—no matter what she told Cal, no matter who she dated or turned down—she wasn't for Joe.

That night he tossed and turned in the big bed that he'd bought after Stephanie had left and that he slept in alone every night. He thought of Emma down the hall. He thought about unwrapping that slinky red robe like Christmas paper on a present. Swearing, he rolled over and pounded his pillow into a lump.

After another hour of sweating and tangling himself in the sheets he gave up in disgust and threw on his clothes. Maybe some fresh air and a quick check around outside would make him tired enough to banish Emma from his thoughts and dreams. It was worth a try.

Failing that, he could always go jump in the horse trough.

Joe picked up a flashlight as he left the house, but he didn't turn it on. He knew the road like the back of his hand. By the time he got to the horse barn his eyes had adjusted to the darkness.

Dolly hadn't greeted him with a low woof and a wag of her plumy tail, so he assumed she was sleeping in the bunkhouse, as she often did since she'd been bred to a neighbor's Irish setter. She wasn't really a watchdog, anyway, liking everyone she met too much to discriminate.

Joe got to the barn and pulled open the door. The shadowy building was almost too quiet. He picked up a crowbar and made his way silently down the wide aisle.

To his surprise, it wasn't the peace of mind he had been seeking that he found in an empty stall, but an intruder curled up on a pile of feed sacks—fast asleep.

"Who the hell are you?" Joe demanded, flicking on the flashlight and shining the beam in the stranger's face.

A head popped up, covered in short black hair. Small fists scrubbed the sleep from eyes that blinked hard in the bright light.

"Please don't shoot me!" the intruder cried in a high-pitched voice, jumping to his feet.

Joe stared, openmouthed. It wasn't a drifter or an out-of-work cowboy, as he had suspected, who stood trembling before him in the pool of light. The figure shaking with fright as he squinted in the glare was only a child.

Chapter Six

"I wasn't doing anything," the boy cried, cowering. "Please don't hurt me."

Joe glanced down at the crowbar he was holding and tossed it aside, feeling like a criminal.

"I'm not going to hurt you, okay?" he said in the same tone he would use on a skittish horse. "I just want to know where you're from and what you're doing in my barn."

The boy, who didn't look more than nine or ten with his big dark eyes, thin face and slight build, swallowed nervously. His gaze darted around the empty stall as if he were searching for answers.

"My name's Kenny," he said in a voice that still shook with fear. "I was just passing through, and I needed some sleep. I didn't bother anything, though. Honest." He looked pathetically earnest. "I was going to be gone by morning, I swear."

Joe leaned against the stall's partition. "Passing through, huh?"

Kenny nodded, his gaze glued to Joe's face. "Yeah. On my way to, uh, my aunt's."

"Where's your aunt live?" Joe wished that Kenny would relax. He looked ready to fly apart.

One of the horses whickered and kicked at the side of its stall. Joe glanced over his shoulder. As he did so, out of the corner of his vision he saw a blur as Kenny tried to dive past him. Without thinking, Joe tackled him, hanging on grimly, and they both crashed to the floor of the stall.

Kenny struggled with desperation, flopping around like a mountain trout on a hook as Joe tried to maintain his grip without hurting the boy.

"Dang it!" Joe finally roared after a few more moments of futile struggle, "quit trying to kick me before I have to do something drastic."

Beneath him, Kenny gave one last buck and went still. Joe could hear the air wheezing in and out of his thin chest. Carefully, without releasing his hold on the boy's collar, Joe shifted off him and came to a sitting position.

"Now," he said, hauling Kenny up to face him. "I want some answers."

Emma wasn't sure what had awakened her, but she sat up in the darkness and listened intently to the silence. Then she slipped on her jeans and a flowered shirt and padded into the hall. Joe's bedroom door stood wide open, but the house seemed quiet. Carefully, so she wouldn't disturb Marian, Emma sneaked downstairs.

She went through the swinging door into the kitchen as Joe burst in from outside, hauling something with him. Joe's face was streaked with dirt.

"Quit struggling!" he growled at the bundle that jumped around like a bag of cats. When he came to a halt in the middle of the room, Emma glimpsed a head of dark hair. What had looked like a bundle of old clothes turned out to be a young boy in jeans and a striped shirt.

"Joe! What happened? Are you okay?" She came forward and then stopped, unsure of what to do. There was a scratch on his cheek, but it wasn't bleeding. "Where did you find him?"

"I'm fine. This is Kenny. I found him in the barn," Joe said, dumping the boy into a kitchen chair. Immediately he popped up again.

"Sit!" Joe roared, and the boy sat. Big brown eyes darted to Emma.

"I didn't do anything," he whined. "Can't you get him to let me go?"

"You aren't going anywhere," Joe said before Emma could speak. "Not till the sheriff gets here and decides what to do with you."

At the mention of the sheriff, Kenny's face went a shade paler and the whites of his eyes expanded with fear. Tears began to dribble down his dirty cheeks.

"Aw, gee," Joe exclaimed, looking helpless. "Don't do that."

Kenny bent his head and sniffled loudly. Emma gave Joe a searching look. What was going on here?

"He was asleep in a stall," Joe explained. "All he told me was his first name and some cock-and-bull story about going to visit his aunt."

"You don't believe him?" Emma asked.

Joe rolled his eyes. "Would you?"

Seeing his point, she transferred her attention to the boy who sat watching them both.

"Hi, Kenny." She tried to smile reassuringly. "I'm Emma and this is Joe."

Kenny stopped sniffling.

"Hi." His voice was barely a squeak.

"Wouldn't he tell you where he was from?" she asked Joe.

His expression was grim. "Not really." He sighed and raked a hand through his hair. Then he hunkered down in front of Kenny while Emma tried not to stare at the way his powerful thighs strained against the worn denim. "Are you hungry?"

Kenny swallowed and made an attempt at bravado.

"Naw," he said. "My mom fixed me a big dinner before I left home."

Emma would have bet he was lying, but she wasn't sure what else to say.

Joe straightened. "As soon as I call Sheriff Hatch I'm going to fix myself a sandwich," he told her. "You want one?"

Something in his expression compelled her to answer in the affirmative, even though she wasn't hungry.

"Sure," she said. "Why don't I make them while you call?"

Joe nodded. "Good idea. Fix plenty."

Understanding dawned. While he called the sheriff without taking his eyes off Kenny, Emma started some coffee. Then she took a ham, some lettuce and a ripe tomato out of the fridge, along with a container of milk. She glanced at Kenny, whose gaze was riveted on the food as he absently licked his lips. Emma began cutting juicy pink slices of ham.

"Thanks, Steve," Joe said after he'd outlined the problem. "I appreciate it. See you shortly." He hung up and turned to Emma. "Steve Hatch, the sheriff, is a friend of mine. He's on his way out."

"Good. The coffee will be ready in a minute."

Joe looked at Kenny and then down at his own hands.

"Come on, son, let's wash up."

"Why?" Kenny asked, balking.

Joe grabbed his arm. "Because you're dirty."

When they got back, Emma noticed that Joe had washed the scratch on his cheek. He watched while Kenny sat back down; then he dragged another chair away from the table. He sat with his long legs stretched out in front of him as Emma assembled three thick sandwiches on homemade bread. She put two of them on plates and set them in front of Joe and Kenny, who looked up with obvious surprise.

"I cut too much ham," Emma said, pouring milk. "If you can't eat that, just leave it. Maybe the sheriff will want it."

Before she could get Joe's coffee, Kenny had taken two bites. While he chewed, Joe winked at Emma. Her face went warm with pleasure as she joined them at the table.

No one spoke again for several minutes.

"Well," Joe said to Kenny, washing down the last of his sandwich with a long swallow of coffee, "if you're done eating, why don't you tell me what you were really doing in my barn."

Kenny drained his glass.

"Thank you," he told Emma politely. "I guess I was hungry, after all."

"No problem." She had to quell the urge to smooth his black hair off his forehead. "The extra ham I cut would have dried out and gone to waste."

Over Kenny's head Joe made a face but she ignored him.

Kenny toyed with his paper napkin, head bowed, while Joe gave every appearance of waiting until the boy was ready to talk.

"If you tell the sheriff I ran away, he'll send me back," he finally muttered.

"Your parents must be worried," Emma told him. "How long have you been gone?"

Kenny began tearing the crumpled napkin into strips. "My folks are dead," he said in a low voice. "A drunk smashed into their car a couple of years ago. He's in jail now."

Her heart went out to the boy, and she wondered how he had managed since the accident. Did he have anyone?

"That's rough," Joe said quietly. "My dad died when I was a kid, too."

Kenny stared warily. "What happened?" he asked.

"He was out looking for stray calves and got caught in a blizzard. He was found too late to save him."

Kenny tipped his head to the side and studied Joe.

"I'm sorry," he said in a small voice.

Surprised by the simple words, Joe found himself blinking sudden moisture from his eyes.

"It's okay," he said gruffly. "It happened a long time ago."

Kenny went back to shredding his napkin. "What did you do when you found out?"

"Cried a lot," Joe said shortly as he struggled with the unexpected wave of emotion. He looked at Emma, who wore an expression of gentle sympathy, and then back to Kenny's bowed head. He seemed like a nice enough kid.

"I cried, too," Kenny admitted after a moment. "I was scared."

Before Joe could reply, a car pulled up outside. As Steve Hatch got out and crossed the yard, Joe's mother pushed open the door from the hallway and came into the kitchen in her robe and slippers.

"What's all the excitement?" she demanded. "I looked out my bedroom window and saw the sheriff coming down the road."

"We've got company," Joe told her, gesturing at Kenny.

She looked him over, and Joe could see her expression soften. "Hello. Where did you come from?"

"That's what we're trying to figure out," Joe said quietly. "I found Kenny asleep in the horse barn."

"Oh, my." Marian sat in an empty chair.

Joe got up and let the sheriff in. Kenny slumped farther into his chair, as if he were trying to hide. Joe made introductions as Sheriff Hatch took off his hat and accepted a cup of coffee from Marian. When Joe introduced Emma, the sheriff shook her hand briefly and smiled into her eyes. Joe wondered if women really thought an overgrown mustache like Steve's was attractive. He rubbed a finger thoughtfully across his own bare upper lip.

The kitchen was getting crowded. Glancing around the table, Joe offered to give Hatch some privacy for questioning.

"No," Kenny protested, looking fearful. "Please don't leave."

Joe, who had been about to get up, glanced at the sheriff.

"You might as well stay." He pulled out a notebook and a pencil stub.

Without thinking about it, Joe rose and stood behind Kenny. He put his hand on the boy's shoulder.

"It will be okay," he said quietly. "No one is going to hurt you. We all just want to help."

Emma watched Joe make the gesture and wondered if he realized how protective he was being. For a man who claimed not to like children, he seemed to understand what they—at least, this particular one—needed pretty well.

Twisting his head to look at Joe, Kenny visibly relaxed. Then the sheriff cleared his throat and began asking questions. At first Kenny refused to tell him anything, even though Joe encouraged him to answer.

Finally Sheriff Hatch got up and glanced at Joe.

"Looks like I'll have to take him in and lock him up," he said in a neutral voice. "Then I'll call around in the morning."

"No!" Kenny wailed. "I don't want to go to jail."

"Then tell me what I need to know," the sheriff said.

Initially Emma didn't think he would.

"I ran away from my foster parents." His high voice was defiant. "And I won't go back. Even if you do throw me in jail." His dark eyes filled with tears, making Emma's heart ache for him. He rubbed them away with his fists. "I hate it there!"

Joe stood watching while Kenny tried to be brave and defiant. If anything, he looked more scared than he had when Joe first found him in the barn. Wondering what Hatch was really going to do with him, Joe tried to think of something reassuring to say, but came up empty.

Sheriff Hatch crouched by Kenny's chair. "If you don't want to go back to your foster parents tonight, you don't have to. But I need to let them know you're okay. If you want, I'll make a few calls, and we'll figure out something else, okay?"

Kenny glanced at Joe, who nodded his encouragement.

"Now, I do need to know your full name and the name and phone number of your foster parents, or I can't help," the sheriff continued.

Again Kenny glanced at Joe.

"Tell him, son. You have to trust someone."

Kenny swallowed and began talking. After Hatch had written the details in his notebook he rose and put his hat back on. Then he motioned for Joe to follow him outside.

"What are you going to do with him?" Joe asked when he'd shut the door behind them. He felt bad for the boy. What a mess.

Hatch scratched his chin, looking sympathetic. "Damned if I know. I'll have to find out where to take him. Poor kid. Some of those foster homes are pretty grim, but there's such a shortage of them. The state really tries, but what can they do?"

Joe thought for a moment, staring down at the toes of his boots. "Why don't you leave him here for tonight?" he suggested, wondering if he might later regret the offer. "You can come back when you have someplace else to take him."

Obviously surprised, Hatch stared hard. "You sure?"

Joe shrugged. "Yeah. Why not? We have room. He's just a kid, and he seems harmless enough."

"Okay. But you're responsible, so keep an eye on him. We don't want him runnin' off again." He stuck out his hand, and Joe shook it briefly. "And thanks for taking him."

"Yeah. Call me when you find out something, okay?" He wasn't sure why he was getting involved, except that Kenny looked so small and scared. Joe felt a certain kinship with him. And Emma's eyes held such tenderness for the boy. Joe wished some of that feeling was for him. Maybe he was just trying to look good to her. He wasn't sure.

After Sheriff Hatch said goodbye and left, Joe went back inside.

"Where's he going?" his mother asked, looking out the window.

"He's leaving for now," Joe said, watching Kenny. "You can stay here tonight."

A smile lit up the boy's face, and he scrambled to his feet. "Really?"

"Yeah. Tomorrow they'll find somewhere for you to stay while this gets sorted out," Joe cautioned him. "I hope that's okay, Mom."

"Sure," she said. "The empty bedroom's made up. Kenny, why don't you come with me and I'll show you where things are? Joe, would you get one of your T-shirts for him to sleep in?"

"Okay." When his mother left, he couldn't resist a quick look at Emma. Her expression was warm with approval. Joe basked in it for a moment, refusing to let himself question why her opinion of him was so important. Then he gave in to temptation and planted a quick, hard kiss on her lips.

"What was that for?" Her voice was slightly breathless.

The taste hadn't been nearly enough for him. He cupped her face in his hands and leaned close.

"Because I can't help myself." The confession was wrenched from his gut.

When Emma didn't pull away he took the kiss he'd been imagining since the last time he had joined his mouth to hers. Her lips welcomed him, parting to allow his tongue entrance. Heat swirled through Joe, urging him to wrap her in his arms and indulge his growing desire. Instead he made himself release her.

Emma's eyes were dark with reaction, her cheeks rosy. He wanted to say something, anything, about his lapse of control, but the most he could manage was a crooked smile. For a moment he feasted his gaze on her face. Then he raced upstairs after the others, full of exuberance. He got the T-shirt for Kenny and told him to stay put until morning.

Back in the kitchen Emma touched her mouth with unsteady fingers and sighed. When the time came, she was going to find it hard to leave Colorado.

The next day Sheriff Hatch called early to ask if Joe could bring Kenny to Caulder Springs.

"The social worker from Sterling is here," he explained. "She's talking to his foster parents now. If she can't work things out with them, she'll have to find someplace else to put Kenny."

Joe agreed to take the boy to town that afternoon. When he got off the phone, Emma was waiting anxiously. As usual, the sight of her made Joe itch to take her into his arms again.

"Was that the sheriff?" she asked.

Joe tried to ignore how pretty she looked in her pink striped shirt and tight jeans. It was getting harder to ignore what her presence was doing to him.

"Yeah, that was Hatch. He wants me to bring Kenny to town later today to see the social worker."

"Could I go with you?" Emma asked hesitantly. "I'd like to be there."

For a moment jealousy surged through Joe as he wondered if she was looking for another opportunity to see Steve Hatch. Then he realized how paranoid he was getting.

"If you want." He strained the betraying bits of anticipation from his voice. "We should leave here at about two. Where's Kenny now?"

Emma glanced around. "I think he's watching television. I was about to ask him to help me in the vegetable garden."

"Good idea." Joe noticed that she was wearing that honeysuckle scent again. He wondered if she had washed her hair with it that morning. "I'll go tell Kenny what Steve said."

"He's been one problem after another," Kenny's foster mother told the social worker, Mrs. Cline, as her husband nodded his agreement. The woman's slightly protruding eyes barely touched on Kenny, while her tone accused him of countless unnamed sins. "We really don't want the boy back." Not once had she called him by name.

Emma's heart contracted at their thoughtless rejection, and she wondered what the court would do with Kenny now. While she watched, he straightened his thin shoulders bravely beneath his faded shirt with the missing button. His apparently indifferent gaze stayed on the far wall. Emma would have liked to reach out and give his shoulder a squeeze, but she knew he wouldn't appreciate the gesture of comfort.

"Don't worry," the social worker told him, her lined face softening slightly. "We'll find a spot for you somewhere."

A sudden thought popped into Emma's mind and she leaned over to whisper a suggestion to Joe, unsure how he'd take it. For a moment his light gray eyes stayed on hers as he appeared to mull over what she had said. Then he surprised her by standing as the social worker was addressing Kenny's foster parents.

"Excuse me, but I might have a temporary solution," he told her. "What would it take for me to get approved as a foster parent?"

The caseworker looked as surprised as Emma felt.

"You'd have to fill out an application, and then we'd do some checking. Why?"

Hope tightened Emma's chest.

"Let's do it," Joe said. "If we can work things out, I'd like Kenny to stay at the ranch until the end of the summer."

"What about the rest of the school year?" Mrs. Cline asked.

"The bus comes right past our driveway," Joe said. "We'll see that he gets to school."

For the first time the caseworker's mask of efficiency slipped and her face relaxed into a real smile.

"Mr. Sutter, I think we might just be able to handle that," she said. "Kenny, if we can, how would you feel about staying on at the ranch?"

Kenny shrugged, his expression indifferent. Emma wondered if she had made a mistake in suggesting that Joe take him. Then a grin broke across the boy's pale face, altering his appearance completely. "Yeah, I guess I'd like that. Thanks, Mr. Sutter."

Joe pretended to flinch. "Maybe you'd better call me Joe."

The other foster parents got up, and the woman's gaze darted to Kenny. Then she looked at Joe and Emma.

"Good luck with him," she said in a tone that predicted failure. She set down a plastic grocery bag. "Here's his stuff." Then she and her husband left without a word or a glance at the boy who had lived with them for half a year.

Emma was relieved when they were gone. How could people remain so unmoved by a child?

Joe had put an arm across Kenny's shoulders while he talked to Mrs. Cline. Since he had sounded so adamant in his feelings toward children, Emma should have been surprised at his generous offer. Instead, knowing Joe as she was beginning to, she thought it sounded like the kind of thing he would do.

All Emma had suggested was that he keep Kenny for a few more days, until another home could be found for him. The rest, apparently, had been his idea.

For the next week, after Marian took Kenny shopping for some decent school clothes, he settled in at the ranch. And he claimed to be catching up at school. Emma helped Joe to finish putting his bookkeeping system on the computer and took more riding lessons.

"You don't need any more instruction," he told her one morning after she had ridden out with him to check on the herd. "Just more practice. But I don't want you riding alone. Too many unexpected things could happen out here."

His eyes narrowed thoughtfully, and she wondered if he was thinking about his father.

"I won't" she promised.

Joe thanked her again for her help with the ranch records. When Emma asked if she could use the computer to print out application letters for a teaching position that fall, he frowned with obvious displeasure.

"Application letters?" he echoed.

"To find a job back in Seattle," Emma explained. "I've certainly left it for the last minute, but I need to start thinking about my future. I won't tie up the computer when you need it, though."

His nod of agreement was brusque, his voice clipped. "Sure. Use it anytime you want."

Emma puzzled over his reaction, wondering if the idea of her leaving could possibly bother him. She hesitated to make any assumptions. Joe would undoubtedly be glad when both she and Kenny were gone and his life returned to normal. A couple of kisses didn't mean anything.

Not to him.

Joe was pleased that Kenny adapted to ranch life pretty quickly. He hung around Joe and Daniel, the foreman, whenever they let him. He didn't talk much, but cowboys wouldn't mind that. Kenny had learned to ride when his father worked on a spread in Wyoming, so Joe gave him the use of an older gelding called Ranger.

Although Kenny helped Marian in the house and Emma in the vegetable garden after school, it was clear to Joe that the boy was happiest shadowing the men.

Dolly, struck with her own case of hero worship, began following Kenny whenever he was outside. At Joe's suggestion, he took over the dog's care—and awaited the birth of her puppies like an excited uncle.

At supper one evening Joe saw that Kenny was already putting a little meat on his thin bones and developing a healthy tan. He still ate as if the meal before him might be his last, but Joe didn't fault a healthy appetite.

"We'll be starting roundup day after tomorrow," Joe announced between bites of roast beef. "Things'll be pretty busy around here for the next week or so."

"Wow," Kenny exclaimed, his eyes wide with excitement. "A real roundup! Will you be roping and branding, like in the movies?"

His excitement was endearing. Joe saw Emma hide a grin.

"Yeah, I guess so," he replied. "We'll be running small herds through the chutes each day, vaccinating, branding and castrating the spring calves, checking the adults over for any problems that need attention."

"What's castrating?" Kenny asked.

Not sure how to answer, Joe glanced at Emma for help. She rested her chin on one hand and raised her brows in silent query, obviously waiting for him to stumble through an explanation. He narrowed his gaze, silently promising retribution before returning his attention to Kenny.

"Castration is turning the male calves into steers," he said briefly, sliding his chair back with the idea of escaping before Kenny could pose another question. "You can come down to the corral and watch the roundup after you get home from school, if you want. As long as your chores and homework get done."

"Maybe I'd better skip class for a few days and help you out," Kenny suggested hopefully.

"Maybe you'd better go to school like you're supposed to," Joe countered. "We'll still be at it when you get home."

"Okay," Kenny replied, his expression unrepentant. "Gee, it sounds neat."

"It will be hot and dusty and smelly," Joe warned him. "The cattle will be hollering for all they're worth when we separate them from their calves. The calves will be bawling. Flies will be everywhere. The work is hard, and we'll be in a hurry to finish. Everyone gets tired and short-tempered before we're done."

Kenny's eyes shone with excitement. "Wow."

Emma almost laughed out loud at Joe's look of consternation.

"Well, you can probably make yourself useful, I suppose," he told the boy. Then he glanced her way. "You can come down, too, if you want. Roundup's kind of interesting if you haven't seen it before.''

"I will," she promised. If Joe was going to be there, it would be interesting enough for her. "As long as Marian doesn't need me," she amended guiltily.

The other woman waved her hand in a dismissive gesture. "Cookie's the one feeding the men," she said. "All I have to worry about is a little extra baking. We can do that early, before it gets hot."

"Perhaps I could help with the cattle," Emma suggested to Joe.

He studied her for a moment, rubbing his sideburn with one finger. "You can watch," he corrected. "You never know what a determined mama cow or a two- or three-hundred-pound frightened calf is going to do next. I'd rather have you on the fence where I don't have to look after you."

Emma made a face but didn't argue. She didn't want Joe getting gored or stomped on because he was distracted. "I'd like to watch," she told him. "Thanks."

His quick grin was her reward. "Don't forget to wear a hat."

Joe had been right about the roundup. It was hot, dusty and unbelievably noisy. When the men started separating the calves from the adult cattle, both groups set up a din of protest that was deafening. Nevertheless, Emma enjoyed sitting on the top rail of the fence with the sun shining down on her as she watched the men.

The man she watched the most was Joe. He worked as hard as anyone, cutting the cows and herding them into the chute while one of the other men worked the gates that sorted them and the calves into separate pens. One cow tried to turn back, and got stuck in the chute. As soon as Joe and Daniel freed her, another cow managed to dash after her calf into the wrong pen. Finally all the animals were sorted. The cries and bellows grew louder.

In the branding pen a wood fire burned and the handles of several branding irons protruded from the flames.

"Some ranches use a gas fire," Daniel explained to Emma as he pulled his mount close to the fence. "And some are experimenting with cold branding, but we do it the old-fashioned way."

"Doesn't it hurt?" Emma asked.

Understanding gleamed in Daniel's dark eyes. She liked the tall, black-haired man. He was normally rather quiet and aloof but she had seen how patient he was with Kenny.

"It only hurts for a minute," Daniel told her. "But it's all necessary."

She didn't reply, knowing that he was looking at it from a cowboy's viewpoint. Instead, she watched the first calf as he was herded from the small holding pen to the calf squeeze chute. Joe had explained to her and Kenny before they started that the calf would be clamped tight and tilted sideways onto a kind of table while he was branded and his ear tattooed. Then he would be castrated and vaccinated before being freed into a new pen.

Emma was amazed at how quickly the men dealt with each calf, turning it loose in only a minute unless the calf managed to escape or to put his front feet through the opening for his head in the squeeze chute. Joe had dismounted and was working over each calf with one of his men while the vet administered shots.

She was thinking how easy Joe made it all look when Kenny, who had just arrived to perch next to her on the fence, shouted with alarm.

Most of the calves trotted into the next pen when they were freed of the chute, but one apparently had decided to charge the men instead. The animal was big enough that no one wanted to be butted by it. Joe waved his hat and yelled.

For a moment the calf hesitated, watching Joe. He stamped his feet and yelled again. The calf pawed at the dirt and lowered its head while Joe waited. Emma braced herself, but then it wheeled around and left.

She took a deep breath, glad no one had been hurt. The incident made her remember how dangerous ranch work could be. The idea of Joe ever being harmed made her stomach tighten with unexpected tension. It was more than the fact that he was Marian's son. It was Joe himself.

Emma looked around the dusty corral. What a singularly unromantic setting for her to realize that she was falling for the often taciturn but always fascinating rancher.

"Hey, did you see that?" Kenny asked, grabbing her arm. "Joe tackled that calf like they was in a rodeo!" His voice rang with admiration.

Emma shook off her private thoughts and looked over to where Joe had indeed grabbed a calf that had somehow managed to get loose. While she and Kenny watched, he threw it expertly. Holding it down, he dealt with the headstrong animal quickly and released it to join the others.

When Joe got to his feet and brushed off the dust, he looked right at Emma. She felt hot all over as Kenny raised clenched fists in a sign of victory. Joe grinned and turned away, while Emma wished she had thought to show her approval, as well.

What might he have done if she had ignored good sense and tossed him a kiss? The image of his probable expression of horror was almost enough to make her giggle out loud. For some reason, the revelation that she was falling for the handsome rancher didn't make her unhappy. Quite the opposite. It exhilarated her mood in ways she didn't begin to understand.

During the week of roundup Emma continued to watch from the corral fence as often as she could. It was almost the only time she saw Joe. He was gone each morning before she was up, eating breakfast at the bunkhouse with the men before work, then presumably joining them there for supper at the end of each day, long after Emma and Marian had eaten. When he came to the house he usually went straight up to bed.

Emma helped Marian bake a steady parade of cakes, pies and cookies, and delivered them to the bunkhouse each day, but Joe was always at the corral with the cattle.

"I'm probably going to forget what my son looks like," Marian joked over one of the quiet suppers the two women shared with Kenny. "Joe always insists on working as hard as the men. Says he wouldn't keep their respect if he didn't."

Emma missed his presence at the table and in the office where they had spent so many evening hours together. One thing she wasn't worried about, though, was forgetting what Joe looked like. If her dreams were any indication, his image must be engraved on her brain.

On the last day of the roundup Emma stayed on her perch on the fence well into the afternoon, watching Joe. She sat, as she had each day, right above the cooler full of water jugs. That way, at least once or twice he was bound to come over for a drink. He would stand for a moment, wiping the sweat from his eyes, and make a comment to either Emma or Kenny.

To Emma, those few moments were worth waiting for. She didn't ask herself why.

Beside her, Kenny talked nonstop about his impressions of the roundup. It was hard to believe she had ever thought him a quiet boy. Listening to his steady chatter with half her attention, Emma kept her gaze on the owner of the Blue Moon. She knew he must be exhausted after a week of long, hard days.

He inspected another of the grown cows, his big body still moving with efficiency and riveting grace. While he checked the animal over for sores or a hoof that might need trimming, the vet forced a syringe of worm medicine down its throat. Then the cow was turned loose to find her calf.

Joe's authority over the men and the animals was absolute. When he was on his cutting horse he moved as one with the animal. On foot he was quick and capable. A natural leader.

An hour after lunch, as the sun climbed higher and the dust rose in a choking cloud, Joe straightened over the cow whose hoof he had been trimming, and peeled off his shirt. Two of the other men had already done so. Emma watched, fascinated, as his bare chest was revealed. She was glad that Kenny had gone to get Daniel another pair of gloves. She wouldn't want him questioning why she suddenly had trouble breathing.

As she continued to feast her eyes on Joe's powerful muscles and sun-bronzed skin, sweat began making paths through the dust on his chest. Her fingers itched to blot it, to take a cool, wet cloth and wipe away the grime, to explore each bulging muscle and intriguing indentation or whorl of dark hair. Emma knew that the image of Joe with his shirt off was going to haunt her dreams that night. She was almost looking forward to it.

She thought of the way he'd kissed her and of the other times she had caught him looking at her as if he might want to kiss her again. She knew he was attracted to her. So what held him back? Was it because she was his mother's friend? Or was it some antiquated code of Western hospitality because she was a guest under his roof? Maybe he just wasn't as interested as she thought. Had mere masculine curiosity, now satisfied, prompted those kisses? Was she mistaken in thinking that something almost alive in its intensity still simmered between them?

Her questions were answered in part later that day. The weather had turned hot, the cattle were cranky and the men more so. Halfway through the afternoon Emma gave up and returned to the house to avoid the worst of the heat. She felt sorry for the men, knew they had to be tired and miserable, and was glad the job was almost done.

While she was in the kitchen the phone rang and Marian answered it. After a moment she turned away from the receiver and asked Emma to take a message to the corral.

"Apparently Doc Preston's beeper isn't working," Marian told her. "There's an emergency and he needs to call his office right away. No one's around to answer the phone in the barn, either. Take my car, it'll be quicker than walking."

"Sure thing." Emma got up from the table, where she had been peeling apples for a pie, and took the keys Marian handed her. She was feeling much cooler and more rational since she'd had a shower and a tall glass of lemonade.

Marian thanked her and turned back to the phone. Emma hurried outside to the car. She planned to give the vet the message and get back to the house without sparing Joe more than a glance. She would die of humiliation if Daniel or one of the other men saw her staring like a lovesick groupie.

When she parked the car Emma saw that the corrals were empty. Daniel was the only one around, and he was picking up some equipment.

"We finished early," he told her when she walked over to where he was coiling up a length of rope. "Joe and the doc went over to the horse barn." Emma had no doubt driven right past them moments before.

Fanning herself with her hat, she thanked Daniel and got back in the car. When she drove to the barn she didn't see Doc Preston's truck but she stopped and went in, anyway. Joe was standing in one of the stalls with a horse that had been kicked during the roundup. His plaid cotton shirt was completely unbuttoned. The sleeves were rolled up to reveal the bulge of his hard biceps, and the tail hung out. He was concentrating on the bay gelding and didn't hear Emma approach.

"How's he doing?" she asked.

Joe glanced up. Beneath the brim of his hat the harsh lines of his face barely softened when he smiled.

"A little rest will put him right." He slapped the horse on the rump and came out of the stall, shutting the door behind him. His narrowed gaze swept over Emma. "What are you doing here?"

She resisted the urge to tug at the legs of her shorts. Her attention slid to the broad expanse of Joe's chest, partially revealed by the open shirt. Up close, she could see that his suntanned skin glistened with moisture and was dusted with swirls of brown hair. Her hands itched to touch him.

"Where's the vet?" she asked, looking around.

"Gone," Joe said. "He left for his office ten minutes ago."

"Oh." She swallowed and tried to think of something else to say. Nothing came to mind. "I had a phone message for him. Guess I'd better get going," she muttered lamely.

"Why?" Joe asked, coming closer. His eyes gleamed as he mopped his face with a bandanna. "What's your hurry?" His mouth was still curved into that enigmatic grin.

"I..." Emma's voice dried up in her throat. Her composure fragmented. Heat began to sweep across her skin. Not the dry heat from outside, but the invasive warmth of a deeper, inner fire. As her senses came alive, her mind had gone blank. A cohesive response to his simple question seemed beyond her.

From the corner of her eye she saw Joe lift his hand. She watched it, fascinated, as it moved toward her. Then he slid his fingers through her hair and gently cradled her head. She shut her eyes against the hunger that surged through her at his touch.

"Emma," he whispered. "Look at me."

She tried to turn away, but he held her firmly. The fingers of his free hand caught her chin.

"Look at me, honey," he repeated softly. "I want to see into those beautiful eyes."

She raised her lids slowly. He was so close she could see the glitter of silver in his eyes and the ring of darker gray around each iris.

"Do you know that I can't seem to resist you?" he mused aloud.

Emma didn't think he expected an answer.

"Why are you trying?" she felt compelled to ask instead.

Chapter Seven

Joe looked taken aback by her question.

"Don't you want me to try resisting you?" he demanded, his fingers tightening on her scalp as his other hand dropped away from her chin. "Or shall I just kiss you whenever I feel like it, then?"

Emma felt her cheeks go pink. Still, some imp within her that she couldn't seem to quell persisted in directing her speech.

"Depends on how often you feel like it, I guess." She arched her brows. "Tell me, do you get the urge often? More than once a day?"

"Sassy, are we?" He leaned closer, his gaze sliding to her mouth. "Maybe I'll just start by indulging myself right now. Okay with you?" His eyes glittered darkly, and Emma felt her burst of bravado evaporate.

She raised her hands to his chest to ward him off, but the moment her fingers touched his bare skin they began stroking and exploring the intriguing contours. With a hiss of surprise Joe released his hold on the back of her skull and folded her into his arms.

"I love it when you touch me," he rasped. "Don't stop."

Emma could feel his heart beating beneath one flattened palm. She murmured his name as he dipped his head. Then his mouth covered hers and she clung to him, returning the kiss. Again and again his mouth merged with hers. His tongue caressed her, his teeth nipped at her lower lip gently and then his warm lips rubbed against hers with the sweetest friction imaginable.

Her arms were locked around his neck, and her body was pressed to his. One of his hands swept down her back and urged her hips closer. She felt his knee nudge her legs apart. When she complied, he slipped his thigh between hers. Emma strained against him. With both hands he lifted her higher on the rigid muscles of his thigh.

A moan worked its way up Emma's throat, and a burning need unfurled itself deep within her. She arched closer, feeling the bulge of his arousal nestled intimately against her. As her breasts rubbed his bare chest, her nipples budded and began to throb. Her fingers dug into the hair at his nape.

Joe groaned and skimmed one hand up underneath the hem of her shirt. He cupped her breast within the confines of her bra and thumbed her beaded nipple. New heat spread through Emma, and she whimpered.

"Please, Joe."

He lifted his head and his eyes blazed into hers. "Please, what?"

She shook her head, unable to put her need into words. Instead, she buried her face in his shoulder, tightened her grip and squirmed against him.

His fingers dipped into her bra and gently teased her nipple. Emma gasped and pushed closer. Joe's other hand splayed on her rounded bottom as he surged against her. Then he gripped her hips and held her still.

"God, Emma, much more of that and I won't even get my jeans off."

His words parted the sensual curtain that had closed around her. She froze, realizing that she had been climbing him like a cat in heat.

"What's wrong?" he asked.

Carefully Emma straightened away from him, trembling as the rough denim of his thigh brushed her bare leg. She let go of his neck. As she did, she became aware once again of their surroundings.

"Anyone could come in," she said, grabbing at the first excuse that came to mind.

Joe released her, looking discomfited.

"You're right. I'm sorry." He dragged in a deep breath and expelled it explosively.

"I'm sorry," he repeated, eyes dark, mouth grim as he gripped her upper arms. "I don't usually lose control like that. You just..." He squeezed his eyes shut as a dull flush darkened his cheekbones.

Emma touched his jaw, and he jerked abruptly.

"It wasn't only you," she said softly. "Please don't apologize."

For a long moment Joe's gaze bored into her. Then he blinked as if he were coming out of a trance. His mouth twisted into a crooked grin.

"The next time, I guess I'd better pick a more private spot," he growled, dropping a quick kiss onto her up-turned lips.

Emma stiffened. Did he think he could indulge himself whenever he wanted for the rest of her visit? And who could she blame if he did?

"Maybe this was a mistake," she said cautiously, part of her hoping he would deny it. Instead, he stepped back and looked into her eyes.

"Perhaps you're right."

"I'm not blaming you, not entirely," she said quickly. "But that doesn't mean I can..." She stopped helplessly.

"I know." Joe sighed. "Believe me, Emma, I'm the last man to make assumptions." He kissed her once more, hard, and then he let her go and looked around.

"Coast seems clear. Perhaps you'd better go now. I guess I'll see you later." His face was full of emotions she couldn't begin to read, but his tone was almost bitter.

At a loss for words, she hesitated and then brushed past him. Glancing back, she saw that he was staring after her. A brief smile curved his mouth but didn't touch his slitted eyes.

"You're something special, Emma," he told her quietly. "Remember that, okay?"

Puzzled at the finality in his voice, she said, "I don't understand."

He turned his face away, but not before she glimpsed a flash of pain there.

"I know you don't." He sighed again and, for a moment, she thought he might explain. When he spoke, it was merely to suggest she go back to the house. "Before someone comes looking for one of us," he added.

Emma made herself keep moving until she was outside. She went to Marian's car and got in, but a little part of her was still back in the barn with Joe. Blinking away a sudden veil of sadness that threatened to descend, she wondered whether she would ever get that part of herself back or if it was lost to her forever.

Back in the barn Joe was wondering the same thing about himself. He had needed her so desperately, and she had responded with such sweet passion. But giving in to the temptation had cost him. He knew he had no right to Emma and feared he would pay a heavy price for the taste of her he had stolen. Pay for it with a long succession of lonely days and nights that were haunted with memories of her touch, her scent and the indescribable feeling of her melting against him.

For a moment he wondered if he would be able to survive the pain. Then, biting down hard on his resolve, he spun on his heel and slammed the flat of his hand into the wall. He had to survive it. For him there was no other choice.

In the days that followed, Emma didn't see Joe alone again. She wondered what might have happened if she had. Watering the vegetable garden on Saturday morning, she was thinking about his changeable personality when Kenny came to her, looking forlorn. Joe was nowhere around. Dolly, heavy with her pregnancy, spent most of her time now asleep in the barn.

"I'm bored," Kenny announced.

"Want to go for a ride when I'm done here?" Emma asked.

Kenny shook his head. "Naw."

"Oh, come on," she urged. "I'd like the company."

Kenny's expression brightened fractionally. "We could go down along the creek," he suggested after Emma had put the hose away, and they headed for the corral. "Daniel told me they were going to move part of the herd to that pasture today."

She could see through Kenny's suggestion. He hoped to run into Joe and the men. She wondered why Joe hadn't taken Kenny with him, as he often did on the weekends, but wasn't sure how to pose the question without causing the boy additional discomfort.

"Or we could ride over to the Granlunds and see if Ruby's baked any cookies," Emma said instead. Kenny had met Ruby and Grover at church, and Emma knew the way to their ranch because she had ridden there with Joe.

Kenny shook his head. "We probably better not."

"Ruby invited us," Emma reminded him as they approached the barn. "She said to come by any time."

Kenny stopped and looked around.

"What is it?" she asked, noticing his worried frown. "What's wrong?"

"I left Dolly here earlier. She was acting kinda funny." Kenny peered through an open doorway. "I wonder where she went."

Emma knew that the dog's time was near. Concerned, she began looking, too. "Maybe we'd better check around."

A few moments later she heard Kenny call her name in a loud whisper. He was standing in the doorway of the tack room as she hurried over to see what he'd found.

There, inside the small room, was a low, narrow cot. On the navy blue spread lay Dolly. She lifted her head and whined, as if inviting the two of them closer.

"Holy moley," Kenny muttered as Emma recognized the squirming bundle beside her. "Dolly's had her puppies!" Slowly he advanced toward the proud mother. "Good girl."

Emma followed. "Don't startle her," she cautioned softly. She could see three small, wet creatures. Apparently unconcerned by Emma's and Kenny's presence, Dolly bent to lick one tiny head.

"Good girl," Emma echoed. Dolly's tail thumped once. Emma touched Kenny's arm. "Let's leave her alone for a little while. She may not be done yet. I'll call the vet."

Kenny nodded. He followed Emma out of the tack room and waited impatiently while she used the extension phone in the barn.

By the time Doc Preston arrived and checked out the situation, Dolly had given birth to five puppies. They all appeared to be in good shape, and so did she. The vet had just left again when Joe walked into the barn looking for the liniment.

"Dolly had her puppies!" Kenny told him. "Doc Preston came out, and he says they look fine."

Joe glanced at Emma and then allowed Kenny to pull him into the room Dolly had made into a nursery. As Emma walked outside to warm herself in the sunshine, she could hear Kenny's excited voice. After a few minutes Joe followed her out.

"That's some litter," he said, sitting next to her on a wooden bench. "Looks like four males and a female."

"Kenny's thrilled." Emma wasn't sure what else to say. She could see patches of fatigue beneath Joe's gray eyes. They made her wonder if his sleep had been as restless as her own. He had been starring in her dreams, most of them embarrassingly erotic.

When he remained silent, she glanced up. He was studying her searchingly.

"How have you been?" The question surprised her.

"Fine." No way was she going to admit the truth.

He let out a deep breath. "That's good to hear."

"Why?"

He removed his hat and slapped it against his thigh, knocking off the dust, while running the fingers of his other hand through his hair. For a moment she didn't think he was going to answer her.

"I didn't want you to regret what happened," he finally admitted, studying the mountains that lay to the west as if he were trying to memorize their shapes.

"Do you regret it?" she had to ask, holding her breath while she waited for his answer.

When he turned his head, his expression was grim, and her heart sank. "Every day."

What Joe didn't say was that he regretted it even more during the long nights when he had to wrestle the nearly overwhelming desire to sneak down the hallway to her bedroom. Once, he had given in to the need that clawed at his gut like some kind of living being, and had opened her door to watch her sleep. She had looked so lovely and untouched that he couldn't bring himself to wake her. Then he'd remembered his mother asleep across the hall and, slowly, sanity had returned. With a sigh he had padded quietly back to his lonely bed.

Now Emma's expression of hurt at his clipped words ran a knife through his heart. He hadn't realized how they would sound to her. Still, he remained silent when she got up, her eyes shimmering with tears, and walked away without a backward glance. Better that she hate him, he told himself as he watched her go back inside to where Kenny watched over Dolly and her puppies. Better that than to give her any more heartache.

Joe built a large, deep-sided box in an empty stall and moved Dolly's little family into it. That way, Dolly could jump in and out when she needed, but there was no worry that the puppies would wander off as they began to explore their surroundings. Kenny spent a lot of time with the puppies and wanted to sleep in the barn, too, but Marian drew the line there.

"You'll sleep in your own bed in the house at night," she told him over supper, in the same tone Joe remembered her using on him years before. "You need your rest for school."

Emma glanced up and Joe winked, wondering if she had read his thoughts. After a moment she smiled back, even though it bore signs of the strain between them.

"No point in arguing when she uses that voice," Joe told Kenny, who looked mutinous. No one complained that the boy spent as much time as he could in the barn, though. So did Emma. She seemed to be captivated, as well.

Joe realized he was feeling jealous of a litter of puppies. He guessed that Emma hadn't been around many baby animals before, living in the city.

"You really like these little critters, don't you?" he asked when he found her sitting on the floor of the stall with her back against the wall. Two of the puppies were asleep in her lap while Dolly nursed the others.

"They're so precious," she said. "And they're growing so fast." There were tears on Emma's cheeks as she stroked one small, silky head. The female was the runt of the litter and Kenny had named her Firecracker because she made the most noise.

Joe hunkered down next to Emma and picked up the other puppy from her lap. He nuzzled it against his jaw for a moment, then returned it to Dolly's side as it began to fuss. He put the other puppy back in the pen, too.

"What are you doing?" Emma questioned sharply.

Joe studied her defiant expression for a moment. Her eyes were wet. He wished he could kiss away her unhappiness. Instead, he seemed bent on adding to it. But a man had only so much willpower, and his was being sorely tested.

"What's bothering you?" he asked, sitting next to her on the floor. "You're crying."

Emma bowed her head. "Nothing's bothering me."

Joe waited, listening to the squeaking of the puppies and the anxious sounds Dolly made as she snuffled and licked each one, checking it over thoroughly.

Finally his patience paid off. Emma sighed and looked up. Her black lashes were clumped with moisture.

"I had a child once," she said softly.

He took her hand and held it between both of his.

"I know, honey. Mom told me about the baby you lost." The thought of her suffering corroded his insides like burning acid. He wished he could take the pain away, but that was something he could never do. A wave of self-loathing at his own weakness where Emma was concerned almost made him sick.

"I miss her." Emma's voice was as clear as silver bells, and just as sweet.

Joe released her hand. He reached up and caught a falling tear with his thumb before it could spill down her face. Without thinking, he touched this wetness to his lips, tasting the salt.

"I'm sorry. I wish I could do something to ease your pain."

Emma searched his strong face. It was etched with concern. Somehow, his words caused her sorrow to ease a little. She felt her body relax and she was able to look at Dolly and her litter and appreciate what they were, nature's constant renewal of herself.

"Thank you for understanding," she told Joe.

His smile was edged with sadness. "I wish I could do more."

While she watched him, the light in his eyes flickered and changed. They began to heat with awareness. The compassion she had seen there moments before was burned away until only need swirled in his gaze, like glowing, molten silver. In response, Emma's senses became alive in a way they did only when he was near.

"Don't punish yourself," he told her as he began to get up.

She reached out to stay him, grabbing his wrist. He hesitated, obviously surprised at her action.

Embarrassed, she dropped her hand.

"Is there something you want?"

"Um, are there things you need to do right away?" she asked, feeling awkward now that the shared moment was over.

"Not really," he admitted. "I just thought it might be wiser if I left." He made no further attempt to get up, but he had to glance away from Emma's quizzical expression. For a few moments he watched the puppies nursing enthusiastically. Dolly's gift to the future. The scene brought a sudden lump to his throat.

Finally Joe got to his feet. He offered Emma his hand. She put hers in it, and he pulled her up slowly. Her lids were lowered, her cheeks pink.

Joe didn't release her hand. As he stared down at her, inhaling her scent, he felt his control shift and begin to crumble. The way it always did when she was around. Damn, but he could hardly look at her without wanting her.

Need roared through him, as all-consuming as a prairie fire. He finally let go of her hand and tipped up her chin. If she had taken one step back, if she had uttered a word of protest or looked away... She didn't.

With a groan of defeat he gave in to the need and lowered his head.

Emma had missed him terribly. She met him halfway, the touch of his mouth igniting all the feelings she had been holding in check. She moaned as Joe changed the angle, deepened the contact. Her hands tightened. His mouth hardened. She edged closer, pulses racing as he crushed her to him. The force of his kiss bent her head back. She was conscious only of his arms around her protectively, his mouth feasting on hers, his heart thundering beneath her hand. As did her own.

"Joe!" she cried when he finally lifted his mouth.

At the sound of her voice an agonized expression crossed his face and he bent to her again.

"We have to quit meeting in barns," she whispered raggedly when they finally broke apart.

Joe was doing his best to ignore his body's urgent demands that he give in to temptation and damn the consequences. He barely heard what she said. Where Emma was concerned, his normally iron will was about as useless as teats on a bull.

He was almost relieved to hear Daniel shouting his name. As Joe poked his head out of the tack room, Kenny came racing down the aisle. He barely greeted Joe and Emma before bending over the puppies.

Emma's gaze met Joe's over Kenny's head. Was Joe thinking, as she was, about what Kenny had almost interrupted? Without another word Joe went out to see what his foreman wanted. Disappointed, Emma watched Kenny pat Dolly and then greet each puppy in turn. She had to smile at his obvious devotion toward the little family.

"I've picked out names," Kenny confided to her as he stroked one finger gently down a plump copper body. The puppy licked his hand with its tiny pink tongue. "Do you think that's okay?"

Emma was grateful that she had been granted a moment for her breathing to slow and her heart rate to descend to normal.

"I'm sure Joe would be happy to have you save him the trouble," she told Kenny. "What names have you picked?"

Before he could answer, Joe stuck his head back in the doorway. He greeted the boy and then looked at Emma as if there was something he wanted to tell her.

"Joe—" Kenny began excitedly.

"I'm sorry, pal. I have to go check on a cow. I'll see you two later." He touched a finger to the brim of his hat in a casual salute. "Bye."

To Emma, the room seemed cooler without him, the light dimmer. Swallowing her disappointment, she redirected her attention to Kenny, who looked as if he had lost his best friend.

"I'd like to hear the names you thought of," she told him.

"I guess I can tell you," he said glumly. Emma was clearly his second choice.

"You'll be able to tell Joe later, maybe at supper."

"I guess." The thought must have cheered him a little. "I named the boy puppies Clancy, Sean and O'Hara," he said. "Because they're Irish setters, you know?"

"Good idea," Emma said, "but you only told me three names and there are four male puppies." She tried hard not to think about Joe and wonder just how he felt about what had happened between them before Daniel's interruption.

"I wanted to give them all Irish names," Kenny continued, "but I don't know any more."

"How about Paddy?" Emma suggested absently.

Kenny wrinkled his nose with obvious distaste. "That sounds like a girl's name."

"It's spelled differently," she explained.

"But the puppy wouldn't know that when I called him," Kenny reasoned, making her chuckle.

"I guess you're right." She thought a moment, but nothing else came to mind. "Why don't you ask Joe?"

Kenny considered the idea. "Yeah, maybe I will." One of the puppies was finished nursing. He began to waddle away from Dolly. Carefully, with one hand beneath the rounded tummy the way Joe had showed him, Kenny picked the puppy up.

"Which one is that?" Emma asked.

He studied the little creature carefully. "I'm not sure. I think it's Clancy, but they're still all pretty much alike."

Emma stayed and watched the dogs for a few more minutes. While she did, she asked Kenny how school was going.

"Fine," he said, tone defensive.

"I'm glad," Emma continued. "You know, you could tell me if you were having any problems."

Kenny eyed her dubiously, as if he was afraid to trust her. "I hate it," he finally burst out.

"Why?"

He looked away, his face closed. "School's dumb."

Emma waited patiently as she petted Dolly. After a moment Kenny put his puppy back and began picking at an imaginary thread on the leg of his jeans.

"The other kids make fun of me, and I can't keep up with the work," he muttered. "I'm going to quit as soon as I'm old enough."

Emma knew the importance of an education. Especially for someone with no family, like Kenny. It could well be his ticket to a better life.

"I used to be a teacher," she volunteered.

He glanced at her curiously. "Yeah?" Then he masked his interest with indifference. "So?"

"I need to get a job in September and I'm thinking about going back to it," she added, feeling her way slowly. "But I'm kinda rusty. Maybe I could practice a little on you."

His expression was definitely suspicious. "Why?"

Emma thought fast. "It's been a long time since I taught," she said. "I'm sort of nervous about standing in front of a roomful of students again."

To her surprise, Kenny's expression softened slightly. "I guess I know what you mean. I hate having to stand up and recite worst of all."

"So, would you help me out?" she asked, pressing her advantage.

"What would I have to do?" His wariness made her heart ache as she wondered how many times he had been disappointed or hurt in his young life.

"Maybe we could go over some of your homework together," she suggested. "Just for a little while in the evenings. I could sort of get a feel for it again."

He thought for a moment. "Would you want to work on math?" he asked. "And maybe spelling?"

She kept her voice casual. "Sure. I could use a little practice with reading, too."

He shrugged. "I guess that would be okay. We can start tonight if you want."

Emma managed to hold in her satisfied grin. "That would be fine." She gave Dolly's satiny head a final pat and rose to go back to the house. "I'll see you later, then."

"Okay."

Kenny seemed bright enough. She suspected it wasn't a lack of brains that kept him behind in school but a combination of low self-esteem and an unsettled background. Joe's attention was helping him with the one thing; perhaps she could make a difference with the other.

At supper that evening Kenny broke the news about helping her brush up on her teaching skills before he even remembered to ask Joe about a name for the fourth male puppy.

Joe looked inquiringly at Emma, and she hoped he wouldn't say the wrong thing. Beneath his bravado Kenny was as skittish as a barn cat in a bright light.

"Are you sure you want to do this?" Joe asked her. "Will you have the time, what with sending out all those job applications?"

"What applications?" Marian asked, looking up from a bite of meat loaf on her fork.

"I've decided to look for a teaching job back in Seattle this fall," Emma explained. "I have to do something to support myself, and that's what I'm trained for."

Marian exchanged a glance with Joe, but all she said was, "Oh."

Emma was relieved when Kenny changed the subject by asking Joe about a name for the last puppy.

"I think that Mickey might make a good name," Joe said calmly, still looking at Emma.

"Yeah," Kenny agreed enthusiastically. "Mickey would be perfect."

Emma finished her supper in silence. A summer spent on a ranch with an attractive cowboy might be great material for daydreams, but when it came to her future and finding a job, going back to teaching was the sensible thing to do. It wasn't as if anything permanent was going to develop between Joe and her, anyway. Despite how appealing that idea might be.

Kenny was still talking about the puppies, naming and describing each one. Finally Joe reminded him that his supper was getting cold, and he took a bite.

"They are getting awfully cute," Emma commented, remembering the feel of their warm, soft little bodies when she held them. "And Dolly is such a good, patient mother."

"You should have children of your own," Marian said.

Emma's expression must have revealed some of her distress at the unexpected comment, because Marian looked immediately remorseful.

"I'm so sorry, dear," she said, her voice full of embarrassment. She covered Emma's hand on the table with her own. "I didn't mean to remind you of anything painful."

Emma tried to put on a brave smile, but watching the puppies in Dolly's tender care had reminded her, too, of the baby she had lost, and her emotions were still close to the surface. She knew she wasn't fooling either Marian or Joe, who watched her closely. Still, she had to try.

"I'm okay," she insisted. "Puppies and kittens are always irresistible, aren't they? I could just cuddle them all day long."

"Why does that make you cry?" Kenny asked as she blinked back the tears that threatened to overfill her eyes.

"Never mind," Joe said shortly.

Kenny's expression immediately crumbled. All it took was a harsh word from his idol to devastate him.

"I'm sorry." He was obviously puzzled by what he had done.

"No, it's okay," Emma told him, darting a pleading glance at Joe. "It shouldn't upset me, and Kenny had no idea."

Joe, who had leaned forward at the table almost protectively, took a deep breath and sat back. "If you're sure," he said. "You don't have to explain anything to anyone, you know."

"I know." Her smile was wobbly around the edges but she was glad to see Kenny's anxious expression fade slightly.

"I didn't mean to make you upset," he said.

"I know you didn't, sweetie." She took a steadying breath, determined not to cry. "I was married once," she explained to him. "And we had a baby."

Kenny was looking at her attentively, a frown puckering his forehead. "Where's the baby now? Did you give it up?"

Emma's heart went out to him. She made herself go on.

"Something went wrong, and the baby didn't live."

Kenny's frown deepened. "That's too bad," he said. "Was it a boy or a girl?"

"Kenny," Joe said in a warning voice, but Emma shook her head.

"It's okay. It was a little girl and we named her Alicia Marie. I still miss her a lot."

"I'm sorry." Kenny pushed his chair back. He came around the table hesitantly and gave Emma a hug. She returned it, holding his thin body tightly for a moment while she got her emotions under control.

"Thank you," she whispered, letting him go. "If I have another child, I'd like him to be just like you."

"Uh, thanks." Cheeks slightly red, Kenny put his dishes in the dishwasher and then turned to Joe. "Can I go back to the barn with the puppies?" he asked.

"I thought you were going to help Emma practice her teaching skills?" Joe's expression didn't give away a thing. Emma realized again how good he was with Kenny.

Kenny turned his pleading gaze on her. "Could I just go for a few minutes first?" he asked.

"It's fine with me," she said. "Just let me know when you get back, okay?"

"Sure." Kenny's attention swiveled back to Joe.

"Yeah, go on," he said with a wry grin. "Tell them their new names."

Kenny was out the back door so fast that Emma almost laughed.

"Is he having trouble in school?" Joe asked her, rising to pour himself more coffee. "Is that what his helping you is really all about?"

"He seems to be," she said. "He said he hates school and wants to drop out as soon as he's old enough."

Joe frowned.

"I think he's got brains," she added hastily, "and I'm sure I can help him."

Joe studied his cup for a moment. "Remember, he's leaving here at the end of the summer."

"So am I," Emma said quietly as she began clearing away dishes. "Probably before Kenny does." Joe's message was plain. Don't get attached to Kenny. Or was he reminding her, in some roundabout way, not to get attached to him?

She felt Joe's gaze on her but he didn't say anything more. Finally, as she was wiping off the stove, she heard him leave the room.

When Joe came back to the kitchen a few moments later his mother was alone.

"Where is she?" he asked.

Her brows rose inquiringly, but she made no comment on his interest in Emma's whereabouts.

"She went outside. You know that I didn't mean to upset her earlier, don't you? I just want her to be happy again, with a husband who'll appreciate her. With children to love. That's what she needs. That's what most women need."

Her words, so ordinary, hit Joe with all the force of a poisoned arrow. Fighting the image of Emma with someone else, bearing another man's children, he managed a noncommittal answer and hurried out the back door, forgetting that Emma had gone that way, too.

She was sitting on the porch in the old swing. When she heard him she looked up. For a moment Joe stood, frozen, as he stared at her. Then, with an effort that bordered on pain, he frowned and clumped down the steps to his pickup. With no idea where he was headed, he left the yard in a cloud of dust.

Chapter Eight

Joe sat on his bar stool at the Watering Hole on the other side of Caulder Springs and nursed his beer. When he had first walked in he had recognized a couple of the other patrons, but he didn't feel like company tonight. He had too much on his mind.

Actually, he had one thing on his mind, and that was Emma. He didn't know what to do about her. Ever since the day in the barn, the fire in his gut had burned hotter than ever. Perhaps, instead of avoiding her, he should just give in to temptation. If she was willing, maybe repetition and familiarity would eventually douse the flames. He doubted it, but anything was worth a try.

Finishing his beer, Joe wandered over to the pool table and watched a couple play eight ball.

"You want to challenge the table?" the man asked.

Joe shook his head. "No, thanks. I'm not in a winning frame of mind."

* * *

After Joe had peeled out of the yard in his truck, Emma stared after him. Why had he left the way he did, as if he were being pursued by demons? Baffled, she went back over the supper conversation, but could remember nothing in particular that could have put that tormented expression on Joe's face.

Was there some financial threat to the ranch that she wasn't aware of? She was no accountant, but the records she had helped Joe put on the computer hadn't seemed to indicate any sort of crisis. What else could be bothering him? Not his apparent interest in her. She knew she had given every indication of returning that interest. Playing hard to get wasn't Emma's style. Even if he had decided, for some reason, to back off, she wouldn't have expected the decision to send him rushing from the house the way he had.

Emma was tempted to question Marian about his behavior, then changed her mind. As long as she had no clue as to the nature of the problem, she couldn't really ask Joe's mother about it without taking the chance of prying into something private.

She finally wandered back into the house, but neither the variety provided by the television and its satellite dish nor the book she had started held any appeal.

"When Kenny comes in, would you send him up to my room?" Emma asked Marian, searching the older woman's face for clues without success. If she was privy to whatever was bothering Joe, she wasn't saying.

"Sure, dear," she replied, glancing up from a glossy magazine.

Emma wandered upstairs to write a letter to a friend in Seattle. Before she was finished, Kenny poked his head in her open doorway. His expression was slightly sullen. Obviously, his earlier enthusiasm for helping her had worn off.

"Do you want to do my schoolwork now?"

Emma rose from the antique cherry writing desk.

"Sure. Get your books and we'll work at the kitchen table, okay?" That way, she would know if Joe got back. She was still concerned about him. Not that where he went was any of her business, she reminded herself, but she couldn't help wondering.

Emma helped Kenny with his math until it was time for him to take his bath and get ready for bed, but Joe didn't come back.

"Do you understand this better now?" she asked Kenny.

"Yeah, I guess. It kinda makes sense the way you explained it," he admitted. "Thanks." Gathering up the books and papers, he raced upstairs.

After the sound of his footsteps faded, Emma returned to the porch swing. Time went by slowly as she sat there watching the twilight deepen into night, but Joe still didn't appear. She grew more anxious about his absence. Where could he be? What was bothering him?

After a while, even though the evening was warm and pleasant, she began feeling like a housemother at curfew so she went inside. Wishing Marian good night, she climbed the stairs to her room, sure she wouldn't sleep until she heard the pickup truck return.

Emma squealed with laughter, barely eluding Joe's outstretched hand as he chased her through the warm surf. The sun was hot. It sparkled against the deep blue water of the lagoon. Joe's eyes had lost their usual icy-silver chill, and his hard mouth curved into a grin as he pulled up short on the fine white sand and settled his hands on his hips. Emma stared admiringly at his powerful body in the revealing suit.

"You can't run forever, Mrs. Sutter," he called teasingly.

Emma heard a rattling noise and looked around to see what it was. She heard it again. The next thing she knew, she was alone in bed, surrounded by darkness.

The noise was coming from the direction of the bedroom window. It sounded like hail hitting the glass.

Still half caught in the lovely dream, Emma lay in bed, listening.

Rattle, rattle. Fully awake and curious, the dream lost to her now, she got up and padded silently to the window. A whisper of air drifted through the opening. From where Emma stood she could see Joe's pickup parked out back. At least he was home. Then she glanced down and saw him. He was bent over, scooping up more pebbles.

Emma leaned out, mindful of her thin cotton nightgown. With one hand on its scooped neckline she called softly, "What are you doing?"

Joe grinned up at her in the moonlight.

"Oh, you're awake."

Emma ran a hand over her hair, pushing back the dark curls. "I am now."

"Get dressed and come down," he urged her, beckoning. "I want to show you the moon."

Emma stepped back, surprised. What was he up to now? Had he been drinking? Another rock pinged insistently against the windowpane.

"Emma?"

At the rate he was going, he'd wake Marian up for sure. Emma leaned out and put a finger to her lips.

"Shh!"

"Are you coming out?" he demanded. It was a good thing that both Marian's and Kenny's rooms were across the hall, on the other side of the old house.

She nodded emphatically and then ducked back in the window, pulling the curtains shut behind her.

Outside, Joe waited impatiently, his gaze on the back door. Finally Emma emerged, wearing a T-shirt and striped shorts. She had sandals on her feet. Her hair was a midnight dark cloud and her long legs gleamed like porcelain in the moonlight.

Feeling the sharp pull of his attraction toward her, Joe went over to the back porch where she stood waiting. When he got close, she started to speak.

"What did you—"

Joe flung his Stetson aside and reached for her. Lifting her off the porch, he stopped her words with his mouth. She struggled briefly, but he was determined. Her lips were warm and soft, her scent as sweet as an old-fashioned rose. When he felt her relax against him, he crowded closer and deepened the kiss.

God, she felt good in his arms, with her hands tucked against his chest. He nuzzled his face into her hair, letting the individual strands caress his skin, and drew in a deep breath. She intoxicated him.

Maybe he had been crazy to try to resist her when nothing could come of the attraction, anyway. After all, she was leaving in a few weeks.

"Joe." Her voice was muffled against his shoulder. With reluctance he set her on her feet and let her go.

He waited for her to repeat her question, but instead she gazed up at him silently. Her lips were slightly parted. Indulging himself, he kissed her again.

It was harder to let her go this time. Covering his shaky control, he said, "I thought you might like to look at the moon with me. The temperature is so mild and the moon is full—and just as pale as a silver dollar. The stars are out, too."

"It's a lovely night," she agreed, looking up at the sky.

Joe still had one arm around her shoulders. He didn't wait for her to change her mind. Freeing her only long enough to grab the blanket he'd taken from behind the seat of his truck, he hugged her close for a moment. And fought the urge to kiss her again.

"Let's go out by the creek on the other side of that rise," he suggested, pointing. "It's not far. We can sit on the blanket and I'll show you the constellations we have in Colorado."

When Emma agreed, her eyes unreadable in the shadows, he walked her toward the stand of cottonwoods. The sound of running water grew louder. Emma was silent, and he wondered what she was thinking.

"Are you tired?" he asked when they stopped. The rise shielded them from the house, and they had gone in the opposite direction from the outbuildings. Around them nothing stirred except an occasional ripple of air. Joe bent to spread the blanket.

"No," Emma replied, looking around, "I'm not tired."

"Me, neither. It's too pretty a night for sleeping." Not sure what else to say, he took her hand and drew her down with him. Lying on his back, he urged her to use his arm for a pillow. She did. For a few moments they both gazed at the sky.

"I think the stars are brighter out here," she murmured. "And I know they're closer."

"That's because they don't have to compete with any city lights," he told her. "And maybe they look closer because you're not seeing them through a veil of smog."

"Seattle doesn't have smog," she said defensively. Her arms were folded across her stomach. Joe reached out and took her hand, lacing their fingers together.

"No?" He'd never been there, but he'd heard how beautiful the city was, tucked between the waters of Puget Sound and the Cascade mountain range. It was a long way from Colorado and the plains. Maybe someday he'd go there, just to see it for himself.

"Well," Emma conceded, "I guess we have a little smog. Nothing like L.A. and other places, though."

"You like it there." It wasn't a question; he could tell from her voice that she did.

He felt her nod against his arm. "As cities go, it's pretty nice, but it's changing. More traffic, more crime, more pollution."

"How do you like Colorado?" he couldn't keep from asking. "It must be quite a change, so bare and empty."

"It is," she agreed after a moment. "But I'm finding that I love the openness. And the ranch, Caulder Springs and the church where you all know each other. It will be hard to leave when the time comes."

Joe caught his breath, and she fell abruptly silent. He wasn't sure why, but her words relieved him. It was good to know that she would leave remembering his country with fondness. He wanted to ask if it would be hard to leave him, but he didn't dare. Instead, he rolled over, facing her.

"You haven't told me about the stars," she reminded him.

He looked into her face, not that difficult to make out in the moonlight.

"Later," he whispered, gathering her closer as he thought to himself that this was a night for fireworks, not stars.

"You never told me how the ranch got its name," Emma said quickly. "Why's it called the Blue Moon?"

Joe grinned in the darkness, savoring the anticipation that was building between them. He stroked the fingers of one hand down her cheek and then spread them across her throat. Her pulse danced beneath his fingers.

"Grandpa named it. He said cattle ranching was truly profitable about once in a blue moon. That you had to live the life because you love it, not for the money. He figured naming the ranch the Blue Moon would keep us in mind of that."

"Oh." Her voice was faint. "I would have never guessed."

"Satisfied?" he asked, propping his head on the heel of one hand as he dipped the fingers of the other into the neckline of her T-shirt and watched her shiver in reaction.

"Well, you told me you were going to teach me about constellations." She peered up at him in the silvery light. "Did you get me out here under false pretenses?"

Sighing in mock exasperation, he rolled onto his back and stared at the heavens. "The only one I remember for sure is the Big Dipper," he confessed after a moment. "See it there?" He pointed upward.

"Even I know that one," Emma said with a chuckle. "This excursion hasn't been much of a learning experience so far."

Joe shifted and rose above her. "Woman," he said with a low growl in his voice, "are you issuing me a challenge?"

Emma slid her hand up his arm. He could see her smile.

"Cowboy," she responded, "would you walk away, if I was?"

At the throaty invitation in her voice, Joe's senses began to vibrate with desire as he bent over her.

"No way, ma'am," he murmured, grasping her chin with one hand. "Not for all the stars in the heavens."

Emma let him pull her beneath him on the blanket. Feeling his big male body pressing into hers, she lifted her mouth to meet him halfway. As her eyelids fluttered shut she felt a tremor race through him. She held his body tighter and gave herself up to the pure joy of being with him. In moments, she was locked into an embrace that nothing would have enticed her to break.

As Joe's breathing grew more ragged and his touch more insistent, he swept Emma into a whirlwind of passion and need. Their clothing disappeared without her quite being aware of it, and the feelings inside her threatened to burst free.

"Emma..."

"It's okay," she murmured, knowing what he was about to ask. "I'm still on the pill. It's okay."

"I wouldn't make you pregnant," he vowed, voice low. His concern moved her deeply. When Joe urged her to touch him as he was touching her, she complied eagerly and sought out his most vulnerable, most sensitive spots. Her hands brushed over the hard planes of his body, her fingers lingering whenever she felt him shudder. Then she continued her intimate exploration as he groaned fiercely.

"You're driving me wild," he admitted through clenched teeth when he had lifted his mouth from hers for a moment. He, too, had been exploring, nibbling and nuzzling, stroking and caressing until Emma thought she might faint from the inferno of heat he roused in her. At his ragged confession, she skimmed one hand downward, across his hard stomach. The muscles shivered beneath her touch as she trailed her fingers into the coarser hair below. She felt his body grow taut, and she hesitated.

"Touch me," he groaned. "Emma, touch me." He was on his back, his body completely open to her. Shifting, she nibbled on his earlobe instead. He sighed, relaxing, and she wrapped her fingers around his pulsing arousal. His body arched like a bow as he hissed the breath back in between his teeth.

Instantly she released him.

"Did I hurt you?"

His chuckle was half-strangled. "It's the sweetest pain," he gasped. "Sweetheart, it only hurts when you stop."

Carefully she touched him again. He groaned, and the rigid flesh jumped beneath her fingers. She stroked lightly down his thick length, and he bit back another groan. Then, as she was contemplating new tortures, he shifted and pressed her down against the blanket.

"My turn now," he promised hoarsely. His wide shoulders blotted out the stars. Then he leaned close, nibbling at her belly with his mouth, licking it with his tongue. Her eyes shut. Her awareness centered on his hot, wet touch.

Joe tormented Emma until she didn't think she could survive another minute without him tangled deep inside her. She begged him to take her, but he shook his head.

"Not yet."

His fingers were tangled in the thatch of downy hair between her legs, his lips skimming up one thigh as she arched helplessly, craving more. Needing more.

And then he gave it to her. He settled his mouth against her and drove her up, up and over the edge. Her fingers dug into his scalp and she hung on, moaning. She pressed herself against him as the world exploded and showered her with all the stars she'd seen above them. Giving her no time to recover, he took her again to the top. He held her there and then set her free.

When she finally went limp and cried, "No more—I can't," he settled himself between her trembling legs, slipped into her throbbing flesh and showed her that she could. One last time, with him.

While she spun away in helpless abandon, his grip tightened. He muffled a ragged shout against her shoulder as his body went still and he, too, found his release.

"Easy, girl. Easy, baby. That's it, just let my hands touch you everywhere."

Emma watched Joe, listened to the low, even tone of his mesmerizing voice as he stroked the skittish piebald filly. He stood with the horse in the small corral adjoining the barn. She was wearing a halter, and Joe had just smoothed a saddle blanket on her black-and-white-spotted back. From

Emma's perch on the top rail of the fence she could see the filly's muscles twitch with nerves. Slowly Joe dropped his hands and took a step back.

The filly, named Polka Princess, rolled her eyes and turned her head to look at him. Then she straightened and blew out a blast of air as he began walking her around in a circle. Emma could hear his voice as he kept up a steady line of chatter.

She shifted her weight on the railing, careful not to do anything that might startle Polka Princess. Joe's patience with the animals always impressed her, especially his way with the young horses. It made her remember his patience with her, and she flushed hotly, glad he couldn't read her mind.

Emma couldn't imagine Joe living anywhere but the ranch, and she loved watching him work the horses. Someday, he had told her, Polka Princess would probably be a cutting horse, or perhaps a barrel racer. Meanwhile, he was gentling her and teaching her the basics.

After a few more minutes he took the saddle blanket off the filly and turned her into an adjacent corral, patting her neck and scratching beneath her striped forelock. Then he came back over to where Emma was perched and grinned up at her. Lines fanned out from his eyes and bracketed his mouth. For a moment she was tempted to lean down and kiss him, but she didn't do it. Since their night under the stars, he smiled more often and his gaze often sought hers. She wasn't about to do anything to jinx the new closeness between them.

"Let's take a ride," he said now, putting a hand on her bare knee below her cutoff jeans, stroking her warm skin with his fingers. "I need to exercise Jet." Jet was a big gelding a neighboring rancher had bought for his daughter and brought to Joe for some polishing. Or, as Joe had explained, the horse's manners needed a little work. He normally didn't take the time for things like this when the ranch was busy, but Jet's owner was a friend.

"Jet's a little too feisty for Penny right now," Joe had told Emma, "but I'll settle him down." She had been relieved to see that his brand of settling involved only a firm hand and a pickup load of patience. Already the horse showed a marked improvement in his behavior.

Now Emma slid down off the fence. "Can I ride Jet today?" she asked. He was a beautiful animal.

Joe looked surprised. "Sorry, honey, but I wouldn't trust him with you. Not yet. He's still got too many kinks in him."

Emma knew Jet's habit of bucking whenever he was first mounted, but she had thought Joe had cured him of that. She was so busy savoring the endearment he had used that she didn't even object to his refusal.

"Okay." She wondered if he realized what he'd called her. One look at his intense expression and she saw that, not only had he realized it, the term had been intentional. His eyes were narrowed against the sun, and he was smiling. She smiled back and he bent to kiss her. Then he pulled her close for a moment before letting her go. Emma cuddled against him, almost losing herself in his heat and power. She blinked, regaining control of her spinning senses with an effort.

"Come on," he murmured. "I've got a horse to ride."

A short while later they were returning to the corral at a slow trot, with Emma riding Belle, as usual. Suddenly two of the barn cats raced under the fence and almost ran beneath Jet's hooves. Rearing, he lurched sideways and crashed into Belle. The horse stumbled as Emma lost her balance. She struggled to stay in the saddle, almost losing her seat. Joe reached out and steadied her with one long arm as he brought Jet under control. In a heartbeat the crisis was past.

Shaken, Emma dismounted. Joe followed, grabbing her. "Are you okay?" he asked.

She drew in a ragged breath. She had fallen before. It wasn't that big a deal. It had all just happened so fast.

"I'm fine," she quavered, then cleared her throat. "Really, I'm all right."

His expression was grim. "I thought you were going to fall," he said. "One of the horses could have trampled you."

Now that she was on firm ground, Emma's equilibrium returned. She felt a little foolish. Trying to distract him, she arched a brow.

"One of Joe Sutter's horses?" she teased. "I heard they were better trained than that. I heard they're forbidden to trample anyone."

Joe's frown of concern melted slowly into a retaliatory smirk. He scooped her into his arms as she shrieked a protest.

"I don't put up with any sass on my spread," he drawled. "I think you need to be cooled off."

"Put me down!" Emma demanded as he carried her to the full horse trough and held her over it. She struggled wildly, hanging on to his neck, but it did her no good. "You wouldn't dare!"

Joe's gaze narrowed and his grin widened. "Are you challenging me, Miss Davenport?" he asked in a dangerous voice.

Emma looked down at the muddy water and then back at him. "Oh, please, Joe," she cooed, batting her lashes flirtatiously. She stroked the front of his shirt with her hand and slipped a finger between the snaps to tickle his bare skin. "I'll do anything if you don't throw me in that horse trough."

He straightened and held her closer to his chest. "Anything?" His voice had deepened.

She nodded emphatically and widened her eyes. "Anything." She let her hand slide along his jaw and teased his earlobe. Then she slipped her fingers into the collar of his shirt, lightly brushing his warm neck. From the corners of her eyes she peeked up at him, head tilted as she slowly wet her bottom lip with the tip of her tongue.

She felt his body tense. His gaze narrowed and a muscle began to work in his jaw. In response, tingles of awareness danced across Emma's nerve endings. Swallowing, she lifted her chin and returned his stare boldly.

"Anything," she whispered again.

Joe's arms tightened around her and his head dipped. His mouth covered hers in a searing kiss. Emma was responding with wholehearted enthusiasm when he suddenly swung her to her feet.

"Damn," he exploded, glaring while she fought to gain her balance on shaky legs. "I have work to do."

"Joe!" she gasped, hurt by his sudden abandonment.

Leaving her in openmouthed shock, her body still throbbing from the hard imprint of his, he grabbed the reins of the two horses and led them to the barn. For a moment she thought he was kidding, getting even for her audacious flirting, but when he didn't look back she realized that his annoyance was real.

"Fine," she muttered under her breath, furious. "*You* kissed *me,* Joe Sutter. If you want to be that unreasonable, you belong with the horses. Take care of both of them, all by your lonesome." Tossing a last frown his way, she stomped up to the house and spent the rest of the afternoon wrenching weeds from the soil of the vegetable garden.

From the open doorway of the barn Joe watched her go. It wasn't Emma that he was annoyed at. Not really. It was his own inability to resist her—no matter where they happened to be at the time—that angered him. That and the dawning realization that letting her go when the time came wasn't going to be as easy as he had first thought.

Jet butted him in the back, hard, and he almost went sprawling. He glared at the horse as it bared its teeth into the semblance of a grin and bobbed its head.

"Watch it," Joe growled. "Laugh at me and I'll see that you end up as a hack-for-hire at a rent-by-the-hour riding stable. And that's a promise." With a last frowning glance down the road where Emma had disappeared, Joe began unsaddling their mounts.

Emma was still seething at his unpredictable behavior when she went inside to shower away the afternoon's grime. The phone started to ring as she was crossing the kitchen. Marian had gone to Tricia's to see how the mother-to-be was feeling, so Emma answered.

"Sutter residence."

"I'm glad to hear that you're still there," said a faintly familiar voice on the other end of the line. "I was afraid you might have already left."

"Who is this?" she had to ask.

The caller's tone warmed a notch. "Now I *am* crushed. This is Cal Banning. We met at the feed store in town. I meant to call sooner, but I've been swamped with work."

Emma remembered guiltily how she had put him off the last time he called. "Hi," she said. "I'm sorry that I didn't recognize your voice."

"No matter. I called to see if you'd like to go to a show in Sterling this weekend. There's a new comedy playing."

Emma thought again of Joe and his hot-and-cold attitude. He hadn't bothered to ask her on a date. Not once. Ordinarily, Emma didn't believe in scheming and manipulating, but perhaps Joe needed a real shock to jolt him into understanding how he was making her feel. Before she could talk herself out of it, she accepted Cal's offer. They made the necessary arrangements, and he said again how much he was looking forward to seeing her.

After she hung up, Emma stared at the phone, regret already sinking in.

"What's the matter, dear?" Marian asked as she walked into the kitchen. "Wrong number? It happens sometimes."

Emma hadn't even heard her car pull up. "No," she said, distracted. "How was your visit?"

It wasn't Cal's fault that he'd called right after she and Joe had argued. She couldn't cancel, not after she had already accepted his invitation. What excuse could she give him?

Emma was barely aware that Marian was talking about Tricia and the baby as she set out the ingredients for supper. Emma didn't have the faintest idea what to do. The only logical thing would be to keep her date. Surely, Joe didn't have any right to object after the way he'd acted. Not that she cared what he thought, anyway.

"You're going where?" Joe set the forkful of food carefully back on his plate and stared at Emma across the table. It was Friday evening and she had just mentioned her plans for the next night, hoping to slip them past Joe's notice.

"Dinner and a show with Cal in Sterling," she repeated bravely. Seated between the two of them, Marian turned her head back and forth as if she were watching a tennis match. Kenny went on eating.

"I think that's a lovely idea," Marian injected into the silence. "After all, you've hardly been anywhere since you came here."

Emma heard Joe make a choking sound.

"Well, we've been to church," she said, not wanting Marian to think that she had been bored at the ranch. She hadn't. "And you and I have been shopping in town. After all, I came to visit you, not run all around the country."

Marian chuckled and cut another piece of roast beef. "I meant that you haven't really had any social life," she amended without looking at Joe. "You haven't been out in the evening at all. Granted, there isn't a lot of nightlife around here, but there are church dances and bingo at the grange hall, not to mention the bowling alley and the Watering Hole."

"What's the Watering Hole?" Emma asked as Joe bit into a roll as if he meant to kill it with his teeth.

"A bar," Marian said, rolling her eyes. "Probably not the kind of place you'd like to go, anyway."

Emma did her best to look thoughtful. "Oh, I don't know," she mused. "If they had live music it might be okay. Maybe Cal will want to stop there on the way home."

"The Watering Hole doesn't have live music," Joe growled. "And it's no place for you to go. If Cal takes you there, I'll..." As both Emma and Marian watched, he stopped abruptly. Frowning blackly, he scraped back his chair and carried his half-empty plate to the counter. In silence he dumped its contents into the garbage and put it in the dishwasher.

"I have to check on a calf," he said, holding himself rigidly. His face was a dusky red beneath its tan. "Thanks for supper, Mom." The door slammed behind him.

Emma exchanged wide-eyed looks with Marian but didn't say anything. Instead, she glanced at her own plate and realized that her appetite had fled. Excusing herself softly, she got up from the table. Tomorrow night, she vowed silently, she was going to have a good time or die trying.

After Emma left on Cal's arm, Joe silently congratulated himself on his superior self-control in resisting the urge to knock the other man's shiny white teeth down his throat. Cal had made Joe want to gag, fawning over Emma like a shoe salesman working on commission. He'd even had the gall to ask if Joe didn't think her prettier than last year's rodeo princess and her whole court combined.

Emma had flushed, her eyes refusing to meet his, while Joe had studied her closely before managing a civil answer. It was a miracle he hadn't cracked his jaw grinding his molars as he had watched Cal escort her to his flashy convertible, his greedy hand on the back of her green dress, and settle her inside as if she were made out of eggshells. After they drove off, too fast in Joe's opinion, he'd noticed that his fists were clenched harder than his teeth.

"That's a neat car," Kenny said.

"I'm sure they'll have a nice time," Marian commented from the kitchen doorway. "I'd forgotten how charming Cal can be. He's always had such lovely manners. His mother was a Finney, you know. No doubt she taught him."

Joe stared at her, narrow-eyed, but she merely gave him an innocent smile in return and wondered out loud if Emma would be too tired in the morning to help her lay out a new sewing pattern.

"She'll probably want to sleep in," his mother mused as she wandered back into the living room.

For the first time in five years Joe wished he hadn't quit smoking. Restlessly he followed Kenny out to the barn. All the boy wanted to do these days was to watch Dolly and her puppies. At the bunkhouse Cookie told Joe that the men had already gone to town. Joe ended up back at the house, watching a television movie he'd seen before and hated. The second time he got up and wandered to the window, his mother put down her knitting and hit the mute button on the remote control.

"Why don't you ask her out yourself?" she demanded.

"Who?" Joe stared hard at the apple tree his father had planted outside the window.

"Emma, of course."

The fury he had managed to contain while Cal was there flared up and threatened to engulf him. He glanced over his shoulder, doing his best to wipe all expression from his face.

"Why would I do a fool thing like that?" he asked in the flat tone that often made grown men suddenly realize they had urgent business elsewhere.

"Emma's such a nice girl. I know you're over Stephanie and you could certainly do worse."

Dammit, Joe wanted to yell at the top of his lungs, don't you think I know that? Instead, he allowed himself one last quelling glance before stalking through the kitchen and out the back door. He didn't trust himself to stay inside without saying something he might regret. Besides, there must be a few hay bales somewhere that needed moving. Tonight he could do the job with his bare hands.

Emma's date wasn't a roaring success, despite Cal's efforts to make it so. The movie was funny, the restaurant he took her to had good Italian food and Cal, himself, was both attractive and flatteringly attentive. He just wasn't Joe.

"I had a nice time," good manners compelled Emma to say when he finally pulled up alongside the blue-and-white pickup.

Cal circled his sporty red convertible to open Emma's door. As he walked her to the house, one arm draped loosely across her shoulders, she glanced around nervously and wondered if Joe was standing in the shadows. She decided he wouldn't bother to spy.

Cal stopped at the base of the back steps. A light on the utility pole on the other side of the house was on, banishing the darkness. Mercifully, the back porch light had been left off.

"I had a great time," Cal said. "I hope you'll let me take you out again."

He was a nice enough man, one Emma might have been attracted to under different circumstances. Now she made herself return his smile, unable to give him a bald refusal even though she knew she wouldn't be dating him again.

"That sounds nice," she said, taking the coward's way out, "but I don't know what my schedule will be. I'm really here visiting Marian, of course, so I don't feel I should make other plans without checking with her." She faltered to a stop, but Cal's smile never wavered.

"I understand. Why don't I give you a call in a few days?"

"Fine." Emma felt that her face had to show the strain she was feeling. Cal leaned toward her and kissed her cheek. Her panic must have showed.

"We country folk might not move as fast as they do in the big city," he drawled, looking confident, "but we usually know where we're headed, even if it does take us longer to get there."

"I see," Emma said breathlessly. "Well, that's probably a good thing." Her conscience threatened to overwhelm her with guilt at deceiving him. "Well," she continued in a rush, smiling brightly, "it's getting late. I'd better go in."

Cal waited as she dashed up the steps, waved quickly and let herself into the house. Only when she finally heard his car drive away did Emma slump against the closed door with a sigh of relief.

Next time, she vowed silently, she would refuse his invitation up front and spare them both. Taking another deep breath, she crossed the mudroom and entered the kitchen, only to yelp with surprise when she heard Joe's voice in the gloom.

"So, did you and Calvin have a good time tonight?" he asked from his seat in the darkness.

Chapter Nine

Emma froze at the sound of Joe's voice.

"What are you doing, sitting here in the dark?" she asked defensively. "Waiting up for me?"

Joe rose to his full, intimidating height. Emma wished she could see his expression, but his face was in shadow.

"Maybe I just wanted to make sure you got home okay," he murmured. "Did you have a good time?"

"I had a fine time," Emma replied, thoroughly annoyed. What right did he have to scare her half to death and then to quiz her about her date? She tried to step around him, but he shifted so that his big body blocked her path. One hand came out to settle lightly on her shoulder.

"Are you going out with Cal again?" he demanded.

Something exploded inside Emma. How dare Joe be jealous after the way he had acted toward her? As if she were some kind of virus he was fighting off.

She thrust out her chin and shrugged away from his touch. "I haven't decided yet."

He came closer, looming over her in the dark kitchen. "Did he kiss you?"

Emma stiffened with anger. "That's none of your damn business! You don't own me!"

Joe wrapped his hands around her upper arms and urged her closer. Tension radiated from him like heat from a bonfire.

"Don't I?" he rasped. "I made you mine, Emma. What we shared was something special, something unique and rare. Don't you know that?"

Suddenly Emma's anger went out like a candle flame in the wind. Her body slumped and she felt Joe's biting fingers release her.

"Of course I know that," she said softly. "What surprises me is to hear you say it. You make love to me and then you go out of your way to let me see how much you regret it."

He stepped back as if she'd slapped him.

"Until you decide how you feel, I don't think you have any right to ask me questions about Cal, do you?"

"Ah, Emma." He sighed. "I *do* care about you. And I'm sorry if I gave you the impression that I don't." He stroked her cheek with his fingertips. "I'm not handling this very well," he admitted. "But I hope like hell that you won't go out with Cal again."

"I—I'll have to think about it." She was fighting Joe's formidable attraction. "I can't decide right now." She waited but he didn't comment. After a moment she walked carefully around him and up the stairs to her bedroom. Tears streamed down her face. Her stomach twisted with the tension that threatened to wrench her in two. Thank goodness that Marian's bedroom door remained shut. Emma could not have borne another confrontation tonight.

* * *

The next evening she spent a couple of hours at the computer, printing off letters of application to the various school districts in and around Seattle. She needed to find a job for the fall term, and soon. When she was finished she brought the letters downstairs.

"I'd like to mail these in the morning," she told Marian.

The older woman glanced up from the television. "Just leave your mail on the kitchen table, dear. Joe can take it out to the mailbox in the morning."

The next day Emma noticed that her letters were gone. At supper that night Joe didn't mention them and neither did she. Determined to keep her feelings to herself, Emma took a big helping of chicken and dumplings and began talking to Marian about the upcoming rummage sale at the church.

She saw Joe sneaking looks at her as he listened to Kenny's chatter about the puppies. School would soon be out for the summer, and Emma knew that he was doing much better since she had begun tutoring him in the evenings. Joe's call to the teacher that afternoon had confirmed it. She expected Kenny to pass everything.

Before Emma could comment on how quickly he was making progress, the phone rang and Joe got up to answer it. He listened for a moment and then glanced toward the table.

"Just a minute, Mrs. Cline. Let me go to another phone."

Emma colored and hastily looked down at her plate. Kenny shifted in his chair as Joe handed the receiver to his mother.

"I'll take this call in the other room."

When Joe came back into the kitchen he still hadn't sorted through his own feelings about the conversation.

"That was Mrs. Cline," he said unnecessarily.

"What did *she* want?" Kenny asked, tone defensive.

The caseworker had been out a week before and told Joe then that she was pleased with the progress Kenny was showing. Despite Joe's assurances, he knew that the boy worried that Mrs. Cline was going to move him to another foster home.

"Relax," Joe said, recognizing the irony of Kenny's concern. She hadn't called to take Kenny away, but to bring out more children. "She wasn't calling about you this time. At least, not directly."

If anything, Kenny looked even more wary.

"Then what did she want?" Marian asked.

Joe took a deep breath. "She wanted to know if we would take two more children."

"Two!" Emma and Marian exclaimed together.

"No way," Kenny cried. "You don't have room, do you?"

Joe hadn't thought about how taking in more children would affect Kenny. Joe had come to like him, and didn't want his feelings to be hurt. He refilled his coffee mug while he thought about the best way to handle the situation.

"There's one more spare bedroom," Marian commented, "but it's down here."

"Having a couple more kids around wouldn't change things that much," Joe told Kenny. "It might even be fun."

Kenny's expression was skeptical, to say the least.

"Mom's right, too," Joe continued. "There is another empty room. In the old days, when this house was built, families were a lot bigger than they are now." His dream of raising sons and daughters on the ranch he loved had died with Stephanie's desertion.

"Why don't you tell us about these children?" Emma suggested.

Joe slanted her a grateful look. "It's a brother and sister, twelve and eight. Their mother checked herself into a drug rehab program, and no one knows where the father is. If we can't take them both, they'll be sent to a group home in Boulder." He repeated what Mrs. Cline had told him. "But the people at the rehab center say the mom would probably do better if they could visit her while she's in treatment."

"Where's the rehabilitation center?" Marian asked.

"Fort Morgan. She'll be there for eight weeks." He drained his coffee mug. "Mrs. Cline needs an answer from us as soon as possible. She'll be in the office for another half hour, so I told her I'd call her back." He looked around the table. "So, what do you think?"

"A group home doesn't sound so bad," Kenny muttered.

"But they'd be too far away to visit their mother," Emma reminded him.

"That's right," Marian added. "If they stayed here, I could drive them to Fort Morgan."

Joe remained silent, as he wondered how Kenny felt. Having kids around was more complicated than he had thought.

When Kenny didn't speak, Joe prodded him. "Think we could handle another boy and a little girl?" he asked, looking right at Kenny.

"What does it matter what I think, anyway? It's your house and you can do whatever you want." Kenny's tone was resentful.

"The decision will affect all of us," Joe said. "That's why we're talking about it now. Your opinion is just as important to me as Mom's and Emma's are." He hoped the women would understand.

For a moment Kenny poked at the food on his plate with his fork. When he looked up, the frown had disappeared from his high forehead. "If the rest of you want them, I guess it would be okay with me."

Joe reached out and ruffled his hair. "Good boy." Then he looked at his mother. "What do you think? You know, once school is out, they'll be here all day. That means more cooking, more laundry and more supervision."

"How do you feel about it?" Marian asked Emma.

Emma looked startled and slightly uncomfortable. "It's not up to me. But if you'd like me to go back to Seattle so you have more room—"

"No!" Joe and Marian both said at the same time. He felt his cheeks go hot at the vehemence of his reply and hoped that his mother's voice had at least partially obscured it.

"I'm sure we can work something else out," Marian said quickly as she glanced at Joe.

He ignored her speculative look.

"Yeah, you're right," he agreed hastily, clearing his throat. "I was thinking that, if Emma wouldn't mind moving to the downstairs bedroom, we could put another bunk in Kenny's room, and the little girl could have Emma's old room." He glanced at Emma. Damn, but he didn't want her to leave, not yet. "Would that be okay?"

"I wouldn't mind at all," Emma said immediately. "You don't want to put any of the children down here alone."

"That's what I thought. Thanks." Joe was relieved. He didn't want the boys tempted to sneak out at night or to cook up any of the other mischief he remembered getting into at their ages, and the sister was too little to stay so far away from the rest of them.

"Kenny, how would you feel about sharing a room?" Joe asked.

Kenny shrugged. "I guess it would be okay. I never had a room of my own before the last foster place. It gets kinda lonesome at night sometimes."

Joe smiled his understanding. "Mom? Are you sure you don't mind?"

"What about you?" she asked.

Kenny wasn't that much trouble. And maybe having a little girl around would be nice. For some reason Joe pictured her with curly black hair and blue eyes. Realizing that he had conjured up a miniature Emma, he said impatiently, "It's fine with me."

His mother's brows rose.

Joe softened his tone. "I promised Mrs. Cline I'd get right back to her. She wants to bring the kids sometime tomorrow morning."

"Tomorrow!" Marian looked startled. "Well, all right. We just have to get some of the furniture moved around."

"A couple of the men can help," Joe told her. "We'll switch the bed that Emma has now with the small one downstairs. The dresser, too."

"Is that really necessary?" Emma asked.

Joe kept his face expressionless. "The one downstairs is a twin bed. It will be fine for an eight-year-old." No one mentioned that it would probably be fine for Emma, too. And he refused to react to the idea of her sleeping on a different floor from everyone else. Instead, he scraped back his chair and picked up the phone.

"I'll tell Mrs. Cline to bring them on out."

Emma thought it was terrific that Joe was willing to take in children that no one else seemed to want. Maybe it was something that he and Marian would make into a regular practice. They certainly had enough room in the big old ranch house. Marian had confided to Emma that Joe had lost interest in remodeling after the divorce. Emma suspected there was room in their hearts, as well. Maybe having foster children around would change Joe's feelings about having children of his own.

Emma didn't want to dwell on that, didn't want to think about him married again someday, with a family.

All three adults were at the house when Mrs. Cline brought Jason and his sister, Rachael, out to the ranch late the next morning. Their clothes were worn but clean. Jason was carrying a battered duffel bag and Rachael clutched a small, scuffed suitcase. She had dark blond hair and hazel eyes. Jason's hair was light brown and needed a trim. Both of them were too thin. Rachael looked scared as she crowded closer to her brother, but Jason's expression was almost hostile.

"Come on in," Emma invited them after introductions were carried out. "Kenny and I will show you to your rooms." She expected that Mrs. Cline would need a few minutes with Joe and Marian.

"This is a big house," Rachael said in a small voice as Emma led them upstairs.

"But it's old." Jason's tone contained a critical element that Emma assumed was mostly bravado.

"The ranch is neat, though," Kenny told them. "There are horses to ride and cats in the barn. And Dolly had five puppies. I like them the best."

"Can I see the puppies?" Rachael asked as Emma stopped in front of the open door to her room.

"They're in the horse barn. Maybe Kenny can take you after lunch," Emma suggested.

"Dolly's a dumb name," she heard Jason mutter as Kenny led him to the room they were sharing.

Emma decided to let the two of them work things out while she unpacked Rachael's pitifully small wardrobe into the child-size chest of drawers that Joe had brought up that morning.

"This room is pretty," Rachael said shyly. "But it's awfully big."

"Your brother will be across the hall," Emma told her. "And so will Mrs. Gray."

Rachael seemed to relax a little as she looked around. There was a pink-and-yellow flowered spread on the narrow bed. The headboard was painted pale yellow, as was the matching chest of drawers and the nightstand. On it sat a pink-and-white lamp with a shade that reminded Emma of a ballerina's full skirts. On the other side of the room was a small white table with two child-size chairs that Joe had brought in from the old barn, and an open bookcase for all the toys and books Rachael didn't seem to have. None of the furniture was new, but it looked nice with the white walls, lace curtains and worn rose-colored carpeting.

"Where is your room with Mr. Joe?" Rachael asked as she switched the lamp on and off.

An image took shape in Emma's mind, of the room she and Joe might share if things were different. If he cared for her as she did for him.

"Mr. Joe's room is that way," she said, pointing. "My room is downstairs. We aren't married."

Rachael frowned for a moment and then her forehead cleared. "Look," she said, pointing. On the wall was a picture of a carousel horse in an ornate frame. "Do you have any real live horses?"

"We sure do. Maybe we can go and visit them one day soon, and feed them carrots."

"That would be nice," Rachael said. She lifted a tattered doll from the bag and put it gently on the bed. "Can I go and see Jason's room now?"

"Sure," Emma told her. "I'm going to help Mrs. Gray with lunch. Come on down to the kitchen whenever you want." She gave the room a last glance, checked on the boys and headed downstairs.

That afternoon Marian decided to take Rachael and Jason shopping while Emma stayed home to do laundry.

"They need everything," Marian said quietly as the two women cleaned up the lunch dishes. "Shoes and tooth-paste, some nightwear and more school clothes. What they have is clean enough, but it's all so worn that it will be fine for play clothes. My heart goes out to them."

Before Emma could comment, the phone rang and Marian answered.

"It's for you," she said, holding the receiver out to Emma. "I have to run upstairs for a minute."

Emma answered warily, suspecting that it was Cal on the other end. When he invited her to go to a cattle sale with him the next day, she made an excuse.

"I understand," he said cheerfully. "I'll call you again soon."

Feeling guilty, Emma thanked him and hung up. A few minutes later Marian came back down, but she didn't ask about Emma's call.

"I think I'll take Kenny with us, and we'll stop for some ice cream on the way home. You don't mind, do you?"

"Not at all," Emma told her. "I'll put on the roast for supper while you're gone."

Shortly after Marian and the children had left, while Emma was putting a load of laundry into the washing machine, Joe slammed into the house. He'd left before lunch to ride out with the men. Now she stuck her head through the laundry-room doorway.

"Hi," she said. "Your mom's gone to town with the kids." She was curious as to why he had come back to the house.

"Hi." He was frowning when he took off his hat. As he turned away to hang it on a hook, Emma noticed that his shirt was torn across his shoulder, revealing an ugly scratch.

"You're hurt!" she exclaimed. "What happened?"

He crossed to the stove and poured himself a cup of cof-fee.

"Caught my shirt on a nail and ripped it."

Emma came out of the laundry room, forgetting about the dirty clothes, and took a closer look at his back.

"That scratch could use some attention," she told him. "It looks like it must be sore."

"It smarts like hell," Joe growled. "Is it red?"

The angry line bisected one shoulder blade. Along the scratch were beads of dried blood.

"The nail broke the skin," she said. "It needs to be cleaned up and have some first-aid cream put on it. Was the nail rusty?"

"Don't worry, mother," Joe drawled. "I've had my shots. I can manage." He started to leave the kitchen.

"Not unless you're double-jointed," Emma told him. "And I don't remember that you are."

Joe stopped in his tracks. His expression made her stomach shiver and her knees threaten to give way. She wondered whether he was remembering the same passionate encounters she was.

"You're probably right," he said finally. "I doubt I could reach it, anyway. Would you mind?"

"Not at all." She followed him upstairs, expecting him to go into the bathroom. Instead, he walked into his room. Emma hesitated in the doorway as he began to undo the snaps on his shirt. With an effort she raised her gaze to his face. He was watching her, his eyes hooded. Suddenly Emma became painfully aware that they were alone in the house.

"I think this shirt is ready for the ragbag," Joe said as he yanked the tail free of his jeans and stripped it off. "Come and doctor this scratch if you're going to, okay?" He turned his back on her and rolled his heavy shoulders as if they ached.

The gesture made Emma wonder if he felt as uncomfortable as she did. Ever since she had gone out with Cal there had been some strain between them, and she wasn't sure how to dispel it without admitting to Joe that she had no intention of seeing the other man again. There was no way she could just blurt it out; she kept hoping that Joe would ask her if Cal had called.

Now her gaze went to the big bed covered with a royal blue spread. She folded her arms across her stomach to suppress the ribbons of desire that fluttered there and tried not to think how long it had been since Joe had last kissed her.

"Come into the bathroom so I can wash it off," she instructed.

He sat on the commode and she dabbed gently at the scratch with a soapy washcloth.

"Why did they go to town?" he asked.

"Marian wanted to pick up some tootepaste and stuff," Emma told him. "Then she's taking them for ice cream on the way home."

"She'll spoil all three of them, given half a chance," Joe grumbled lightly as he watched Emma in the bathroom mirror. She smoothed medicated cream on the scratch and then bandaged it.

"Did she spoil you?" she asked, meeting his gaze in the glass.

His voice grew husky. "Every chance she got."

Emma lowered her eyes and wet her lips. Joe felt his control slip another notch with each touch of her hands. He had been a fool to let her near him. He should have asked Cookie's wife to fix him up, instead. She was a nice woman but her touch didn't burn him like Emma's did. With Marian and the children gone, there was no protective buffer between Emma and his own urgent desire for her.

As Joe continued to watch her reflection, she finally looked at him again. What he saw in her deep blue eyes made the breath stop in his throat. He felt her fingers tense against the skin of his back, her nails digging into him, and he realized that his own hands had knotted into fists.

Emotions that Joe had done his best to ignore poured through him. Possessiveness. A passion that transcended mere physical lust. He had no right. But, by all that he was or ever hoped to be, he didn't think he could go another day, another hour, without holding her again. Without absorbing that special scent that made his head spin, or tasting her mouth or touching the skin that was as soft as the muzzle on a day-old foal.

All Joe's resolutions to leave Emma the hell alone lay in shreds at his feet. His will to resist what shimmered and burned between them was gone.

"Emma," he murmured as he studied every tiny detail of her face in the mirror. Lord, she was a beautiful woman.

When he said her name, her expression of fierce concentration softened. Her eyes darkened and her lips parted tenderly.

Joe uncoiled his body. Slowly he faced her in the small room.

"You know I'd never willingly hurt you," he said. It was the only promise he could make. How he wished he could claim her openly, show his interest in her like any other man. But some things weren't meant to be.

The thought made him falter. Claim her like a man, a real man. Chilled by an icy blast of reality, he brushed abruptly past her and crossed the hallway to his own room, intent on escape from the temptation he couldn't seem to resist.

Chapter Ten

Joe might have been able to resist Emma if she hadn't followed him back across the hall, lingering in the doorway of his bedroom. Apparently she hadn't noticed anything odd in his behavior or his statement about not hurting her.

"That scratch should be fine," she said. "Someone could put more cream on it this evening, if you want."

"Thanks." Joe's mind wasn't on the scratch. "Come on in." His voice sounded rusty to his ears. He waited tensely for Emma to make up her mind, to take that one step that would bring her across the threshold and into his waiting arms. He had never used force on a woman and he never would, but he knew that he was dangerously close to the limits of his control.

He knew, too, what letting Emma go would cost him. And let her go, sooner or later, he must. But at that precise moment he would have given the ranch, his life, even his soul to make things different. He closed his eyes on the sudden, devastating pain.

"Joe? Are you okay?"

He opened his eyes again and saw Emma come into the room, concern on her face. It was all the encouragement his tormented soul needed—the spark that turned the smoldering desire trapped inside him into an all-consuming blaze.

Joe reached past her to shut the bedroom door. The click was as loud as a rifle shot in the silent house.

"You should have gone while you could," he told her, his hand still braced against the closed door. "But it's too late now. Don't ask me to let you go. I need you too much." The confession was surprisingly easy to make.

"I need you, too," Emma admitted in a faint voice. "I don't want to leave." And then she walked into his embrace.

"I'm sorry," Joe whispered after his arms had closed around her. "I know I'm not being fair to you, but I can't help myself." His voice broke and he buried his face in her hair. There were no pretty promises he could give, nothing he could say that would make any difference in the long run. Desperately he tried to keep a lid on the raging hunger that threatened to consume them both.

He felt Emma's hands curl trustingly about his neck. His whole body went still as he absorbed the sweetness of her touch. There were no sounds in the room except for the ticking of his alarm clock and his own ragged breathing. No scent he was aware of except the faint odor of honeysuckle. He looked down and saw his own stark need reflected in Emma's eyes. His control shattered like glass, and he took her mouth in a desperate kiss.

Over the course of the next few days Emma spent time with Rachael after school. They worked together in the vegetable garden and in the kitchen. The child was lonely and she talked often about her mother and what the two of them would do together when they got home.

"We'll play old records on the stereo and sing," she said. "Mom knows all the words." They would walk to the neighborhood store together and make cookies and have a tea party.

"Jason doesn't come to our tea parties," she added, "but he always eats the cookies."

"That all sounds like fun," Emma commented. Listening to Rachael's chatter helped her to keep from dwelling on Joe. She knew she was getting too deeply involved with him. There was more going on than their attraction to each other. Joe was clearly reluctant to trust—in his own feelings or in her. Emma wasn't sure which. All she knew was that she was leaving in a matter of weeks and she no longer knew if she wanted to or not.

"I wish my daddy would come back," Rachael announced, breaking into Emma's thoughts.

Not sure what to say, Emma gave the little girl a hug instead. No matter how she felt about Joe, her heart couldn't help but respond to Rachael's obvious need for love.

Jason, on the other hand, didn't seem interested in Emma's feelings, in getting along with Kenny or in helping with the chores. He declared that the puppies were dumb and the ranch was stupid. More than once Emma overheard him say something unkind to Kenny, but, when she questioned the younger boy about it later, he always remained silent. The only thing that Emma saw Jason take any interest in was Joe's computer.

"Hey, neat," he said when he came into the office while she was running the printer. "Do you have any computer games?"

"I don't think so, but you could ask Joe," she responded.

Jason immediately lost interest. "No big deal."

Watching Jason leave, Emma was beginning to wonder if Joe might have any regrets about taking in the two extra youngsters. She was sure that Jason's attitude must try his patience as much as it did her own.

When she told Joe about the boy's brief show of interest in the computer, his expression became thoughtful.

"Computer games," he mused aloud. "I should have thought of that myself."

As a matter of fact, Jason *had* been trying Joe's patience to the limit. He "forgot" the chores Joe asked him to do, he bullied Kenny and teased him about the puppies. Jason had made Kenny cry by telling him they would probably have to be put to sleep at the animal shelter.

It had infuriated Joe to see the younger boy hurt like that. After wiping Kenny's tear-streaked face, Joe finally convinced him that good homes would be found for all of Dolly's puppies. Once Kenny was calmed down, Joe asked him to send Jason to the corral.

When Jason wandered over and leaned a negligent shoulder against the fence, Joe had begun working a yearling pinto. "Don't you like it here?" he demanded in a low voice.

"I guess."

"Don't you like Kenny?"

Jason flushed a dull red. "He's okay, I guess."

"What you told him about the puppies upset him," Joe continued, holding firm to his patience.

"That's what happened to our puppies," Jason said. "My dad took them to the shelter, and they killed 'em."

"And how did that make you feel?" Joe asked, feeling a little sorry for the boy.

Jason ducked his head. "Bad."

Joe figured he had made his point. He asked what Jason would like to do if he had the choice.

"I dunno," he replied after a silence that began eating into Joe's even temper like acid. "Sleep, I guess."

"You can't sleep all the time," Joe replied, keeping his voice low and even as he worked the pinto on a lead rein.

Jason didn't reply. Joe resisted the urge to march over and throttle him, reminding himself that a young boy took at least as much patience and gentling as did a young horse. The idea of Jason trotting at the end of a lunge line even had a certain dark appeal to it.

"If you think of anything other than sleeping, let me know, okay?"

Again Jason didn't answer. Exasperated with the one-sided conversation and the boy's unwillingness to cooperate, Joe redirected his attention to the yearling filly. For a few moments he murmured encouragement as she walked and then trotted.

"Why do you move so slow and talk so quietly? Afraid you'll scare her?"

The question startled Joe, who had assumed from the silence that Jason had gone back to the house.

"That's exactly right. The first thing I have to do is to win her trust. Otherwise, she won't be willing to learn from me." Joe explained how easy it would be to spook the young horse. After he answered a few more questions, walking the filly to cool her down, he turned her into an adjacent corral, scratching beneath her forelock and praising her softly. Then he walked back toward the horse barn. Jason was still there, thumbs hooked into the waistband of his jeans.

"Do you like the horses?" Joe asked as he coiled up the lead rope.

Jason frowned, and Joe could almost see a smart-alecky answer forming. Then he hesitated.

"I can't ride or anything. I guess I like the young horses, though. I like watching you training them." He scuffed the toe of his shoe in the dust. "I guess it's kinda neat the way you teach them stuff without yelling at them. And how you're careful not to scare them." He picked at a thread on the hem of his T-shirt. "I wonder if I could do that. I mean, get them to trust me."

"If you were patient," Joe said, bracing one booted foot on the bottom rail. "I bet you could if you tried. If the horse is scared, he won't learn. It's faster to break them, like they did in the old West, but you get a better horse if you take the time to gentle him and win his trust."

He watched Jason carefully, wondering what torments the boy had been through in his young life. "Maybe you could help me out," Joe suggested. "I could show you how to gentle a couple of the yearlings, how to get this year's crop of foals used to humans. We could work in a few riding lessons if you wanted." He was surprised at the way Jason's face lit up.

"You mean it? You'd trust me with them?" His lip had lost its scornful curl and his expression was actually animated.

"Sure," Joe said. "It's important to start them out right, though. Otherwise, it takes a lot of time to undo the damage."

While he watched, Jason's face changed. "What if I made mistakes?" he asked. "I could ruin your horses, and they're probably worth a lot of money."

His lack of faith in himself made Joe want to thrash someone. "Sure, they're worth a lot," he agreed, "but I'd be there at first to help. You like the horses. You're smart. I bet they'd like you fine. Why don't you give it a try?" Just what he needed, when he was so busy, he thought. More lessons. Then he realized that if it made some kind of difference with Jason it would be well worth the time.

The boy agreed cautiously. "I guess I could try. See how it goes. If you really mean it?"

"I really mean it," Joe told him. "And I have another idea, too, if you're interested."

He watched the battle between curiosity and indifference. Finally curiosity won out.

"I dunno. What is it?" That wary look was back. The one that made Joe sad for him.

"If you'd muck out the stalls in the horse barn every morning until school's over and then this summer, we could see about a game for the computer when we go to town."

Jason looked surprised.

"You'd probably have to show me how to use it, though," Joe added.

"You mean I'd have to shovel sh—"

Joe held up a warning hand. "You'd be mucking out stalls," he repeated.

After a pause a reluctant grin broke across Jason's face. "Yeah," he agreed. "Sounds like a deal. As long as I get to pick out the game."

That evening Emma was sitting in the porch swing watching the twilight fade when Joe came out and asked if he could join her. She hadn't seen him until supper and there hadn't been a chance to say anything personal, even if he had wanted to. She had caught him looking at her several times, though, and had wondered what he was thinking. Once, he had winked. Emma wondered if it was because of his divorce that Joe seemed so reluctant to trust his feelings.

Now, as they sat together on the porch swing, Emma speculated shamelessly.

"I had an interesting conversation with Jason this afternoon," Joe said, interrupting her thoughts about him. Then he told her about the agreement he had arrived at with the boy.

"It's probably a good thing he insisted on picking out the game," she teased after he recounted the whole conversation. "Hey," Joe protested lightly. "I don't know why he didn't want me to pick one out. They must have some kind of computer chess or at least a good poker game." His expression was one of exaggerated hurt. Emma batted at his arm.

"Boys Jason's age aren't interested in chess or poker."

"What games do they play?" Joe asked.

Emma thought for a moment. "I have no idea," she admitted. She was glad to hear that Joe had made some progress with Jason. The boy probably needed a man around even more than his sister did.

She hoped that Joe might invite her to take a walk, or turn the conversation to a more personal subject, but he did neither. Instead, he seemed content to sit on the porch, talking idly and giving the swing an occasional push with his booted foot. Too soon it was time for Emma to go in and help Kenny with his schoolwork.

She figured that Jason would give the younger boy a hard time about the evening lessons, but he surprised her.

"Would you have time to help me, too?" he asked when he saw her working with Kenny. "I get math okay, but English and writing about stuff makes my head ache. Maybe you could explain it so I understand."

"School's going to be out in a few days," Kenny reminded him. "What good would it do you now?"

Jason bristled. "I plan on going back in the fall, dummy."

"None of that," she told him.

After a moment he said, "I'm gonna get held back. If you helped me this summer, maybe I could pass for sure next year."

The change in his attitude was a relief, and Emma was pleased that he was looking ahead.

"Sure," she said. "We can work together as long as I'm here."

Jason gave her a real smile. Then he confided that Rachael was having trouble with reading, so on the last day of school Emma picked them all up in Marian's car and took them to the tiny Caulder Springs library. In return for her tutoring, Jason and Rachael were to water the vegetables when needed.

Between tutoring, caring for the garden, her job search and helping Marian out, Emma was busier than she had been in a long time. She didn't mind; being busy helped to keep her from thinking too much.

The next time Joe went into town Emma begged a ride to the fabric store with Rachael. They were going to sew a dress for her to wear to church.

"I'm going to the vet's, and I'll pick you up in a half hour," Joe told Emma after she and Rachael had climbed out of his truck.

As Rachael clung to her hand, Emma grinned up at him through the open pickup window. Sunglasses hid his eyes.

"Buying fabric is a pretty serious undertaking," she informed him. "Thirty minutes may not be time enough."

"We have to find the very prettiest dress material," Rachael chimed in.

"You're already the prettiest girl I know," Joe told her, making her giggle and duck behind Emma. "Tell you what, if you don't keep me waiting too long, we'll have time to stop for ice-cream cones on the way home."

"Oh, boy!" Rachael exclaimed. "We'll hurry."

"You've got a deal." Without thinking, Emma held out her free hand. Joe reached down and took it, enfolding it in his and holding it longer than was necessary. Then, just when she thought she couldn't stand his touch for a moment longer without revealing what his warm, rough grip was doing to her, he released her. She wished she could see his eyes behind the tinted lenses—to see if he had been affected half as much as she had.

"See you," he said, touching his hat before he looked around and backed out into the street.

Shaken, Emma glanced at Rachael. "I guess we'd better hurry."

"Joe's nice," Rachael said, following her. "And I think he likes you."

"I like him too," Emma told her. "And I like his mother, Marian. She and my mother were school friends a long time ago." She hoped to distract Rachael, but was less than successful.

"Maybe you'll get married and stay at the ranch," Rachael commented as they walked between rainbow rows of fabric. All three children knew she was leaving before school started in the fall.

"I don't think so." Emma sat her down with a pattern book, determined to change the subject.

"Don't you want to stay?" Rachael asked with all the simplicity of a young child.

Emma blinked rapidly, to avoid sudden tears. "We need to hurry," she reminded her small companion. "Or we'll miss out on the ice cream." She turned the page. "Here's a nice dress."

By the time they had picked out a pattern and some cotton fabric sprinkled with daisies, the pickup was back outside.

"Hurry," Rachael said as Emma paid for their purchases. "I want to show Joe what we got."

After Joe had admired the dress pattern and the flowered material, they went to get the promised ice cream. On the way home, with Rachael sitting between them, Emma couldn't help but wonder what it would be like to ride in the truck with Joe and their own child, back to the ranch they shared. The image brought new tears to her eyes and she hastily wiped them away, glad that she was wearing her own sunglasses. She looked out the window while Joe talked to Rachael, and wished she could see into his head. Or his heart.

A few days later Marian was driving the children to Sterling to see Mrs. Cline. Before they left she told Emma they would probably stop for hamburgers and a movie afterward.

"Do you want me to go with you?" Emma asked.

"No, dear. We'll be fine, and I know you have other things you'd rather be doing this afternoon." Marian's glance strayed in the direction of the horse barn, but Emma pretended not to notice. It had been a while since she and Joe had found the time to go riding together.

"I need to cut out Rachael's dress," she said instead.

The smile on Marian's face dimmed. "Would you mind fixing something for supper for Joe and yourself? There's leftover roast in the fridge if you want to cook some potatoes and make hash. Joe likes that with ketchup."

Emma agreed to feed Joe, knowing there was no polite way to refuse. She didn't expect to see him before supper was ready, but he surprised her by showing up at the house only a short time after Marian left.

"Where's Mom going? Were the kids with her?" he asked as he stuck his head in the open doorway of Marian's sewing room. Emma had been carefully cutting around the pattern pieces of Rachael's dress.

"They went to that appointment with Mrs. Cline," Emma reminded him. Then she told him the rest of Marian's plans. "You're at the mercy of my cooking, I'm afraid."

He looked so appealing in his work clothes and with his hair finger-combed that she could hardly keep away from him.

"What are we having?" he asked.

"Steak-and-kidney pie with artichoke hearts on the side," she told him, straight-faced.

His mouth dropped open. It was all Emma could do to keep from laughing.

"Are you always this gullible?" she teased. "We're really having roast beef hash, biscuits and a green salad."

Joe's eyes crinkled at the corners as his mouth curved upward into a grin. "I'm relieved to hear it," he said. "For a moment I thought I'd have to fill up on peanut butter sandwiches again."

His comment surprised a chuckle out of Emma, who was relieved they could joke about her first fiasco in his kitchen.

"I don't know," she said, expression sobering. "You haven't tasted my hash yet."

He was still grinning when he shook his head. Emma thought he would leave, but he surprised her by sitting in the maple rocking chair.

"What are you doing here?" he asked, glancing at the length of fabric she had spread out on the table. "Isn't that the material you bought for Rachael the other day?"

"Yes," Emma all but stammered. Somehow having Joe this close when they had the house to themselves was doing strange things to her. She had gotten used to having the children as a buffer between them, and she couldn't keep her mind off the fact that they had hours of privacy ahead of them.

"I was going to cut out the pattern pieces so Rachael and I can start sewing her dress. She wants to wear it to church as soon as it's done."

Joe's eyes narrowed. "Are they making too many demands on you?" he asked. "You know, I didn't expect you to turn into a combination nanny and teacher while you're here. And I'm sorry Mom's been so busy with them, too. Not much of a visit for you."

"I don't mind," Emma said, lowering her head. "I'm glad to help." She repositioned a pin in one of the pattern pieces. "I heard what you said about not wanting children," she rushed on, "but you're so good with them. Surely you can see now that a man like you should have children of his own."

To her dismay, Joe rose and turned away, but not before she caught a glimpse of his harsh expression.

"You don't understand," he said in a low voice as he walked from the room.

"Joe!" Emma went after him. She was determined to clear the air between them and find out where he stood. He stopped but kept his back to her.

"Emma, leave it alone."

She crossed the space between them and caught his arm. Pulling him around, she pleaded softly, "Then make me understand. Please, Joe. Tell me what's bothering you."

Joe looked into her lovely blue eyes and was tempted almost beyond bearing. The shameful secret he'd carried for so long hovered on his lips. Then he remembered the expression on Stephanie's face when she told him why she was leaving, and the tone of her voice when she tried to convince him that she didn't blame him. Not really.

No, he couldn't tell Emma. Instead, he gazed into her pleading face and hardened his heart against the entreaty in her eyes.

"There's nothing bothering me," he said firmly. "Nothing." Ignoring the pain welling up inside him, he pulled his arm free of her grasp and walked away.

Chapter Eleven

"Joe, don't leave," Emma cried.

He looked at her, and she could see the battle that was taking place within him. It showed on his face and in his eyes. There was anguish there, pain she ached to share and a sadness she longed to banish from his heart forever. If only he would tell her.

"Please, Joe," she said again, sensing that he wasn't ready, wondering if he ever would be. "Sit back down. Keep me company for a little while. Tell me what's been going on around here, while I cut out Rachael's dress." She waited to see what he would do.

Hesitantly he came back into the room. He glanced at the broad piece of material pinned with tissue pattern pieces. Without warning he bent and scooped Emma into his arms.

As she smothered a gasp of surprise he said, "I have a better idea." He dropped into the rocker, still holding her close. She felt a sigh work its way up from somewhere deep in his chest. She thought she felt him place a kiss against her hair but wasn't sure.

"Isn't this nice?" he asked, cuddling her against him.

"Mmm. You're right."

He rocked the chair gently. "You're so sweet," he murmured, his breath warm on her neck. He stroked her arm with his fingers, then laced them with hers and brought her hand to his mouth. His lips burned against her sensitive skin. Emma shivered with reaction. He felt her response and his arms tightened.

"Don't you have to go back outside?" she asked breathlessly, even though, only moments before, she had been encouraging him to stay. She tried to resist the urge to forget everything except his touch, his kiss.

"Trying to get rid of me so you can cut out your material?" Joe asked. "I thought you wanted me to keep you company?"

She touched his rough cheek. "I'm not trying to get rid of you." She wondered what he was thinking.

He nuzzled her neck, his breath tickling. "I'm the boss, remember? I don't have to go back at all today if I don't want to."

Emma wondered if she could somehow reach him with her love. She slipped her arms around his neck and gazed into his face. "And do you want to go back?" she asked.

His eyes began to glow. "What do you think?" he whispered, lowering his head.

He gave her no time to answer. Instead, he covered her mouth with his in an openmouthed kiss full of aching tenderness. Emma responded with all the feelings she had for him, running her hands across the width of his shoulders and then stroking his warm skin above the collar of his shirt.

He lifted his mouth and changed the angle, holding her chin with his fingers as he plunged again and again. Emma could feel him harden as his breathing became harsh and shallow. Her own body was heating in response to him, the passion that simmered beneath the surface coiling tightly within her. Perhaps all he needed was her unconditional love, her unselfish giving of all she was and had. Maybe that would be enough to convince him that whatever was troubling him could be dealt with together if he would only trust her enough.

"Joe," she murmured, breathless. "We need to talk."

"Later," he replied. "Later." Again he kissed her. Urgent, passionate kisses she could no more resist than life itself.

Hope poured through Emma, along with a fiery need she couldn't deny. She shifted on his lap, squirming to get even closer. Suddenly Joe's arms tightened around her, and his thighs flexed powerfully as he rose from the rocking chair, still holding her cradled against his chest. Emma buried her face in his shoulder as he carried her up the stairs and down the hall to his room. He held her effortlessly, not even breathing hard from the exertion.

Kicking the door shut behind him, he laid her gently on his big bed. Silver eyes clouded by passion, he followed her down.

Afterward, Joe held Emma tenderly while she stroked his damp chest with her hand. He had to care for her; no man could make love the way he just had without his emotions being involved. Whether or not he realized it. Even if, for some reason, he wasn't willing to admit it. To her or to himself. He loved her. Emma believed that strongly enough to take a big risk of her own.

She clasped his big, work-roughened hand in hers and brought it to her lips. After nibbling at his knuckles she whispered, "I love you" as she pressed a kiss to his palm.

She didn't expect Joe to return the sentiment. Not right away. Neither did she expect him to go tense, to pull himself into a sitting position and grip her upper arms with his hands. But he did. He looked into her eyes and calmly broke her heart.

"Emma," he rasped, "we both got what we wanted here. And what we have together is damned good, better than I've ever known." He swallowed, his gaze never wavering. She knew there was a *but* coming. She could hear it.

"But I never meant for you to get the wrong idea," he continued, as hope drained away, leaving her feeling humiliated. "I can't make a commitment to you." He let her go and swung his legs over the side of the bed. "I'm too much of a loner to settle down again. I tried it once, and it just didn't work."

His words were like arrows, piercing her with deadly accuracy. How could she have been so wrong? How could she have made love with him again, allowing him to put off her questions, her need to talk?

For a moment Joe buried his dark head in his hands. Then he turned back to her, real concern on his face. Emma pulled the sheet up to cover her bareness. Words wouldn't come. Her throat was blocked.

"You don't love me," he insisted. "You can't. It's just that you're here and everything is so different from what you're used to, that's all. We get along and there's real electricity between us. Let's not make something of it that it isn't, okay?"

She wasn't about to beg or to argue. She knew how she felt, but she wasn't going to defend those feelings. There was something wrong here, some note that rang untrue, but she was too upset and hurt to find it. What she needed now was to get away.

"I see," she said in a thin voice. "I hope that my declaration didn't embarrass you."

Joe reached for her and then let his hands drop. "No," he said, and his voice was shaded with elements she couldn't interpret. "Of course not. You honored me. And I swear that I never meant to hurt you, but I can't return those feelings." For a moment he looked almost stricken. Then the harsh expression faded to one of calm concern and earnest sincerity. "I'm sorry," he said, turning away once again. "But I won't give you promises that I can't keep. It's for the best, believe me."

For long moments after he had pulled on his jeans, Joe stood at the window and looked out at the land that rolled away from the house in grassy waves, as far as the eye could see. He listened to the sounds of Emma dressing. Then he listened to her soft footsteps as she crossed the room and closed the door gently behind her. Only when he was sure she was gone did he dare turn around.

It had taken everything in him to keep from pulling her into his arms and begging her to forget every lie he had just told her. Only the knowledge of how badly they would both be hurt if he gave in to that weakness kept him from spilling the truth.

The truth that he adored her and wanted nothing more than to tell her so and keep her by his side forever. But forever would last only until she found out that he was less than a whole man, until she began hating him for what he couldn't give her. And that he could never bear. Seeing her love turn to hatred or, worse, to pity would surely kill him.

His mother had been more right than she knew. Emma needed a family. Her loving nature cried out for one. And a family was the one thing Joe could never give to her or to any woman.

The doctors had told him it was most likely a boyhood infection that had left Joe sterile. His inability to father a child had destroyed his first marriage. Once the test results were in, Stephanie swore she didn't blame him. But she couldn't get away fast enough. She had packed her bags, left for Denver and let a lawyer clean up the mess.

Joe didn't blame her. She had a right to a whole man. So did Emma. But he suspected that Emma was the kind of woman who would try to convince him and herself that a family didn't matter. She would stay until she longed for what he couldn't provide. Better that both she and his mother believed he preferred to remain alone.

Joe's shoulders slumped when he looked at the rumpled bed. The bed where he'd held Emma and absorbed her fiery responses as if their heat could warm his lonely heart. The bed where, for a few moments, he had forgotten that all he could ever hope to have with her was now. And after today, even that might be taken from him.

He had seen the hurt in her eyes when he'd told her the lies that were so necessary to protect them both. It had been all he could do to force them out. But he had to. The same way he had to let her go before she discovered the truth.

Emma fixed dinner as she had promised Marian she would, automatically going through the motions. She heard Joe overhead in his office. When the food was ready she went to the base of the stairs and called him. They sat down and she ate the hash and salad without really tasting it. Neither of them said much. He watched her, concern etched into his hard features, while she made inconsequential conversation.

He insisted on helping her clean up. As soon as the kitchen was tidy, she murmured her thanks as she hung up her flowered apron.

"I'm going to walk down to the corral where the foals are," she said, not quite meeting his eyes. Let him worry if he wanted. She needed to be alone for a little while.

When she got to the corral she bent and pulled up a weed stalk, nibbling the end of it while she leaned on the fence. Several of the mares came over to see if she had brought them anything, but her hands were empty.

"Sorry, gals," she said, patting a neck and an inquisitive nose before they drifted away to resume grazing. "I left the house in a hurry, and carrots were the last thing on my mind."

No, she had been thinking about Joe and what he had said. He'd warned her off, but what he apparently didn't realize, despite her passionate declaration, was that his warning came too late.

She loved him. The time had passed when she might have escaped unscathed. The puzzling thing about the whole mess was that she had really, honestly believed that Joe loved her, as well. Part of her still did. He was too decent a man to sleep with a guest of his mother's because she was available, and then casually discard her. Emma had to believe that.

She thought about the way he cared for his mother, the affection with which he treated the three young charges the state had entrusted to him, even the way he looked after the many animals on the ranch. Joe was not a man who didn't know how to love. None of this made any sense.

She tossed away the weed stalk she had been chewing. Was she allowing her own emotions to color reality? Perhaps what she needed to do was to cut short her visit and go home. Even though Marian told her constantly how much she enjoyed having Emma here and what a tremendous help she had been, was there really a reason to stay on? Not if Joe was telling the truth, there wasn't.

When Emma got back to the house Marian and the children were unloading the car. "Well," Emma asked with a smile that was only slightly forced, "did you all have a good time?"

"Yes. It was fun. I got a nightie with a gray kitty on the front," Rachael said, stopping to give Marian a hug.

"Yeah, I had fun. Thanks," Kenny added.

Jason shoved his hands into his pockets and glanced at Emma. "I guess I liked the movie." He shrugged. "It wasn't bad." He edged toward the back door. "Can I go now? I want to change my clothes so I can get some stuff done in the barn."

After Marian had sent him on, she looked again at Emma. "How are you doing?"

"I'm fine."

After a silent moment Marian addressed the two remaining children. "Why don't you get changed and put your things away?"

She waited until they had gone upstairs. "What's wrong?" she demanded, looking as if she meant to stand there until her curiosity was satisfied.

"I think I'd better go home," Emma said. "It would be better if I left right away."

"Better for who?" Marian asked, surprising Emma with her vehemence. "Not for me."

"Better for me," Emma said. "Better for Joe."

Marian's expression became sympathetic. "Maybe better for you," she conceded, "but I doubt it would be good for my stubborn son."

"Do you know why his marriage broke up?" Emma asked quietly. "I mean the real reason. I'm not trying to pry. . . ." She faltered to a stop, realizing that prying was exactly what she was doing.

Marian held up a detaining hand. "I know you aren't." Her smile was gentle. "I'm not blind, dear. I've seen the way Joe looks at you, even if he does think he's hiding it." She leaned closer. "And I'd be happy if you two got together. But I'm through interfering."

Emma wasn't sure what to say.

"As to why his marriage broke up, I wish I could tell you, but I can't." She glanced around them, apparently sorting through her thoughts. Emma tried to wait patiently. "It's just that I don't know," she continued. "I was living in Arizona with John at the time. I knew things had been a little rocky between Joe and Stephanie the last time we saw them, but I never dreamed that she would actually leave. Joe never told me exactly why they'd decided to separate." She paused. "He's never been willing to talk about it since, except to say once that it was his fault and that he totally understood why she left. When I tried to question him, he clammed up."

Emma glanced at the back of the house guiltily. "I see." She was disappointed. "I was hoping you could help me figure him out." She hooked her thumbs into the back of her belt and studied the toes of her shoes.

"Don't give up yet," Marian said. "And don't leave early. Not unless you really have to. The kids and I need you here."

Her sincerity made Emma's eyes grow moist. "I'll think about it," was all she could promise.

"That's the spirit," Marian said firmly. "I knew you had staying power. Well, good luck. And if you want to talk..." Her voice faded. "Well, I'm here if you need me."

After thanking Marian for her support, Emma went back into the house to run another load of dirty clothes. Was she a fool to hang around? Or did she, as Marian said, have staying power? Either way, Emma knew she was in danger of getting hurt. The only question left was which would ultimately hurt her more, staying or going?

Joe did his best to keep his distance from Emma, waiting to see how she would treat him. To his surprise, she acted as if nothing had happened. Slowly, gradually, he was drawn back into the warm circle of the family. It was especially difficult to stay detached around the kids. He played the new computer game with Jason and Kenny, and usually lost, when they weren't challenging each other. He answered

Rachael's endless questions about the animals when she tagged after him. He admired her new dress at great length the first time she wore it to church. Even the boys complimented her. Later, she confided in Joe that she had a crush on Kenny.

Taking each day as it came, Emma neither advanced nor retreated. Acting as relaxed and normal as she could under the circumstances, she waited as patiently as possible for him to make the next move. On one unseasonably hot afternoon, after Emma got back from driving Rachael and Jason to see their mother, he called from the horse barn to tell Marian that he was on his way. Emma walked down the road to meet him, taking a cold soft drink with her. When he stopped the pickup, Joe was grinning.

"Looking for someone?" he asked as Emma strolled over to the open passenger window in brief cutoffs and a halter top. His warm, approving expression was almost her undoing. She swallowed and her hand trembled when she held up the can.

"I'm looking for a thirsty cowboy."

Joe pushed back his hat and leaned forward. "You found him. If you want a ride, I'd be happy to oblige."

It was all the invitation that Emma needed. She got into the truck and slid over, handing him the can. As Joe popped the top, he offered her the first drink.

"No, thanks." She could see drops of perspiration trickling down the side of his face as he tipped back his head and swallowed. "Mmm," he said, nestling the can in the V of his legs before he shifted gears, "that hits the spot. Thanks."

"You're very welcome." They drove the rest of the way to the house in companionable silence, Emma's pulse beating in double time as she watched him out of her peripheral vision. When they got out of the truck, Joe rested a hand on her shoulder.

"Thanks again for the drink."

"My pleasure."

He left his hand on her shoulder as they walked through the kitchen, greeting his mother. Marian didn't say anything, but she winked slyly at Emma behind Joe's back.

"I'm going over to Jerry Kaylor's to borrow a nail gun," Joe announced at supper. "Emma, want to ride along?"

"I do," Rachael said before Emma could answer.

Joe reached over and tugged on the end of her ponytail, making her giggle. "Next time," he said. "Okay?"

"Okay," Rachael answered, looking momentarily disappointed.

"Emma?" he repeated. "How about it?"

"Okay, sure." The invitation surprised her. He hadn't sought her out since she had confessed her feelings for him. Maybe she was making progress. In the truck she told him about taking the kids to the drug rehab center.

"It's a pretty cheerful place," she said. "Not like I pictured at all. I waited out front while they visited her, but they both seemed to be in good spirits afterward. All the way home they were making plans for after she gets out."

"I hope she doesn't disappoint them," Joe said gruffly.

"Me, too." Emma was surprised at the depth of her attachment to them. When she and Joe got to the neighbor's, she waited in the pickup while Joe went to get the nail gun. The other man walked back to the truck with him. He pumped Emma's hand when Joe made introductions.

"Enjoying your visit?" Jerry asked.

"Yes, I am." She glanced at Joe. "It's been a real education." When his eyes widened she colored and added hastily, "I mean, staying on a working ranch. I grew up in the city."

After a few more moments the neighbor, an older man with gray hair, bid them goodbye and waved as they drove off.

"He seems nice," Emma commented as Joe downshifted and turned onto the main road.

"Yeah, he's always ready to lend a hand."

A companionable silence fell between them. In what seemed to Emma like less time than it took to sew a straight line, Joe drove into his own yard.

"Emma," he said softly when he pulled the truck up, "just a second, okay?"

She managed not to tremble as he slid one tanned arm along the back of the wide bench seat and curled his hand possessively around the back of her neck. Her last rational thought as his head tipped toward hers was to wonder if Marian and the kids were all watching from the windows. Then he kissed her lightly and she forgot to worry.

When they broke apart he didn't speak, only smiled in the way he had that sent her heart into her throat. "Go on in," he said. "I've got to take this tool to Daniel and talk to him about tomorrow. I'll be back in a while. I'll see you then."

"Okay." She opened the passenger door. "I enjoyed meeting Jerry."

"I enjoyed showing you off," he replied, leaving her to wonder how he meant that.

As Joe drove down to the bunkhouse he asked himself just what he thought he was playing at. As usual, he couldn't seem to stay away from Emma, no matter how hard he tried.

"Did you get the nail gun?" Daniel asked when Joe finally spotted him at one of the hay sheds on the other side of the bunkhouse.

"Yeah." Joe climbed down from the truck and handed him the nail gun. He hesitated, torn between eagerness to get back to Emma and the certainty that he was only making things more complicated.

"So," Daniel said, lighting a cigarette and taking a drag. "How's the house guest? I haven't seen her around lately. Is she getting bored with ranch life?"

"No," Joe said slowly. "I don't think so. She says she likes it. She's gotten pretty involved with the kids, tutoring all of them even though school's out for the summer, and sewing for Rachael. Yesterday she took Rachael and Jason to see their mother at the drug rehab center."

Daniel stood smoking and looking around at the stillness of the evening. "What do you think of her?" he asked after a moment.

Joe frowned. His foreman wasn't usually one to ask personal questions, even though he and Joe had worked the ranch together for a long time and had gotten to be friends.

"What exactly are you asking me?" Joe asked, crossing his arms over his chest.

Daniel knocked the ashes from his smoke and grinned, dark eyes narrowing beneath the wide brim of the black hat he always wore. The band was a strip of turquoise stones set in tooled silver, but Joe didn't know if the workmanship was indicative of Daniel's own tribe. Joe had never asked, and Daniel had never said.

Now the foreman studied the glowing tip of his cigarette before he answered. "Just curious," he said finally. "She's a beautiful woman. You're a red-blooded man. I thought the two of you might hit it off."

For a moment Joe wished he could confide in someone. "You're right," he said slowly. "She is beautiful, and there is something between us."

"Thinking about asking her to stay?" Daniel asked lightly. "She's nice. You could do worse."

"No." Joe was adamant. "I won't be asking her to stay. She's leaving in a few weeks. It's for the best." He ignored Daniel's skeptical expression. "I'll see you in the morning," he said as Daniel ground his cigarette beneath his boot heel in the dusty path.

As Joe walked back to the pickup he heard the other man's casual good-night and waved without turning. In the privacy of the truck he hit the wheel with his fist and muttered a curse before twisting the key in the ignition.

When he got back to the house a little while later, he saw Emma in the kitchen with Rachael. They were baking brownies, and the little girl promised to bring him some as soon as they were cool enough to cut. The boys were watching television and arguing about one of the actors.

Listening to them squabble, Joe realized how much he enjoyed having all three children around. They added another layer to the fabric of his life. For so long, the knowledge that he would never have heirs, never have the houseful of children he had once imagined, had been such a constant pain, like a splinter that had festered. Now it occurred to him that the foster children, even though they didn't share his blood, had dulled that pain. If it hadn't been for his feelings for Emma he might have hoped to find some measure of peace.

One Sunday morning after the service, while Emma was waiting for the rest of her Colorado family to finish visiting, a man about Joe's age hurried up to their small group. He wore a wide grin on his handsome young face.

"Joe Sutter!" he exclaimed. "How the heck have you been, buddy?"

"Eric!" Joe greeted him, returning his smile and stretching out his hand while Emma watched curiously.

"I haven't seen you in a long time," Joe continued. "How's Denver?" The two men shook hands enthusiastically. Emma wondered if they had grown up together and been schoolmates.

Before Joe could introduce her, the man he had called Eric motioned to a young woman who had been standing back a little way.

"Honey, you remember Joe, don't you? He was at our wedding." Eric urged her forward. She was a pretty blonde, and she was carrying a tiny baby in a crocheted blanket.

Eric carefully took the swaddled infant from his wife's arms. "I want you to meet my daughter," he said, voice full of obvious pride. "She's only three weeks old."

"Uh, congratulations," Joe said while Emma watched. He barely glanced at the baby. "That's great." His hands were at his sides and he backed up a step.

"Here," Eric said, thrusting the baby at him while his wife beamed. "Go on and hold her for a minute. She's so tiny, you won't believe it. We named her Victoria Caroline, after our mothers, Vicky for short." He was still holding out the tiny bundle. Emma could see the strain on Joe's face, a muscle in his jaw twitching, as he attempted to ward off the baby.

"No, that's okay," he said quickly. "I don't want to drop her. She's cute, though."

To Emma, the desperation in his voice was clearly audible. Concerned, she moved forward. Joe looked pale under his tan.

Emma could see the puzzlement begin to seep into Eric's proud face. Joe's expression was an odd mixture of yearning and pain. Time stretched awkwardly as he held up his hands in apparent defense.

Emma thought only of rescuing Joe from an awkward situation. She darted forward. Smiling up at Eric, she cooed, "Oh, may I? I just love babies."

Eric nodded. A gigantic fist squeezed Emma's heart as she scooped up the sleeping infant. Victoria Caroline's mother watched proudly as Emma inspected the tiny features and touched the dainty waving hand.

The baby frowned in her sleep.

"She's precious," Emma said with a catch in her voice. Almost as precious and only a little bigger than her own tiny daughter had been, except that this baby was warm and pink and, no doubt, extremely healthy. While Emma held her, little Vicky's dark blue eyes fluttered open and she made a smacking sound with her tiny mouth. Emma's heart lurched and a wave of pain threatened her composure. Trying to appear as normal as possible, she glanced at Joe.

He was watching her closely.

"Isn't she sweet?" Emma asked.

Apparently he had recovered from whatever had bothered him. His expression bore only mild curiosity. "Yeah, she's going to be a heartbreaker." He grinned at the baby's mother and shook Eric's hand yet again. "You did good, buddy."

Emma handed the baby back to her mother. "She's lovely."

"Thank you."

Eric saw someone else he knew in the crowd. With a hurried goodbye he swept his little family away.

Marian was still talking to the Granlunds. Emma could hear Grover expounding on a new strain of beef cattle.

"Are you all right?" she asked Joe under the cover of their neighbor's booming voice.

"I'm fine. What about you?"

"I'm okay," she asserted, still a little shaken by the experience of holding an infant for the first time since Alicia, but she would survive. On the other hand, she wasn't so sure about Joe. Before she could ask him about his strange reaction to the baby, he interrupted Grover's monologue to ask something about his hay crop.

While Grover elaborated on its quality, Joe watched Emma through lowered lids. The eager way she had reached for Eric's child had convinced him, beyond any doubt, how badly Emma needed another babe of her own to fill her arms as well as the empty place she must still have in her heart. If it was the last unselfish thing he ever did, he would find the strength to let her go, so she could get over whatever attachment she thought she felt toward him and find a man back in Seattle to give her what she needed.

Of that, Joe made himself a solemn oath.

Chapter Twelve

Pain and self-loathing were tearing Joe apart. Each time he saw Emma he remembered every kiss, every touch they had shared and the sweet, wild way she responded to him. He wanted nothing more than to scoop her into his arms and hold her close to his heart, while he poured out his feelings for her.

Instead, he avoided her as much as he could. It wasn't difficult; there was plenty to do on the ranch to keep him busy. Often he ate at the bunkhouse. He left the house in the mornings before anyone was up and came back after they had gone to bed. On a couple of nights he even slept at the bunkhouse, returning home before dawn to change clothes, and then leaving again. Each time he did that he would find himself outside Emma's bedroom door, listening for the slightest sound from within. One side of his brain insisted that he slip soundlessly into the downstairs room and join her in that warm, soft bed, taking what he so desperately

needed and giving in return what he ached to share with
Emma and no other woman. The other, more rational side
of his brain reminded him that he had no right; *his* best fell
far short of what Emma longed for and deserved.

His avoidance was obvious to her. In addition, he was
around so seldom that the children were starting to ask what
was wrong. Neither she nor Marian knew what to say, except that he was busy with ranch business. Nor did Emma
know how to break through the icy shell that Joe had managed to build around himself. He was inapproachable.
When she did try to talk to him, he very politely froze her
out. It was as if he had closed a door on the feelings she had
been so certain they shared. She wanted to fight for him, for
them. But she couldn't do that if he was never around.

On one especially hot afternoon, when the children had
gone off swimming with a neighboring family, Marian sent
Emma to look for Joe and give him a message from a business associate.

"Just tell him to call Adam Davis," Marian told her.
"He'll know what it's about. And take my car. It's too hot
to walk."

"Okay, sure." Emma didn't ask whether the call was
something that could wait for Joe to show up at the house.
The afternoon was so unusually warm and muggy, her mood
so low, that she almost didn't care whether Marian was still
trying to get them together.

Missing Joe had turned into a dull ache—a part of Emma,
like her blue eyes and the black hair she had always considered too curly.

Lifting the limp strands off her neck as she started the car,
she felt sorry for the men working under the unforgiving
sun. There didn't seem to be a breeze anywhere.

When she reached the horse barn she saw Joe's pickup
parked outside. It was covered with dust. She pulled the car
up next to his truck and got out, the butterflies in her stom-

ach starting to dive bomb like kamikaze pilots. Taking a deep breath, she wiped her damp palms against her shorts and went inside. She recognized the sound of water splashing on the concrete floor as she called Joe's name.

As she walked down the wide aisle she saw him near the other door. His bare, broad back was turned toward her. Apparently the water gushing from the hose in his hand had drowned out the sound of her voice. His hat, boots and discarded shirt lay in a pile a couple of feet away from his bare feet. Water streamed onto his wet head and cascaded down his torso, wetting his jeans. While Emma watched, he raised the hose and splashed more water over his shoulders.

Emma had stopped in her tracks, mesmerized by the sight of him beneath the stream of running water. In the subdued light of the barn, his wet body gleamed like a fine bronze statue. His wide back was, in itself, a work of art.

Her breath caught in her throat as her gaze traced the path of his spine. Its fluid curve separated his torso into two perfect halves and then dipped into the low-riding waistband of his jeans. Below his wide leather belt his tight, blue-clad buttocks flexed as he shifted his weight.

Emma must have made some sound in reaction; he pivoted slowly. His chest was as perfect as she remembered— broad, powerful, elementally male. Curling hair spanned the expanse from one small, distended nipple to the other. The dark thatch of hair narrowed and ran down his flat stomach, past his navel, disappearing beneath the open snap of his jeans.

His unbuckled belt hung open, framing the bulge in his fly that proclaimed his sex. Emma stared and swallowed.

Joe's hand holding the hose had dropped to his side. The barn was silent except for the splash of water onto the cement floor and, after another drugged moment, Emma managed to raise her fascinated gaze past his chest to the hard lines of his face.

His expression was alive with some barely suppressed emotion. His eyes smoldered as he returned her helpless stare.

Emma wet her lips with her tongue and forced them to form words.

"I brought you a message."

"What is it?" Joe's voice was harsh, impatient.

"Adam Davis wants you to call. Marian said you'd know what about."

Joe's head jerked in affirmative response. "I'll get back to him later. Thanks."

Rational thought fled as Emma continued to look at the man standing before her, poised warily on the balls of his feet—as if ready to defend himself against some unseen threat. If he had asked why else she had come, she couldn't have answered.

"Emma," he rasped instead in a voice she barely recognized as his. "If you know what's good for you, you'll go back to the house."

"But I . . ." She blinked, confused by his hostile tone.

He tossed his head, his nostrils flaring like those of a stud horse at the scent of a mare. "Emma, do as I say. Do it *now*."

With one last glance at the raw passion stamped on his face, Emma obeyed him without question. She turned and fled.

She was already outside, blinking in the bright sunlight, when sanity returned. Everything she wanted was in that barn. Was she running away from a chance to break through Joe's wall of ice? It was a chance she had to take.

Drawing in a deep breath, Emma willed herself to stop shaking. She walked slowly back to the barn. She slipped inside and the well-oiled door shut noiselessly behind her.

Joe was standing where she had left him, holding the hose up so the water poured directly onto his bowed head and down over his face. Beneath the flow, his mouth was open and gasping, his eyes squeezed shut.

With complete disregard for her dry clothes, Emma reached up and took the nozzle from his hand.

Joe froze and his eyes popped open. Like twin flames they blazed into hers. Watching him intently as he towered over her, dripping wet, Emma adjusted the spray to a fine mist and began to play it across his chest.

"What are you doing?"

She smiled gently. "Cooling you off."

After a timeless moment in which Joe continued to stare, a muscle throbbing in his tightly clenched jaw, he dipped his head in apparent surrender and closed his eyes. While she held the hose on him, he rotated his powerful body slowly, raising his arms so the water caressed his sides and underarms. Then he turned his back and Emma smoothed water over it, her hand remarkably steady despite the turmoil going on inside her.

His jeans were soaked, and Emma's shirt was getting splashed. No matter, she was hardly cold.

Turning again to face her, Joe held her gaze with his as he pushed back his wet hair. Then, without blinking, he grasped the unfastened top of his jeans with one hand and lowered the zipper with the other.

Emma swallowed but remained silent as he shucked them off and kicked them aside. The water quickly dampened his shorts, gleaming white against the tan of his thighs, until they clung like another skin.

She couldn't help herself. She glanced down at the blatant proof that he was anything but cooled off.

Joe took the hose from her unresisting fingers and aimed the nozzle away from them.

"Your turn," he said with a toss of his wet head. His silver eyes flashed. While he waited, unsmiling, Emma raised her hands to her shirt and began slowly freeing the buttons.

His obvious desire fueled her own. Perhaps the heat between them would melt his wall of ice.

Joe watched, breath lodged in his throat, as the creamy swells of her breasts were bared above the delicate lace of her bra. When her shirt hung open she stopped and let her hands fall to her sides.

Joe reached behind him and turned off the faucet. The flow of water stopped abruptly. As the silence in the barn wrapped around the two of them like a cocoon, Joe tossed the hose to the floor. Unable to help himself, he leaned forward and pressed his mouth to hers. She made his head spin.

"You're so lovely," he murmured, pushing the shirt from Emma's smooth shoulders with hands that weren't quite steady. The cuffs caught on her wrists and he unbuttoned them. Before the shirt could fall to the wet pavement, he scooped it up and tossed it carefully onto a nearby barrel. Then he slipped one bra strap from her shoulder and kissed the slight mark it had left on her skin.

Her scent, a mixture of honeysuckle and sunshine and pure, sweet Emma, filled his nostrils. He touched her with his tongue and savored her taste. She moaned. Joe trapped the sound with another kiss. Her hands gripped his shoulders, her touch hot against his cool skin. He deepened the kiss and pulled her close, sliding one thigh between her legs. She trembled.

He bit back a groan.

When he finally loosed his hold on her and raised his head, he looked down to see that the sheer material of her bra was wet from the contact with his chest. Her nipples were puckered, pushing at the fabric and drawing his attention. Deeply moved by her response, he looked into her face.

Emma's eyes were wide and dreamy, her mouth full—softened by his kisses. Joe's control began to fray. He brushed his thumb across her full lower lip. Another thread of that tenuous control broke.

He skimmed his fingers down her throat. She arched her neck and closed her eyes. Another thread snapped.

He traced a path between her breasts. She moaned, and another thread broke free.

Glancing around the deserted barn, Joe handed Emma her shirt and picked up his wet jeans.

"Come on," he murmured, tucking her against his body with one arm. His skin burned wherever it touched her. He expected her to balk or at least to question his intent. Instead, she slid her arm around his bare waist, fingers slipping beneath the band of his shorts, and went with him to the empty stall where he had first found Kenny.

Dropping his jeans on the straw-covered floor, Joe shut the door behind them and plunged the small area into shadow. Then he brushed a hand over the pile of worn feed sacks.

"I wish—" he began.

Emma pressed two fingers to his lips and shook her head. "Don't," she murmured, sinking to her knees on the rough pallet. "I'm right where I want to be."

Everything in Joe reacted as he knelt and faced her. His anguished vow to leave her alone was forgotten. Forcing himself to be gentle, he lowered the other bra strap and watched while the sheer material slid downward, catching on the beaded tips of her breasts. Emma reached behind her and unhooked the bra, letting it fall completely away.

Joe groaned at the sight of her bared before him and cupped the weight of her breasts in his trembling hands. His thumbs brushed her nipples and she arched her back. A whimper escaped her lips. Needing no further encouragement, he bent his head.

Beneath the heated onslaught of his lips and tongue, Emma felt a reaction that echoed deep within her awakened body. She buried her hands in his damp hair and held him close.

Releasing one nipple, Joe strung kisses across to the other breast. He drew the tip deep into his mouth while Emma gazed at his lowered head. His eyes were shut, his short, thick lashes shadowing his weathered skin. Her heart ached with a tenderness that rivaled the burning need growing inside her. Gently, lovingly, she smoothed a hand through his wet hair.

Then Joe released her breast and let the tips of his fingers skate down her back while her sensitized skin danced with reaction to his touch. His hand slid beneath the waistband of her jeans to caress the sensitive spot at the base of her spine while his mouth nibbled a trail back to her lips.

The kiss he took was rougher, his mouth hotter. More urgent. His breathing was faster, his touch more demanding. His manhood pressed into her stomach as Emma reveled in his unbridled hunger.

Joe broke the passionate contact with her mouth and leaned down to nibble at the skin above her waist while he fumbled with the fastening on her jeans. Emma arched away, allowing him greater access. He parted the denim, revealing her red satin panties. She wondered if he could see their color in the gloom of the stall.

"Mmm," he murmured, answering her unspoken question, "I sure do like you in red." Then he placed a kiss on the sheer fabric, dazzling her senses, before rising and pulling her to her feet.

Disoriented, Emma held tight. He grasped her hips and pulled down both her jeans and the underwear in question, marking their progress with a trail of sizzling kisses.

She giggled raggedly when he kissed her knees. Then she steadied herself with her hands on his shoulders and stepped out of the last of her clothing. He laid it aside and pulled her down to the nest of feed sacks.

"Emma," he murmured, "you're exquisite. I want you so much. I can't wait."

"Don't wait." She reached out and freed him from his shorts. He hissed in a breath at the loving touch of her hands. Then he began tracing patterns up and down the length of her with the tips of his fingers. Each stroke ended on her thighs, coming closer to the center of her femininity. Finally, when she thought she might cry out with impatience, he caressed the gates of her most private place.

Her legs fell helplessly open to his questing fingers. When he stroked her there, light, teasing movements, she moaned and her hands gripped him tighter.

He bent and kissed her lips, his mouth burning against hers, his tongue plunging deep as he continued to rub and caress her intimately.

She moaned when he hesitated, almost wept with relief when he touched her again. Then he spread one hand across her stomach, his expression fiercely possessive, his touch a brand. When he came to her, she urged him on. He knelt between her legs and trembled on the brink of taking her.

His eyes burned with an inner fire.

"Good God, Emma," he groaned, "I can't tell you how much I want this. How much I need you." He slid one hand beneath her. Then he leaned forward with a harsh sigh and buried himself to the hilt of his masculine power.

Imprisoned within her tight, hot grip, Joe paused, letting her adjust to his size and strength. She felt so good, so incredibly good. He withdrew with agonizing slowness and buried himself yet again. And again.

Emma began to come apart in his arms, grasping him tighter, rising to meet him at each stroke, holding him close with her hands and her legs. Welcoming him deeper and deeper until she finally exploded like a dying sun.

Feeling her shiver and tremble around him, he thrust one last time, deeper than ever. His body arched, muscles clenching, and he reached his climax.

Emma held him tight as he poured his life force into her. Afterwards he sprawled beside her, cradling her close to his heaving chest. Her pulse was still racing, her heart soaring with wonder at the way he had made her feel and the heights to which he had taken her.

"Joe," she murmured, "you're wonderful."

"No," he whispered hoarsely. "Not me. You." He raised her hand to his lips and kissed her fingers. "You're the wonder."

After a few moments, when he didn't say anything else, Emma became more conscious of her nakedness and their surroundings. Someone could come into the barn at any time and see Joe's boots and hat. Marian might wonder what had happened to her.

Emma shifted restlessly and then got up.

"What is it?" Joe asked sleepily.

"I'd better go." She reached for her clothes. Beside her, he sat up in the gloom and wrapped an arm around his bent knee. "What's the matter?"

Emma found she was unable to look him in the eye as she hooked her bra and began yanking on her panties. What had she expected, a declaration of eternal love? Hadn't he warned her about that?

As she glanced around at the stall and the feed sacks, the ugly phrase "roll in the hay" came to mind. With clumsy haste she pulled on her shirt and fumbled with the buttons. Joe brushed her shaky hands aside gently and fastened them himself.

"Emma," he said as he did, his tone more insistent, "talk to me. What thoughts are going through your head?"

She shook her bowed head. "Nothing. I just don't want your mother to worry about me."

Joe appeared to consider that for a moment.

"No," he drawled finally, standing and reaching for his jeans. "I don't suppose she'd think this was a very good idea."

His casual words cut her to the quick. What did all they had just shared mean to him? Anything? Did *he* think it was a good idea? Fear of the truth kept her from asking. Instead, she wiggled into her jeans. Before she could fasten them, Joe lifted her to her feet.

"At least your pants aren't wet," he grumbled, holding out his own sodden mass of denim.

Emma found that she could force a smile at his disgruntled tone. "True."

He caught her in his arms and pulled her close for a long, tender kiss that left her shaken.

"Damn," he muttered half to himself as she felt him harden against her. "I want you again." He buried his face in her hair and breathed her scent. "Will I ever get enough of you?"

She shifted restlessly. What was he really asking?

"I think you know," he continued quietly, "after you walked back in here just now, nothing could have stopped me. I tried to warn you away."

She relented and touched his cheek with one hand. "I disregarded your warning," she confessed.

Joe kissed her again with aching tenderness. "And now perhaps you'd better go before I get caught with my pants off," he said, only half-joking.

He had hardly been able to believe his eyes when she had walked back into the barn and taken the hose from his suddenly nerveless fingers. All his resolutions to keep her at a distance had gone up in a blaze of passionate need he had seen mirrored on her face.

Those same resolutions remained shattered when he looked into the deep blue of her eyes and knew that, for him, escaping with his heart in one piece was no longer an option—had not been for weeks. He had tried to resist, had meant to spare her. Now he reached out with greedy hands to snatch what happiness might remain. He wanted to experience everything he could with her before she left. He wanted to spend every available minute storing up memories to linger over when she was gone.

"I guess it seems a little backward, asking you now," he said slowly, "but I'd like to take you out. On a real date."

When he saw the light of happiness blossom on Emma's face, his own heart lifted.

"Oh, Joe," she said, smiling.

"Let's do it up right," he suggested, making a sweeping gesture with one hand. "What would you like to do?"

Head tipped to one side, she thought for a moment. "Could we go to Denver?" she asked. "I only saw a glimpse of it, from the air and then from the window of the bus." She threw her arms around his neck in a burst of excitement. "Oh, Joe, could we? It would be so much fun to go back there with you."

She must have felt him stiffen, because she immediately dropped her arms and stepped back. "We don't have to go that far," she said quickly. "Sterling or Fort Morgan would be fine. Or even Caulder Springs, if you'd rather."

Her exuberance was contagious, and he hated to see it fade. He hastened to reassure her. "No. Denver is a great idea. Let's start with dinner somewhere nice. We can stay the night if you'd like to, and do some sight-seeing the next day before we come back. How does that sound?" Denver was a big city. What were the odds of running into his ex-wife, anyway? Probably a million to one.

Emma nodded happily, her eyes sparkling again. "It sounds heavenly." Then her smile faltered a little and his heart tipped. "But what will your mother think?" she asked.

Joe brushed aside the voice of reason. "Don't worry," he told Emma. "I'll talk to her. It will be fine."

For the next week Joe spent every moment he could with Emma. If he had to ride out, she rode with him. His men accepted their new, closer relationship without comment. They took the children on a picnic to the river. They held hands and went on romantic walks in the twilight. One night they again made love under the stars. On a hot, quiet afternoon Joe took her to the old barn and locked the doors. There he seduced her in the sleigh that was stored there. And every night, when the house was silent, Joe came to Emma's room and lingered in her arms until dawn.

They talked of everything except their feelings. Marian beamed at them and Kenny and Rachael teased them, giggling when Joe pretended to chase them away. When Jason interrupted them necking like teenagers, he rolled his eyes and made gagging noises while Joe chased him, laughing. Emma basked in the love that deepened within her each day and suspended her letter-writing campaign.

The night before their trip Joe dreamed that they ran into Stephanie and she screamed accusations at him. When he and Emma checked into their Denver hotel he searched the lobby surreptitiously, half expecting his ex-wife to appear from behind a potted plant. He couldn't relax at dinner, even though he knew that Emma had to be aware of his bizarre behavior.

Despite Joe's nervousness, the meal was a success. Emma must have decided to ignore his strange mood, because she chatted easily about Seattle and teaching. Over dessert she encouraged him to talk about growing up on the ranch, about school and college. Gradually, while they discussed one nonthreatening topic after another and he saw only strangers, Joe finally began to relax.

Emma was more beautiful than ever in a strapless dress made of some shimmery blue fabric. Tiny sapphires twinkled on her ears and a matching pendant hung on a gold chain around her throat. Joe couldn't wait to get her alone.

"Would you like to go into the lounge and dance?" he asked, prolonging his own torment. He wanted the evening to be perfect for her. Just being with Emma made it perfect for him.

"Would you?" she countered with a knowing smile.

Joe set aside his own need to claim her. "If I don't get you in my arms, one way or another, I'm liable to make a scene," he teased. "A slow dance might cause less of a stir than a steamy embrace at the cashier's station."

Emma slid back her chair and put her napkin on the table. "What are we waiting for?" she asked in a throaty purr that sent Joe's pulse rate into warp speed. "I'll take your first offer, and then I'll take your second," she promised as he rose to grasp her hand.

Driving home the next day in the sleek sedan, Emma stroked the hand Joe had rested on her thigh since they had left Denver.

"Did I tell you that I had a wonderful time?" she asked.

"Tell me again." Without taking his eyes from the road, he leaned closer so she could kiss his cheek. She wanted to be sure he knew how much she loved being with him. Everywhere they had gone, from the tall, modern building that housed the art museum to the state capitol with its shining, gold-plated dome to Victorian-style Larimer Square where Emma had shopped for souvenirs, she had seen other women looking covetously at Joe and giving her envious glances. She was proud to be with him, and even more delighted that he was apparently oblivious to anyone but her. True, he had been unusually withdrawn when they had first arrived in Denver, even tense, but that had faded at dinner.

She had made sure that nothing controversial had come up in their conversation, and finally Joe had relaxed completely. The light in his eyes and his possessive touch when they had danced together had exploded into passion the moment they'd entered their hotel room.

That night Joe had turned to her again and again. In the morning, waking up in his arms had been a bittersweet experience for Emma, but she had determined not to let thoughts of the future mar the wonder of their time away together. Now she floated on a golden cloud of happiness, only slightly affected by the necessary return to the ranch and reality.

"I had a terrific time, too," Joe said as he glanced at her warmly. "Especially last night and this morning..." He looked back at the road. "I'll never forget them," he finished, his hand turning over to tighten on hers before he shifted it to the steering wheel.

Emma was bereft at the loss of his touch. The way he spoke sounded almost as if the weekend had been more of a goodbye than the promise of the lingering hello she had hoped it might be.

After they got home and settled back into the routine with Marian and the children, Emma continued to puzzle over the incident with the baby at church and Joe's insistence that he didn't want children. She couldn't shake the idea that there was something more that she was missing, something hidden in his resistance that was crucially important.

At least Joe continued to be more open in his feelings for her. He smiled often, held her hand in front of the rest of the family and, one morning, had even kissed her goodbye while his mother stood by, beaming.

Emma didn't know where any of it was leading, didn't dare speculate. She only knew the idea of going back to Washington was getting more and more painful.

* * *

Emma had planned to ride out to the southeast pasture and meet Joe, but the phone detained her. This time, when Cal called, he accepted her excuse that she didn't feel right about leaving Marian again when she was the one Emma was here to visit.

"If things change, let me know," he said cheerfully. "Otherwise, have a good visit."

After Emma thanked him and hung up, she felt as if a small weight had been taken from her shoulders. Hurrying, she went down to the corral to saddle Belle. When she got there she was surprised to see Tulsa, the big gelding Joe usually rode.

"Where's Joe?" she asked, stroking the animal's neck. Tulsa blinked his big brown eyes, and Emma heard the sound of a child crying. It was coming from the horse barn. Quickly she left the horse and rushed inside.

"Rachael!" she called. "Is that you? Are you okay?"

"She's in here," Joe shouted back as Emma hurried down the center aisle.

Relief that he was there took the edge off Emma's fright. Joe would take care of things, no matter what. The door to the tack room stood open, and the light was on. Inside, Joe was holding Rachael, whose cheeks were streaked with tears. Kenny stood by, watching anxiously.

"What happened?" Emma demanded when she reached them.

Rachael thrust out one bare, tanned arm. "I got scratched." Three red furrows marred her skin.

"They aren't too deep," Joe told her, his face as tender as Emma had ever seen it. "They won't leave a scar."

Rachael examined the wounds more closely. "I might like a scar," she said.

Emma took her hand gently. "Let me see." The scratches weren't deep, but they had drawn blood.

"She picked up that big black-and-white cat when he was sleeping," Kenny volunteered.

"How did you ever sneak up on him?" Emma asked. The barn cats always fled when she tried to make friends.

Rachael shrugged. "He didn't wake up."

"Here, honey," Joe told her as he held up a white tube with his free hand. "This won't hurt." He glanced up at Emma. "I already washed them out. This will prevent any infection."

Emma turned a big smile on the little girl he was holding with his other arm. "It looks like Joe is fixing you all up."

"We keep a first-aid kit in the tack room," he explained. "Around here, you never know who might need it."

"I suppose," Emma agreed.

"Would you like a Band-Aid on that?" he asked Rachael.

"Do you have good ones or just plain ones?"

Joe poked through the small white box. "Just plain ones, I'm afraid. They're all the men will wear."

"That's okay," she replied, wiggling to get down. "I don't need one. Thank you, Joe." When he set her down on the concrete floor she grabbed his face between her hands and gave him a kiss on the cheek. To Emma's amusement he colored as he hugged her.

"You're welcome." His voice was gruff. "Remember what I told you about the barn cats. They're pretty wild, so the best thing is to leave them alone unless they come to you first." He glanced up at Emma. "A couple of the older ones are friendly enough, but the younger ones think they're little mountain lions."

As Rachael and Kenny left, Joe called after them, "Remember, the old barn is off-limits. Stay out of there."

"We remember," they chorused as the two of them disappeared around the corner.

Joe shook his head as he put the first-aid kit away. "A couple of minutes ago she was crying as if she had been mortally wounded. Now she's forgotten all about it."

"That's kids, I guess." Emma looked at him closely. "How are you holding up?"

Joe saw her concern and grinned. He remembered the jolt of fear that had hit him like a sucker punch when he'd first heard Rachael's anguished screams—and his relief upon discovering that she had only been scratched and not half-killed. It could have been much worse, a scratched face or even a damaged eye.

Joe's first violent reaction on seeing the angry red streaks had been to get rid of all the cats so they couldn't harm the children again, but common sense had immediately super-seded that rash impulse. It had been pure luck that Rachael had managed to sneak up on an old tom that was almost deaf. Joe hoped the experience and his warning would be enough to dissuade her from doing it again. She might sur-vive it, but he had doubts about himself!

The nightmare Joe had experienced before the trip to Denver finally came true when he and Emma stopped at the video store in Caulder Springs after lunch at the town's only café.

"Hello, Joe," said a familiar voice at his elbow as he waited in line to rent a movie. Half-certain that his recent thoughts must have conjured her up, he straightened reluc-tantly and looked into the face of his ex-wife. She was as pretty as ever, with her blond hair long and silky straight around her heart-shaped face.

He was surprised that he felt nothing toward her—except a churning fear that she might expose his shameful secret.

"Hello, Stephanie." He glanced around to see that Emma was looking at her curiously. His heart began to pound with irrational fear. "What are you doing in Caulder Springs?"

"My husband, Ben, and I are visiting my parents," Stephanie said. Her hand, adorned by a sparkling set of rings, smoothed over the stomach that Joe saw was swollen by her advanced pregnancy. If Joe hadn't been so anxious, he might have been curious. He glanced around but didn't see a man in tow.

"I just ran in to rent a copy of *Casablanca*," she added, then colored slightly. She must have remembered, as Joe did, how the two of them used to watch that movie, and others, cuddled together in bed.

"Stephanie," he said, feeling painfully awkward, "this is Emma Davenport. Emma, my ex-wife, Stephanie...?" He glanced at her with raised eyebrows.

"Anderson," she supplied.

"Stephanie Anderson," he repeated. Then he watched, heartily wishing her back to Denver, as the two women exchanged greetings and polite smiles.

"Nice to meet you."

"You, too. When's your baby due?" Emma asked, while Joe contemplated a quick escape. Deep down, he didn't really believe that Stephanie would be vindictive enough to reveal the reason for their divorce, but he was terrified she might let something slip. Something that would replace the love he saw shining in Emma's beautiful eyes with the sickening glaze of pity.

"It's due in about three weeks," Stephanie was telling Emma. "That's why we came home for a visit now."

"How nice," Emma said, darting a glance at Joe.

This must be awkward for her.

"We have to get going," he told Stephanie. "Nice to see you again." As he was turning away to make his escape, his hand on Emma's back, he felt the cold touch of Stephanie's hand on his arm.

With a sinking sense of impending disaster, he hesitated. Emma stopped, too.

Joe wanted to shout at her to run for the truck. Instead, he waited, feeling as helpless as a deer trapped in a beam of light.

"I want you to know that I'm sorry how things ended up between us," Stephanie said, her voice soft with sincerity. "I have everything I want now, especially this baby." She hesitated and Joe hoped desperately that she was through. Instead, she added, "I'm ashamed now that I left you so abruptly. At the time, well, I couldn't deal with what we found out, I guess. But I hope you've found some happiness, too." She glanced at Emma.

"I'm fine," Joe said gruffly, face burning. To him, Stephanie's meaning was obvious. And Emma had heard every damning word. She was a smart woman—smart enough to figure out the rest. She looked puzzled, but, soon enough, the ugly truth would come to her.

"Goodbye," he told Stephanie. He couldn't have smiled or said more to save his own life. He could see Emma casting him worried glances, but he ignored her. He laid down the video and stalked out to the pickup, leaving her to follow as best she could. All he wanted to do was to get back to the ranch, saddle up Tulsa and ride. Alone. The way he should have stayed in the first place.

Chapter Thirteen

"She's pretty," Emma ventured on the way home from the video store. From Joe's silence and his unwavering stare through the windshield of the pickup she wasn't sure he heard her. "Stephanie, I mean. She's an attractive woman."

"Yeah." As responses went, it wasn't much.

Emma tried to ascertain just how upset by the meeting Joe really was. He hadn't even stayed long enough to rent the movie they'd picked out. For a moment Emma had been afraid he was going to drive off without her. "I can see how running into Stephanie so unexpectedly could be, um, a little unsettling,"

"Can you, now?" There was an edge of sarcasm in his voice that Emma had never heard before.

"Sure," she said, pressing on. "I'd probably be a little shook if I ran into Bob, my ex. And I'm over him." She hoped that Joe would tell her he was completely over Stephanie, too. Was that the real reason he hadn't been able

o make a commitment to Emma? Because he was still in
ove with his ex-wife? But she had remarried and she was
regnant, for God's sake. Wouldn't that be a little, well,
isillusioning?

Joe hadn't responded to her last comments. His expres-
ion was bleak. Emma wasn't sure if she should feel terri-
ly hurt and disappointed, or just plain mad that he hadn't
een honest with her from the beginning. Tears were defi-
itely out; a woman had her pride. Emma went with anger.

"You could have warned me that you were carrying a
orch," she told him.

To her surprise, she finally had his full attention. His head
napped around and his expression was incredulous.

"A torch!" he hollered. "Have you been eating green al-
alfa?"

"What?"

"In other words, are you crazy?" he translated with ex-
ggerated patience.

"Am *I* crazy?" Emma exclaimed. "I'm not the one who's
till emotionally involved with a remarried, very pregnant
x-wife!"

To her utter astonishment, Joe began to chuckle. True, it
as a singularly humorless sound as expressions of mirth
ent, but at least it was a reaction. Then he sobered. "Is this
ome kind of smoke screen?" he demanded as he slowed
nd turned onto the road to the Blue Moon. "Are you try-
g to distract me?"

Now Emma was truly lost. She threw up her hands and
azed out the side window. "As if I could."

"You were there." Joe's tone was bitter, his face grim as
e glanced at her and then back at the road. "You heard
hat she said."

He lapsed into silence as Emma tried to recall the brief
onversation in the video store. Something about Stepha-
ie being sorry she had left him the way she had. Nothing

significant, as far as Emma could tell. Oh, and that she ha[d]
found happiness. Was that it? Emma gazed at Joe throug[h]
narrowed eyes.

Was he upset that Stephanie was happy?

"I thought I heard what she said," Emma mutter[ed]
slowly. "I must have missed something."

Joe pulled up by the house and braked the truck. "Sur[e]
you did. Well, it's too late to try to make me feel better, s[o]
you might as well give it up." He drummed his fingers on th[e]
steering wheel. "Go on in," he said finally when Emm[a]
continued to sit there, trying to make sense of this conver[-]
sation. "I need to ride out and check something in the nort[h]
pasture."

"Okay. I guess I'll see you later."

As she shut the pickup door and watched him drive awa[y,]
he grunted something that might have been an agreement [or]
merely another clue she couldn't decipher.

"You two have a nice lunch?" Marian asked when Emm[a]
went inside. She was playing Monopoly with the three chi[l-]
dren.

"Yes, we did," Emma said truthfully. Lunch *had* bee[n]
nice, although it was difficult now to recall the cozy, flirt[a-]
tious way they had teased each other then. How long ag[o]
that seemed!

"Uh, can I talk to you?" Emma asked Marian, wh[o]
looked up from counting her play money. "Alone."

Marian immediately got up. "I'll be right back," she sai[d.]
"Don't steal my hotels while I'm gone."

Rachael giggled. "We won't."

As soon as Marian followed her into the other roo[m,]
Emma told her about running into Stephanie.

"Joe acted like she said something terrible," she co[n-]
cluded. "And I have no idea what he's talking about, but [it]
really upset him."

Marian looked as baffled as Emma felt. Together they went over as much of the conversation in the video store as Emma could recall.

"I can't imagine what he means," Marian said.

"Hey, hurry up," Jason hollered. "It's your turn."

"Be right there." Marian made a helpless gesture. "I can't believe that Joe is still hung up on her. It's you he cares about. I'd bet the ranch on it."

"Well, something upset him. I think I'll saddle Belle and try to find him," Emma decided. "We need to have this out."

"Maybe you're right," Marian agreed. "How long should I wait before I send out a search party?"

Emma smiled at the older woman's efforts to cheer her up. "Until you see the buzzards circling overhead."

Marian wrinkled her nose. "Ugh." She gave Emma's arm a squeeze. "Good luck, dear."

"Thanks," Emma called over her shoulder as she dashed upstairs to change into boots and jeans and to grab her hat and riding gloves. "Something tells me I'm going to need it."

When Emma passed back through on her way out, Marian said, "If the two of you aren't back for supper, I'll keep something warm." Her words might be mundane, but her expression told Emma she was behind her all the way.

"Thanks." Emma leaned over and gave her friend a peck on the cheek. As she went out the back door she could hear Kenny asking what was going on.

Joe had taught Emma weeks ago how to saddle her own horse. All that remained now was to find him.

She had expected to see him riding with his men, or driving a small group of the red and white cows and their calves, not sitting alone on a grassy rise, staring into space.

Joe heard the sound of Belle's hoofbeats and turned to see Emma riding his way. Before she got within shouting distance he resumed his original position, staring at the eastern horizon.

Behind him Emma reined in and dismounted as Belle nickered a greeting to Tulsa, who was grazing nearby.

"Joe?" she asked in a tentative voice. "Are you okay?"

He might have guessed that she would come after him. "Yeah." He knew he should look at her, smile, reassure her that his strange attitude in the truck had been temporary. It was almost more than he could summon the energy to do. Finally he rose and walked down the small swell in the landscape to where she waited anxiously below, twisting her hands together.

"I'm okay," he repeated. "What's up?"

"I was worried about you." Emma chewed on her lower lip. Joe remembered the feel of those small white teeth on various parts of his body. As always, he was drawn to her, like one magnet toward another.

"I guess I should thank you for worrying."

"You don't have to," she replied quickly. "You didn't ask for me to worry, you didn't invite it." He saw her swallow. "You probably don't even want it."

He hated seeing the pain in her eyes. Eyes that he had once thought he would call indigo if he was trying to be poetic. Even then, the first time he saw her, he had known she was going to be trouble. He closed his eyes and tipped his head back, breathing deeply—imagining that even out here he could smell the honeysuckle scent of her.

Yes, she was trouble. He had known, but he'd reached for her anyway. And now he was paying. And, even more unfair, so was she. Tired of the pain he always seemed to be causing her, Joe made a sudden decision. As much as he might wish that she was his and that the young charges staying at the ranch were their own, his and Emma's together, it wasn't to be.

He owed her an explanation.

"I kind of enjoy having you worry about me," he confessed in response to her earlier statement. "I'm sorry if I made you think otherwise." He extended his hand. After a brief hesitation Emma put hers in it. Joe walked her back up the rise to where he had been sitting before she rode up.

"What's over there?" she asked, pointing.

"Nebraska."

If she thought it strange that he had been so absorbed, she didn't comment.

"Almost time for Dolly's puppies to go to their new homes," he said, to break the silence. All but one, Kenny's favorite, had been spoken for. Joe planned on keeping it.

"I'll miss them," Emma said. "So will the kids."

"They'll still have Mickey to play with." He glanced at the sea of grass around them. "Be time to start haying soon."

"I bet you'll be busy then." She dropped down onto the soft grass.

"Yeah," Joe said as he stretched out beside her and propped his head on one hand. "Things will be hopping around here until the hay's all baled and safely stored in the sheds." He squinted up at the sky. "As long as the weather doesn't do us in. Always that chance, though. Gotta get the cows bred with next spring's calves, too, pretty soon."

Emma glanced around, content for now to let him lead the conversation. Perhaps he would give her some clue as to what had upset him so. She was pretty sure it wasn't anything to do with haying, breeding or any of the other seemingly unending ranch chores.

"Emma," he said after a few moments, and his voice had deepened. She noticed that he was plucking blades of grass, frowning at them as if he were totally absorbed.

"Yes, Joe?" Her voice came out smooth and steady, despite the fact that her heart had risen to her throat—where it threatened to choke her.

Suddenly he surged to his feet and walked down to where his horse stood grazing with hers. Resting his arms across the scarred western saddle, he appeared to study the line of fence that stretched clear back to the cattle sheds.

Emma thought he looked unbelievably handsome, standing there in his black Stetson. A man of the West. As always, his big body in traditional cowboy gear and snug, faded jeans took her breath away. Just as it seemed that he might never turn and speak, he gave his horse a pat on the rump and walked back to where Emma was waiting.

"This isn't easy for me to say," he told her in a low voice. His face was all harsh lines and angles, as if pain had honed away the softer tissue, leaving only bone and the steely strength that underlined his character.

Emma got to her feet and held out her hands. To her surprise, Joe took them in his. His grip was hard, almost painful, but she held on, sensing that he needed a lifeline. Willing that lifeline to be her love for him.

"You can tell me anything," she said, trying to encourage him.

"Ah, Emma." He sighed, looking away as if the very sight of her was more than he could bear. He released her hands and, bending his arms at the elbows, linked his fingers behind his neck. He stretched as if trying to alleviate some tension.

"I've been so unfair to you," he continued, dropping his arms. "I had no right to touch you, but I couldn't help myself."

His words threw her into total confusion.

"What do you mean, no right?" she asked. He wasn't married or engaged. Marian certainly would have told her if he was. Was he about to confess that he had never gotten over Stephanie? That he loved her still, despite the fact that she was no longer his?

Emma didn't think she could bear to hear that his heart belonged to someone else. She folded her arms across her chest, trying to prepare for news that would devastate her.

"Stephanie and I had no children." Joe's voice was flat and emotionless, but his eyes, glistening with moisture, held all the feelings he was trying so hard to suppress. "She wanted them. So did I."

His admission confused Emma even more. "But you said—"

"I know what I said. Maybe I was lying, even to myself."

"Why would you do that?" Her voice was rough with empathy. She longed to reach out and take away his pain.

Then, suddenly, she knew. Knew what he had been too ashamed to admit. Knew why he had pretended not to want children. Knew what he had been terrified that Stephanie would somehow reveal in the video store. An icy chill went through Emma.

"Joe," she said, grabbing his arm. "You don't have to do this. Don't say any more." She could feel the tears filling her eyes, could see the answering sheen of moisture in his. She ached for his pride, for the loss to the world of the children he would never father.

For a long, silent moment he returned her stare. Then he shook off her hand. "Let me finish." His voice was hoarse.

"It's not necessary," she insisted, sure she could somehow convince him that it didn't matter.

"It's necessary to me." He set his jaw and blinked away the hint of tears so that Emma was no longer sure if they had even been there.

"Stephanie and I waited to start our family. When we decided it was time, we tried but nothing happened. She got impatient. I guess that fertility problems in women are much tougher to diagnose, so I had the test first."

Emma wished he would stop, knew he couldn't.

"After we got the results, there was no reason for her to go in." He shifted away and bowed his head.

"Oh, Joe," Emma murmured, wanting to hold him in her arms. "I'm so sorry." She couldn't think of anything else to say.

He lifted his face, and she could see two lonely tear tracks down his tanned cheeks. The sight broke her heart. His defenses were laid bare, and she hated to see him humbled.

Now she did put her arms around him. "It doesn't have to matter," she said quickly. "It doesn't matter to me."

He twisted away from her. "No! Don't say that." The violence in his voice made her tremble. Not for herself. She knew better than to be afraid. But for him. For his hopes and dreams. For his lost chance for a son, an heir.

"I know it's a disappointment," she went on, "but—"

He gripped her shoulders hard, his eyes blazing down at her. "Don't say it," he warned through gritted teeth. "Don't say that it doesn't make any difference to you, because it will. Someday it will. Mom was right. You need another baby, a child of your own to love and to care for." Another tear, as painful to see as a drop of blood, trickled down his cheek. He ignored it.

"No!" she protested and he put a finger across her lips.

"Shh. Don't say it. Because I want to hear that lie, Emma. You don't know how much I want to hear it and believe it. So don't say it. Don't tempt me like that."

She stared at him, stricken.

"I can't give you babies. Not ever." He was shouting. "And it does matter." He sucked in a deep breath. "Believe me, it matters one hell of a lot."

"No," she argued, desperate. She felt more tears gather in her own eyes and impatiently wiped them away. "It wouldn't have to matter. We could adopt—"

"Stephanie suggested that, too, but I wouldn't listen."

Emma knew that if she lost him now, she lost him forever. "Joe, do you love me?" she demanded.

His expression was incredulous. "Love you? Hell, yes." He fisted one hand until the knuckles went white. "I may have no right, but I couldn't help myself. I love you so much...." His voice trickled off as he stared at her.

"I love you, too," she told him, eager. "And I'd rather have you than ten children. Joe!"

His expression told her that he didn't believe her. *Wouldn't* believe her. Her spirits nose-dived.

"You'd hate me," he said, voice already distant. "You believe what you're saying now, but eventually, you'd hate me." His voice dropped to a whisper. "And that would kill me."

"No, I'd never hate you, never blame you," she insisted, but she knew she had already lost.

"I don't want your pity," he said wearily. "I won't let you settle for less than all you deserve—a man who's whole."

"I need *you,*" she insisted, desperate. "You're the only one I want."

"That will change, and then you'll thank me." He looked down at her and his silver eyes were empty, his tears dry. "We'd better go back."

"Joe!" she cried as he mounted his horse. "You're wrong. How can I convince you that you're so wrong?"

He glanced down at her and his expression made her shiver. It was as if his soul had retreated, somewhere beyond the pain. Somewhere she couldn't follow.

"You can't convince me," he said. "I know I'm right. Someday you'll see that."

As Emma scrambled into Belle's saddle he rode slowly away. For the first time since she had met him, his shoulders were slumped in exhaustion and defeat.

* * *

Joe hadn't told Emma how having Kenny, Rachael and Jason at the ranch had made him realize that he could care for children who weren't of his blood. For it didn't change the fact that Emma deserved to have her own family, and to carry each precious babe in her womb. She shouldn't have to miss that just because he couldn't deliver.

As Joe rode into the yard by the old barn, Jason came running out, his face pale and his eyes wild behind his tears. He saw Joe and his face turned red, his expression becoming an uneasy blend of guilt and relief.

"What's wrong?" Joe demanded, reining in hard. Emma was right behind him.

"It's Kenny!" Jason choked out. "He fell and he's hurt bad."

The old barn was only used to store ranch vehicles and equipment. Nobody went up to the loft anymore; the ladder was rickety and in need of repair. Keeping the barn locked was impractical, so Joe had warned the kids away and assumed they would mind. Now a sickening feeling balled in his gut. He knew too well the attraction to what was forbidden. If Kenny had fallen to the cement floor—

Quickly, shaking, Joe dismounted, and so did Emma.

Jason followed them into the barn. "We didn't mean to climb the ladder," he said. "We were just playing and . . ."

Vaguely Joe heard Emma comforting Jason. Kenny was lying at the foot of the ladder, ominously still. One arm was bent awkwardly, and his eyes were shut. Rachael was kneeling beside him.

"Is he okay?" Emma asked, hovering, while Joe checked for a pulse and made sure he was breathing.

"He's alive." Joe's heart thundered with relief. "But he's unconscious, and his arm is broken. Jason, how far did he fall?"

The older boy swallowed, fresh tears streaming down his face. "He was almost at the top," he whispered. "The rung gave way and he just dropped right down. He's so still. I was going to call Marian on the horse-barn phone."

Joe knew better than to move him.

"Emma," he said, glancing into her worried face, willing her to listen and not to panic. "Call an ambulance. The number's on the phone. Jason, go with her and get some blankets from the tack room." Joe gripped Kenny's hand in his, wanting desperately for the boy to wake up, to be all right.

"What can I do?" Rachael asked tearfully as the others hurried away.

Joe looked up, startled. He had almost forgotten about her. Rachael's eyes were red, and she was still crying quietly. He felt like crying, too. Since his less-than-auspicious arrival, Kenny had become very special to Joe. Now he was so pale and so still.

"Stay here with me," Joe told Rachael, taking her hand in his free one. "I need you, okay?"

She managed a watery smile. "Okay, Joe. I'll keep you company." She squatted down beside him and put her other hand on his shoulder. Together they watched Kenny and waited.

The ambulance attendant took Kenny's vital signs and then contacted the trauma unit at one of the hospitals in Denver. Emma had called Marian from the other barn, and she came rushing over. She stopped when she saw Kenny.

"Oh, the poor boy," she murmured.

"The hospital is sending a helicopter," the attendant announced. "It should be here in twenty minutes." He and his partner immobilized Kenny and monitored his vital signs while he remained unconscious.

Emma was upset, but she was even more concerned about Joe. Usually a rock for others to lean on, he was pale and silent as he watched the medics work on Kenny. When Emma wasn't darting anxious glances at Joe or watching the boy who lay so silent and still, she did her best to comfort Rachael and Jason.

"Will he die?" Rachael asked.

"Don't be dumb!" Jason's voice was filled with anger. "He's not going to die, is he?" he asked Joe.

Joe blinked and looked up. "What? No, of course not." His expression was grim. Emma put a hand on his shoulder, but she didn't know if he even felt it.

"How did the accident happen?" she asked Jason. "Why was he on the ladder?"

Jason's face reddened and he turned away, head down. Rachael watched him with a worried expression on her round face. "Don't tell," she whispered loud enough for Emma to overhear. "They'll send us away."

Jason glanced at Emma, who quietly took both of the children aside. "You'd better tell me," she urged. "If you don't tell the truth, the state might think Kenny's fall was Joe's fault. Then they *would* take you away."

Jason hesitated and glanced at his sister, who shook her head emphatically. "Don't tell."

There were tears in Jason's eyes. Emma wanted to hug him, to reassure him, but couldn't do anything.

"I dared him," he confessed miserably. "I knew we were supposed to stay off the ladder. We all did. We were just playing a game, and I dared him." Without warning, Jason flung his thin body at Emma, who caught him in her arms and gave him a hard hug.

"What if I killed him?" Jason choked.

"Shh." She tried to soothe him while smiling reassurances at his sister. "He's going to be all right. I know he will."

Poor Jason. Poor Kenny! She wished the chopper would hurry up. After what seemed like an unbearably long time, they heard a faint but unmistakable drone.

"There it is!" Jason cried, pointing to a small, growing dot in the western sky.

In remarkably short order the chopper had landed and loaded Kenny's still form, secured to a stretcher.

"The rest of you will have to follow by car," said a man with short blond hair. "Report to the trauma unit as soon as you arrive."

"Mom?" Joe asked. "Will you stay here?"

"Of course," she said. "Jason, Rachael, Mrs. Cline is on her way. She'll want to talk to you about the accident."

Jason looked at Emma. "Just tell the truth," she said. "And everything will work out. You'll see."

"What did Jason tell you?" Joe asked as soon as he and Emma were on their way to Denver in the sedan.

They had each thrown a few things in a bag in case they had to stay over. Emma refused to think that far ahead. Kenny was going to be fine. He had to be!

"He admitted that he dared Kenny to climb the ladder. He's terrified that Kenny will die, and it will be his fault. And Rachael is afraid that the state will put them somewhere else."

"I hadn't thought of that," Joe admitted, his eyes glued to the road. "Do you think they will?"

Emma wasn't sure. "Accidents happen," she told him. "I think they'll take that into consideration."

The drive seemed to take forever. "Do you know where the hospital is?" Emma asked when they hit the outskirts of Denver.

Joe nodded. "I visited a friend there once. It isn't far now."

Emma sent up prayers that Kenny would be okay. When she wasn't thinking about the boy, she went over her talk with Joe, looking for arguments to convince him that his sterility didn't have to be a problem between them.

Beside her, Joe's thoughts were too jumbled for him to manage any coherent prayers. Instead he just willed the boy to come through this. He gripped one of Emma's hands in his, squeezing it as he looked at her.

"He'll be okay," she said, smiling tremulously. "Little boys are tough."

"Yeah," Joe croaked hoarsely. "They have hard heads." He couldn't make himself return her smile. By the time they finally pulled in to the hospital parking lot and found the trauma unit, a nurse told them that the doctors were with Kenny.

A man in a suit came over.

"Joe Sutter?" he asked.

"That's me."

The man introduced himself as Frank Harrison and explained that he was from the child protective division. "Kenny regained consciousness for a few moments during the flight," he said. "Right now they're doing some tests and X rays. Then someone will be out to talk to us. Meanwhile, I'd like to ask some questions so I can fill out my report. Can we sit down?"

Joe introduced Emma. She and Harrison exchanged greetings.

"Come on," Joe said, indicating a row of chairs. She followed and they all sat down. Harrison took a long form and a clipboard out of his briefcase. He pulled a pen from an inside pocket and asked a lot of questions. Joe and Emma answered them the best they could. As he was finishing up, he was paged to take a phone call.

"Excuse me," he said as he got to his feet. "I'd better answer that."

"What do you think?" Emma asked Joe after the other man had walked away.

"I don't know. Why don't they tell us something about Kenny?"

After another wait that seemed to last forever, Frank Harrison came back.

"I talked to Mrs. Cline." His professional demeanor had thawed slightly. "She interviewed the children who witnessed the accident." He glanced down at his clipboard. "Jason and Rachael Williamson."

"What's going to happen now?" Emma asked, gripping Joe's hand tightly.

"Our findings don't indicate any problems," he said. "You must understand, though, that we can't be too careful."

Joe's gut clenched. He knew what Harrison meant. They had to rule out any chance of neglect or actual abuse. His stomach heaved at the idea of anyone harming a child.

"I understand." His voice sounded rusty. "Thanks."

Before Harrison could say anything else a doctor came down the hall.

"Kenny's awake," she said after introductions were made. "There's some bruising and swelling of the brain, but his responses seem normal. The arm has a simple break and should heal without any problems. We'll be watching him closely."

"How long will you have to keep him?" Joe asked.

"Probably for a few days. Until the swelling goes down and the tests are all normal."

Joe let out a sigh of relief, feeling the hard knot in his gut begin to unravel, and gave Emma a hug.

"That's so good to hear," she said.

"When can we see him?" Joe asked the doctor.

"As soon as Mr. Harrison is done speaking with him, you can go in for a couple of minutes each, one at a time."

Joe shook her hand and thanked her. Harrison followed the doctor back down the hall.

"Don't be too long, now," Joe heard the doctor tell him.

"You go in first," Emma said to Joe.

"Thanks. I won't really believe he's okay until I see with my own eyes."

"I understand." Emma's expression was gentle, making Joe realize how very much he loved her. "You care a lot for Kenny, don't you?"

"Yes," he said, shifting his thoughts with effort. "I guess I do."

They had a party when Kenny came back to the ranch. Joe and Emma hadn't stayed that first night in Denver. Instead, Emma had returned to the hospital the next day with Marian. She had seen little of Joe, and that was probably easier. She still hadn't thought of anything more to say about what he had told her.

"Boy, are we glad you're back," Jason said when Kenny followed Joe into the house.

Kenny looked around, grinning. "I'm glad to be here."

Emma stepped forward to give him a hug. She had to blink rapidly to keep the tears from her eyes, and she hoped that no one had noticed. Glancing up, she saw Joe give her a conspiratorial wink.

"We made a chocolate cake!" Rachael exclaimed. "And there's lemonade and ice cream."

"That's right," Marian added. "Rachael helped with the baking, and Jason blew up the balloons. What do you think?"

Kenny looked at the festooned room and the neatly laid table. Tears came to his eyes. "Thanks, you guys," he said, ducking his head.

"It's good to have you home," Joe told him. His voice was hoarse and he cleared his throat. "Okay, let's eat."

Wondering if Joe realized what he had just said, Emma served thick wedges of cake as Marian dished up the ice cream.

"Sit here," Jason suggested to Kenny, putting his arm around the younger boy's shoulder as if they were long-lost buddies. "Next to me."

When they had finished eating, Emma got to her feet to pour more coffee. As Joe watched her, he suddenly remembered the day's mail. He had laid it down next to the stove when he and Kenny had come in.

"Emma," he said now, "I almost forgot, but there's a letter for you. It's on the counter, with the rest of the mail."

She picked up the long envelope while he watched, assuming it was another negative response to one of the applications she had sent. He watched idly as she opened it and scanned the contents.

Emma's expression changed from mild curiosity to shock. "It's from a school district in Washington," she exclaimed. "They're offering me a job."

Chapter Fourteen

"I hate to see you cut your visit short," Marian said, punching down the bread dough on the floured cutting board. "There were so many things I wanted to do that we just never got to."

Emma leaned back in the kitchen chair. Joe had taken Rachael and Jason to visit their mother, and Kenny was watching a rented movie on the television. Except for an occasional complaint about his arm, he seemed fine.

"I'm hardly cutting my visit short," Emma said. "I've been here for weeks. It's been good of you to have me for so long."

"Nonsense." Marian's tone was brisk as she picked up the dough and slammed it down. "I don't know how I would have managed without you, especially with the children."

"Rachael wants to wear her new dress to church again this Sunday," Emma commented. She had gone back to the fabric store for more material the other day. Sewing helped to keep her mind occupied.

"It was nice of you to stay up hemming it last night so she could wear it today. She looked so pretty when they left." Marian put the dough into a large bowl. "I hope their mother appreciates those kids."

"Mrs. Cline said she's doing very well in treatment," Emma commented, idly tracing one of the squares on the checkered tablecloth with her finger. "I wish I had time to sew a few more things for Rachael." She sighed, blinking back tears. It wasn't just Joe she would miss when she left, although he was the one who would be keeping the biggest piece of her heart when she flew back to Washington.

Deliberately Emma pasted a smile on her face and began talking about the teaching job in Forks, on the Olympic Peninsula. She had to let the school board know by the next day whether she was going to accept the position.

"Well, there are advantages to teaching in a small school," Marian agreed. "I imagine that Forks is pretty in the summer, being near the coast and all."

"Yes, I'm sure it is." Emma forced some enthusiasm into her voice. "I'm looking forward to a fresh start. It probably won't take long to meet everyone in town."

She was still sitting at the table visiting with Marian when Joe drove up outside and, moments later, the two children burst into the house.

"How's your mom?" Emma asked.

"Okay," Jason replied on his way to the living room. "Is Kenny still watching that movie?"

"I think so."

"Cool." He helped himself to a cookie and kept going. He never said much about those visits. Emma thought he was embarrassed that his mother was in drug rehabilitation, but when she had tried to point out how hard the other woman was working to make a better life for him and Ra-

chael, he didn't say anything. Maybe his mother had disappointed him so many times that he was afraid to hope.
Emma didn't know much about her, only that she was doing well in treatment. Anything more was confidential.

"Hi, Emma," Rachael said, coming over to give her a
hug. "Mom liked my dress." She rested her head on Emma's shoulder. "I hope she gets out pretty soon."

"She will," Emma told her. "As soon as the doctors
think she's ready."

"I miss her," Rachael said with a sigh. She went on for
several minutes, repeating everything she could remember
about the visit and telling Emma that her mom had promised to buy a sewing machine as soon as she got a job. "Or
if my dad comes back," she added, making Emma sharply
aware of the difficult situation that Rachael took for
granted. If her father was a drug user, too, it might be better if he stayed away.

Emma would have been sad to see the children leave the
ranch, but she was happy they were looking forward to being home with their mother. Maybe their lives would work
out this time. She hoped so.

"I'm going outside to cut some flowers," Marian said.
"Rachael, do you want to come with me?"

"Sure."

Emma stayed seated at the table after they had left, idly
listening to the sounds from the television set in the living
room. Joe hadn't come in with the others. He must have
gone straight on to saddle up Tulsa or to take a Jeep out to
check on the cattle.

She didn't expect him for lunch, and he wasn't there. After a noisy meal with Marian and the children, Emma did
some work in the vegetable garden. While she was on her
knees in the dirt she couldn't help but note all the things she
wouldn't be around to pick and eat as they ripened—the
tomatoes, the beans and the squash, among others.

She had to call and accept the job in Forks, and make a plane reservation back to Seattle. She would need to pack up the things in her apartment.

Here in Caulder Springs Tricia hadn't yet had her baby; Emma would have liked to be here for that. Cal had finally stopped calling, but she wouldn't really miss him. She would be sorry to leave the Granlunds and some other new friends she had made at church. It would be difficult to say goodbye to Marian and the children. And hardest of all was leaving Joe.

Sighing, Emma straightened from the row of carrots she had been thinning and sat back on her heels. As if her thoughts had conjured him up, she saw Joe walking toward the house with Daniel. The two men could have just passed through a time warp from the old West. Both wore dusty Stetsons, jeans and battered boots with their faded plaid shirts. Daniel might have looked equally at home in buckskins, with his long black hair and enigmatic eyes, but she wouldn't change one thing about Joe.

Except for his stubborn male pride and his absolute refusal to listen. He was too intent on saving her from himself to believe that the last thing she wanted was to be saved.

"Hi," she called, realizing that she would even miss Daniel. She didn't see him that often, but he had been patient and kind to her. Now he smiled and waved back.

"Going to open a roadside stand?" he asked.

Emma got to her feet and brushed the dirt from her knees. She glanced at the rows of healthy plants with pride.

"No roadside stand," she felt compelled to say. "I'm going back home to teach school."

She couldn't see his expression below the brim of his hat, but she did see him angle his head to glance at Joe before answering.

"That right? Where are you going to be teaching?"

"In a small school in a little town on the Olympic Peninsula," she told him as he and Joe came closer. "I'm looking forward to it."

"Good luck, then." Daniel had a devastating smile. Emma wondered if the women in town were aware of what a handsome foreman Joe had working here. She wondered if Daniel's Indian blood made a difference, although it shouldn't. It might to him, though.

He was nice, polite, hardworking and undeniably attractive—as tall as Joe and only slightly leaner in build, but still fit and well muscled from the hard physical work. Of course, he wasn't as appealing to Emma as Joe—no one was.

"A one-room schoolhouse?" Daniel asked, pausing to examine a hill of seedless watermelon plants.

Emma was keenly aware of Joe standing off to the side, waiting. Undoubtedly impatient to get on with whatever the two men had been doing. To get away from her. Perversely, she wanted to drag the conversation out.

"It's not quite a one-room schoolhouse," she told Daniel. "But I will be teaching a combined classroom if I take the offer. First and second grades together."

"Haven't you accepted the job yet?" Joe asked, speaking for the first time.

Emma had too much pride to let her smile waver. "It's all over but the phone call," she said. "I have to let them know tomorrow. Then I'll have to sign a contract."

Joe glanced at Daniel. "Can you find those records yourself?" he asked. "They should be right on the desk in my office."

Daniel's black eyes shifted to Emma. She could have sworn they were twinkling, even though he must have sensed the tension between her and his boss. "Sure thing," he told Joe. "I'll manage. Maybe I'll have a glass of your mom's emonade before I come back out, too. Might take me a few minutes," he drawled.

"And have some of Emma's oatmeal cookies, while you're at it," Joe suggested. "She just baked them last night."

"Okay." Daniel's enigmatic gaze rested on Emma for a moment before he touched his hand to the brim of his Stetson and told her, "I'll see you before you leave."

"Why did you send him on?" she asked Joe as soon as the other man was out of hearing distance. "I like Daniel."

Joe stared down at the toe of one scuffed boot. "You didn't have to sound so delighted about the job offer," he grumbled perversely, ignoring her question. She could have had a few misgivings, he thought dourly. Even though this was what he wanted, he didn't have to like it. Neither did he.

"Of course I'm excited," Emma insisted as she stabbed at a weed with the hoe. "I was a good teacher, and I'll be glad to get back to it." She paused, her smile fading.

"After all, there's nothing for me here," she added in a quieter voice as her gaze searched his face. "You've done your level best to convince me of that."

Her words made him ache. The pain surprised him. He had been so busy persuading her she had no future with him that he hadn't really thought about what his own life was going to be like without her. Hadn't let himself think about that.

"When are you leaving?" he asked, dreading the answer.

"Soon," she said. "In a few days, I guess. There are a few people I'd like to say goodbye to first."

He thought about saying goodbye. Knew if he could get through letting her go without breaking he could deal with anything. Sighing, he looked away.

"That's probably for the best." Well, it might be for Emma, but it sure wasn't for *his* best. His resolve wavered, and he gripped it firmly. Held on tight. It was too late now, anyway. Had probably always been too late for them. Since way before he met her. Since his life had been decided by a test tube and a doctor's chilling words.

"No chance of fathering a child."

Emma was only doing what Joe had told her to do. Nothing had changed between them. Nothing *would* change.

Without saying anything more he gave her a tight smile and went on into the house.

It was late that same evening when Joe padded back downstairs in his stocking feet, trying to be quiet. He had just finished working in his office and wanted a fresh cup of coffee and a couple of Emma's cookies before subjecting himself to another restless night in his big, empty bed.

As he got to the bottom of the stairs and turned on the hall light he thought he heard a sound from Emma's room. Silently he went over and stood outside her closed door, as he had so many other nights. This time he was surprised to hear the sounds of muffled crying coming from inside the room.

Without thinking, he opened the door. Emma, who was sitting up in bed hugging a pillow, let out a squeak of protest.

"Who's there?" she demanded in a tremulous voice.

Joe realized that with the light at his back she couldn't really see him.

"It's just me," he said in a rough whisper as he came farther into the darkened bedroom. The light from the hallway spilled around him, illuminating Emma's bed. The bed he hadn't occupied for way too long.

"What do you want?" she demanded. "It's late."

Ignoring his body's instant response to her, Joe sat carefully on the very edge of the bed.

"I heard you crying," he said quietly. "Are you okay?"

"Of course I am," Emma blustered, chin thrust forward, as Joe smiled despite himself.

"And you wouldn't tell me if you weren't," he guessed.

For a moment Emma looked taken aback. Then she glanced down at her hands gripping the pillow. "I guess I wouldn't."

Joe sighed and raked a hand through his hair. "No reason for you to," he muttered, half to himself. "Not after the selfish way I treated you."

Instantly she became defensive. Not of herself, which would have been understandable, but defensive of him.

"Don't you talk like that, Joe Sutter," she scolded. "You never did anything I didn't want you to do. You bent over backward putting my welfare ahead of your own. You might be misguided, but you're far from selfish."

Her quick defense of his motives moved Joe deeply. No matter how much he had hurt her she was determined to see only the good in him.

"Are you upset about leaving here?" he asked with a small measure of hope as a new thought formed in his head.

"Maybe," she admitted slowly as she peered hard into his face. Joe realized that, although he could see hers in the light from the hallway, he was sitting in shadow. "What if I am? My feelings are no mystery to you."

Nervously Joe began to pick at a loose thread on her bedspread. He didn't stop to consider whether the question he was about to ask would help the situation between them or make it worse. He only knew he didn't want Emma to leave Colorado, not entirely. Just knowing she was around, knowing he might accidentally run into her, would either keep him sane or it would drive him right over the edge. Right now he didn't much care which.

"I was wondering if you'd given any thought to looking for a teaching job here," he said, studying the design of the bedspread with utter fascination.

"Here? You mean here in Caulder Springs?" she asked.

"Well, somewhere in northeastern Colorado," he corrected her in a low voice. "I was wondering if teaching might fulfill you enough."

"Enough for what?" Her voice had turned sharp, and he was beginning to feel like a fool, never knowing if he was going to blow hot or cold next.

"Enough so that you wouldn't miss having children," he burst out. If he was going to look like a fool, too, he might as well go all the way.

Emma stared at him in the silent bedroom. She was quiet for so long that Joe wondered if she was going to answer him at all. What *did* he want, anyway? For her to become an old-maid schoolteacher because of him? He wasn't sure himself.

Just when he thought that Emma wasn't going to speak, she said, "I'm not sure how to answer that. I don't know what you're asking."

Well, that made two of them, Joe thought.

Emma couldn't have been more surprised if he had suggested she open a brothel outside of town. She had no idea what he was thinking, or what he was getting at, but she knew she had to be honest with him. It was too late for anything less.

"No, it won't be enough," she said clearly, straightening and tossing aside the pillow she had been hugging. As soon as she did, she became conscious of her clingy red nightie. Well, it wasn't as if Joe hadn't seen her wearing less. And he always said he liked her in red.

She stared harder, wishing she could see his face. She knew he was disappointed with her answer, but she didn't understand why.

"Teaching someone else's children won't be enough," she repeated. "I want to raise them myself, to have a family, even if it isn't one of my own blood. I want children who would be a part of my life, no matter where they originally came from. I don't want to have to say goodbye to them at three and hello again the next morning. Can you understand?"

"Yeah," Joe said in a voice devoid of feeling. "I understand."

"No! You don't," Emma burst out, then immediately lowered her voice. "I don't think you do. I know you said that you wouldn't consider adoption, but *I* would. In a heartbeat. I know how I've come to care about Kenny, and Rachael and Jason. It isn't so important to me that my children grow in my body, but only that I can keep them in my heart—and give them a home, a happy home with the man I love."

"I didn't say I wouldn't consider adoption," Joe said again in that same expressionless tone. "Only that I wouldn't consider it when Stephanie brought it up."

Emma was confused. "Have you changed your mind?" she asked.

Once again he began twisting a loose thread in the bedspread. She wanted to slap his arm and demand an answer. Instead, she made herself wait with a semblance of patience she didn't come close to feeling.

"I guess I learned a few things from having the kids here this summer," Joe said slowly, without raising his head.

"Like what?" she prompted when he again fell silent.

"Like finding out how nice it's been having them around," he continued. "And discovering how good it feels to know they like me and depend on me. To know there are things I can teach them and share with them. Important things." He shrugged and glanced up at Emma. "It didn't matter that they aren't mine. Hell, it doesn't even matter if I get to keep them forever or not." Again he fell silent.

Emma willed him to go on. She was afraid to speak for fear he'd clam up entirely. Maybe sitting there in the nearly dark room made it easier for him to talk about these things.

"And playing that dumb computer game with Jason," he added, his voice a little warmer. "He was so proud when he beat me, but he must have told me at least once every time we played that I better not let him win. He didn't want me to think he was some little wimp who couldn't take losing. I think Jason's lost too many things in his life." Joe sighed and his fingers became still against the bedspread.

"And when Kenny was hurt." He stopped again, and Emma could hear the pain in his voice. He bowed his head. "I couldn't have been more afraid for him if he had been my own flesh and blood," he whispered raggedly.

Tears came to Emma's eyes. "I know," she agreed. "I felt the same way."

When Joe didn't say any more, she spoke again. "So tell me," she asked in a sensible voice, "why won't you give me the same credit you claim for yourself?"

Joe's head snapped up. "What do you mean?" he demanded.

"Well," Emma went on in the same reasonable tone, "you can love children who aren't your own, but you won't believe that I could do the same."

If Joe saw the trap she was laying for him, he chose not to avoid it. "You lost a baby," he said hesitantly. "You know what it's like to feel a child grow inside you."

"That's right," she said. "I do know. And I also know I can survive, even flourish, without having the experience again." She made an impatient gesture. "Sure, I'd like more children. Most women in my situation would. But I don't need that at the expense of the man I love.'' She leaned across the bed and caught Joe's hand in hers.

"Do you hear me, Sutter?" she demanded. "I love you. That's the most important feeling in my life. You can send me away, sacrifice both our lives and our happiness, but that won't change anything. *I love you.*"

For a moment, she thought she had finally broken through to him. Then he got to his feet.

"No, Emma," he said sadly. "You may believe that now, but it won't work."

Infuriated by his stubbornness, Emma scrambled from the bed and snapped on the nightstand lamp. The sudden brightness made them both blink.

"I'm not Stephanie!" she cried, forgetting that there were people sleeping above them. "And you, Joe Sutter, are the closest thing to a blind, dumb, braying, stubborn mule that I've ever had the misfortune to argue with. When you get an idea in your head, God forbid that anyone should even *try* to shake it loose."

Joe looked so dumbfounded that, under other circumstances, she might have been tempted to laugh. His mouth was hanging open and a slow flush was crawling up from his neck, across his stark cheekbones.

"A mule?" he echoed.

"A blind, dumb, braying, *stubborn* mule," she repeated, emphasizing each word. Then, without warning, her eyes filled with tears at the injustice of the situation.

"Don't you understand?" she cried as she dimly became aware of a door opening upstairs. "I *never will* have children to raise, not mine or anyone else's. I *will* have to settle for teaching them and sending them home at three o'clock. And it's all your fault!"

"My fault," he repeated. "Why?"

"Because," she wailed, rubbing her streaming eyes with her fists. She grabbed a tissue from the nightstand and swiped at her nose. "I won't raise children without a father. If you, Joe Sutter, don't marry me, I won't have *any* children from *any* biological background." She didn't care what he thought anymore. She was beyond measuring her words.

"I'll never have children because I'll never marry without love, never raise children without a husband—and I'll never love anyone else but you." She sucked in a deep breath. "Now do you understand?"

She had to stop to blow her nose. Before her in the light from the lamp Joe looked as if he'd been kicked by a steer. "I'll never have children without you," she repeated. "What you're so afraid of happening is *going* to happen and it will be all your fault." She drew in a shaky breath, knowing that this was her last chance.

"So if you don't ever want me to have those children you've decided I can't live without," she said tearfully, "then walk away from me now. And it will all come true, just like you feared."

Exhausted, out of breath, Emma finally became silent. She watched Joe, who looked stunned by what she had said.

"So if I don't marry you, you won't have children, anyway," he finally repeated, as if trying to understand the convoluted reasoning of a female. "Because you'll never love anyone else enough to marry them." Halfway through the sentence his voice had gotten hoarse. Emma could see that his eyes were moist.

Then, while she watched, afraid to breathe, his expression began to take on the look of a man who had been dealt either a mortal blow or a winning hand. He blinked so hard that two lone tears ran down his cheeks.

"Emma," he said in a voice drowning in pain and hope. "I didn't know. I swear, I didn't know."

He opened his arms, and she launched herself into them. As he folded them around her, she grabbed his neck and tugged him hard. While she did, he began to laugh—a soggy chuckle, but nonetheless, a genuine one.

"I guess I'd better marry you," he whispered thickly. "Or I'll be doing just the thing I was ripping out my own heart to avoid."

Immediately Emma leaned back and studied his face. "Do you mean it?" she demanded, hardly able to believe that, *finally,* she had gotten through to him. "Do you really mean it?"

His smile widened. The confidence she had come to expect returned to his expression, along with an aching tenderness that made her want to start crying all over again. His eyes glowed and he looked like a man who had been handed a reprieve from a death sentence.

"Promise me that you'll call Forks in the morning and tell them you've accepted another position," he said in a hoarse, low voice. "The position of Joe Sutter's wife."

Emma nodded, fresh tears filling her eyes. Tears of joy this time. "I promise," she whispered.

Joe pulled her close. "I'll make you happy," he vowed fiercely as he kissed her. And Emma knew he would. He was her life, and she was his.

When he released her, gray eyes shining, he said, "Let's wake Mom and tell her. If she's managed to sleep through this, she'll want to know she was right all along."

"Did you know she brought me here hoping you and I would get together?" Emma asked, surprised.

His grin was devilish, his face finally relaxed. "I knew the moment I saw you," he admitted. "And I knew she was right. That's what's made me so mad."

Emma slipped on her wrapper and linked her arm through his. "I'm never going to let you go," she confessed.

Joe wrapped his arms around her. "Lady," he breathed, "that's one promise I'm going to make sure you keep."

As he lowered his head, the last thing Emma saw was that the ice had finally melted from his silver eyes.

*   *   *   *   *

Share in the joy of a holiday romance with

1993

SILHOUETTE

Christmas

STORIES

Silhouette's eighth annual Christmas collection matches the joy of the holiday season with the magic of romance in four short stories by popular Silhouette authors:

**LISA JACKSON
EMILIE RICHARDS
JOAN HOHL
LUCY GORDON**

This November, come home for the holidays with

Silhouette

where passion lives.

Silhouette

SPECIAL EDITION
™

WHAT EVER HAPPENED TO...?

Have you been wondering when a much-loved character will finally get their own story? Well, have we got a lineup for you! Silhouette Special Edition is proud to present a *Spin-off Spectacular!* Be sure to catch these exciting titles from some of your favorite authors.

FOREVER (SE #854, December) *Ginna Gray*'s THE BLAINES AND THE McCALLS OF CROCKETT, TEXAS are back! Outrageously flirtatious Reilly McCall is having the time of his life trying to win over the reluctant heart of Amanda Sutherland!

A DARING VOW (SE #855, December) You met Zelda Lane in KATE'S VOW (SE #823), and she's about to show her old flame she's as bold as ever in this spin-off of *Sherryl Woods*'s VOWS series.

MAGNOLIA DAWN (SE #857, December) *Erica Spindler* returns with a third story of BLOSSOMS OF THE SOUTH in this tale of one woman learning to love again as she struggles to preserve her heritage.

Don't miss these wonderful titles, only for our readers—only from Silhouette Special Edition!

Silhouette

SPECIAL EDITION™

WILD RIVER TRILOGY

by
Laurie Paige

Come meet the wild McPherson men and see how these three sexy bachelors
are tamed!

In HOME FOR A WILD HEART (SE #828) you got to know Kerrigan McPherson.

In A PLACE FOR EAGLES (SE #839) Keegan McPherson got the surprise of
his life.

And in THE WAY OF A MAN (SE #849, November 1993) Paul McPherson
finally meets his match.

Don't miss any of these exciting titles, only for our readers—and only from
Silhouette Special Edition!

When the only time you have for yourself is...

STOLEN *moments* ™

Christmas is such a busy time—with shopping, decorating, writing cards, trimming trees, wrapping gifts....

When you do have a few *stolen moments* to call your own, treat yourself to a brand-new *short* novel. Relax with one of our Stocking Stuffers— or with all six!

Each STOLEN MOMENTS title is a complete and original contemporary romance that's the perfect length for the busy woman of the nineties! Especially at Christmas...

And they make perfect **stocking stuffers**, too! (For your mother, grandmother, daughters, friends, co-workers, neighbors, aunts, cousins—all the other women in your life!)

Look for the STOLEN MOMENTS display in December

STOCKING STUFFERS:

HIS MISTRESS Carrie Alexander
DANIEL'S DECEPTION Marie DeWitt
SNOW ANGEL Isolde Evans
THE FAMILY MAN Danielle Kelly
THE LONE WOLF Ellen Rogers
MONTANA CHRISTMAS Lynn Russell

HSM2

 **WORLDWIDE LIBRARY**®

SILHOUETTE.... Where Passion Lives

Don't miss these Silhouette favorites by some of our most popular authors!
And now, you can receive a discount by ordering two or more titles!

Silhouette Desire®

#05751	THE MAN WITH THE MIDNIGHT EYES BJ James	$2.89	☐
#05763	THE COWBOY Cait London	$2.89	☐
#05774	TENNESSEE WALTZ Jackie Merritt	$2.89	☐
#05779	THE RANCHER AND THE RUNAWAY BRIDE Joan Johnston	$2.89	☐

Silhouette Intimate Moments®

#07417	WOLF AND THE ANGEL Kathleen Creighton	$3.29	☐
#07480	DIAMOND WILLOW Kathleen Eagle	$3.39	☐
#07486	MEMORIES OF LAURA Marilyn Pappano	$3.39	☐
#07493	QUINN EISLEY'S WAR Patricia Gardner Evans	$3.39	☐

Silhouette Shadows®

#27003	STRANGER IN THE MIST Lee Karr	$3.50	☐
#27007	FLASHBACK Terri Herrington	$3.50	☐
#27009	BREAK THE NIGHT Anne Stuart	$3.50	☐
#27012	DARK ENCHANTMENT Jane Toombs	$3.50	☐

Silhouette Special Edition®

#09754	THERE AND NOW Linda Lael Miller	$3.39	☐
#09770	FATHER: UNKNOWN Andrea Edwards	$3.39	☐
#09791	THE CAT THAT LIVED ON PARK AVENUE Tracy Sinclair	$3.39	☐
#09811	HE'S THE RICH BOY Lisa Jackson	$3.39	☐

Silhouette Romance®

#08893	LETTERS FROM HOME Toni Collins	$2.69	☐
#08915	NEW YEAR'S BABY Stella Bagwell	$2.69	☐
#08927	THE PURSUIT OF HAPPINESS Anne Peters	$2.69	☐
#08952	INSTANT FATHER Lucy Gordon	$2.75	☐

AMOUNT	$	_____
DEDUCT: **10% DISCOUNT FOR 2+ BOOKS**	$	_____
POSTAGE & HANDLING	$	_____
($1.00 for one book, 50¢ for each additional)		
APPLICABLE TAXES*	$	_____
TOTAL PAYABLE	$	_____
(check or money order—please do not send cash)		

To order, complete this form and send it, along with a check or money order for the total above, payable to Silhouette Books, to: *In the U.S.*: 3010 Walden Avenue, P.O. Box 9077, Buffalo, NY 14269-9077; *In Canada*: P.O. Box 636, Fort Erie, Ontario, L2A 5X3.

Name: _____

Address: _____ City: _____

State/Prov.: _____ Zip/Postal Code: _____

*New York residents remit applicable sales taxes.
Canadian residents remit applicable GST and provincial taxes.

SBACK-OD